EARLY PRAISE FOR BABY SHARK

"BABY SHARK reels you in and keeps you in its jaws. A grabber from page two with a killer ending. A great read and highly recommended."
    —Gregg J. Haugland, Allbooks Reviews

"Baby Shark's Kristin is my kind of woman, a combination of Uma Thurman and Jennifer Garner. High-energy entertainment. Great fun!"
    —John Dykstra, Academy Award winning Filmmaker

"Kristin Van Dijk, Baby Shark, is one of the most refreshing heroines to come around in a very long time…she not only swims with the bigger fish, but outsmarts them as well…a must for your summer reading list."
    —Judy Miller Snavely, *Devil's Disciple:*
    The Deadly Dr. H.H. Holmes

"…I found I could hardly leave Baby Shark until I'd read it through."
    —Alan Paul Curtis, Who-dunnit.com

"His heroine may be tough, smart, and a talented pool player, but there's a vulnerability about her that keeps her likeable. Other characters are just as wonderful, the dialogue snappy, the pace a-mile-a-minute in this can't-put-it-down-till-the-last-page thriller."
    —Sheila Lowe, *The Complete Idiot's Guide to*
    Handwriting Analysis

"Baby Shark is a smart, spirited page-turner about a young woman out for revenge—it's not for girliegirls."
    —Jill Diamond, Chair, North American Boxing Federation
    Women's Division

"Robert Fate has created characte
all the darkness, *Baby Shark* is ul
ment to the resiliency of the hum
    —Richard Walter, *Escape Fror*

BABY SHARK

BABY SHARK

ROBERT FATE

CAPITAL CRIME PRESS
FORT COLLINS, COLORADO

Copyright © 2006 by Robert F. Bealmear

First edition published in the United States by Capital Crime
Press. Printed in Canada. Cover design by Nick Zelinger.

Capital Crime Press is a registered trademark.

Library of Congress Catalog Card Number: 2006920762
ISBN-13: 978-0-9776276-9-1
ISBN-10: 0-9776276-9-1

www.capitalcrimepress.com

For Fern

My deepest appreciation to my comrades-in-arms Bruce Cook, Sheila Lowe, Gwen Freeman, and Bobbie Cimo for their willingness to share their time and expertise. And to Robin Bright for his loving and critical eye.

And thanks to Don Chastain whose affection for the good ol' cowboy ways has influenced my view of the time and place.

"Another girl might have given up, blocked it out of her memory…or just rolled over and died."

Otis Millett, PI, Fort Worth, Texas

1

October 1952

THE RUMBLE OF the machines stopped everything cold. No one spoke, but everyone knew what was next.

My dad was in the back of the room talking to Henry Chin, the owner of the place. He turned at the sound of the Harleys, we exchanged our glance, and I jammed my book in my jacket pocket.

Motorcycles didn't automatically mean trouble, but I was a seventeen-year-old girl, and my dad and I had been in enough poolrooms to know the law of averages.

The regulars knew the score. They racked their cues and prepared to leave.

As the men in black leather pushed into Henry's, I ignored their weathered faces and started for the door. But I was aware of their stares, the reek of sour sweat and tobacco, and the same old rude comments as they brushed past me.

I heard Henry's son Will call out, "We're closing, boys. Only time for one beer."

The bikers growled obscenities as the door closed behind me, and I was outside with the others who'd abandoned Henry's.

They pushed up their collars against the sharp night air and crunched gravel to their cars and trucks, not hurrying, not loitering either at that isolated crossroad. I beelined to the security of my dad's Cadillac, got in, and locked the door.

I nursed the last of the Dr Pepper I'd brought with me and watched across the way as a big rig lumbered out of the filling station onto the dark highway.

It headed west. Its colored lights outlined its shape as it moved away. It picked up speed, and soon was nothing more than a lightning bug in the long black distance.

Dad was taking a long time. I glanced over my shoulder and saw a shadow just before a big man broke into the car. Glass from the side window went everywhere.

He reached in, got the door open, and jerked me from the Cadillac. Sounds like firecrackers were coming from Henry's.

"Oh, Christ," I choked out, trying not to stumble, as the man dragged me by my ponytail.

I heard the crackle of more pistol shots and the earsplitting blast of a shotgun as he shoved me ahead of him, back into the old building. I took it in, the angry shouting, the acrid stench of gunpowder, someone falling, glass breaking. I took it all in fast.

Henry was sprawled face down on the floor, covered in blood. His son Will was slumped over the counter, his skull blown open, a smoking sawed-off shotgun near his lifeless hand.

A biker sat on the floor panting and whimpering, holding his guts in with both hands. Blood everywhere.

I saw my dad kick a scarecrow-thin guy in the groin so hard he never got up, and turning, he broke a cue across the face of a young guy with scraggly blond hair. The guy who'd dragged me in shoved me aside, grabbed my dad by his throat, and put a pistol to his head.

That brought things to a stop.

The only sounds were the whimpering from the biker who'd taken a load of buckshot in his belly and the pitiful soprano squeal coming from the guy holding his crotch.

I tried to control my shaking.

The blond guy, who had the stained hands of a mechanic, waved the shattered end of the cue, eager to attack my dad. But he waited. He snuffled blood and watched the sandy-haired guy with blue eyes.

The guy with blue eyes spoke to my dad in a voice that I would never forget. It was crude, bold, confident.

"You don't remember me, but I remember you in your baggy salesman suit and worn-down shoes. Your Coupe de Ville."

"Oh, I remember you," my dad said. "Never forget a brain that works as well as yours."

Blue Eyes said, "Think you can fool everybody like you just dropped in for a game. You're a fucking hustler. That's what you are."

"That might be so," my dad said. "While you're at it, look around at what you're doing here, genius. Is this the work of an intelligent human?"

"I was smart enough to know we'd meet up again. Sometime, somewhere. I knew I'd get you back for the way you screwed me over. The way you pretended to be surprised when you kept winning."

My dad smiled and responded in a voice so reasonable it surprised me. "If that's what this is about—my arrogance or my duplicity or my whatever—why take it out on these others? Let's shoot some pool. We won't quit until you say so."

The gut-shot biker let out a belch that pulled everyone's attention. He groaned and puked blood as he toppled over and died, his startled eyes wide open.

While the bikers all watched the show, Dad gave me a hard glance that told me to run. But I couldn't. I couldn't leave him.

When the leader of the thugs brought his attention back to my dad, he told the room, "The hustler says we should shoot some pool. He thinks he's in charge."

The bear of a man pushed his pistol hard into my dad's temple and displayed his yellow teeth as Blue Eyes took his time and looked at me.

"We'll shoot some pool all right," he said.

What I felt in the pit of my stomach was unlike anything I'd ever experienced. The gas station across the highway. I could run there.

"I know where there's a lot of money," my dad said. "I can take you to it. Let's talk."

"See? There you go again," Blue Eyes said. "Thinking I'm just a poor hick. It was never the money. I've always had more money than I need, and that's all the talk you get."

The man with blue eyes lifted his chin a fraction of an inch, and the longhaired mechanic wailed like a lunatic as he rammed the broken cue stick into my dad's chest. The big bear of a man stepped away from the erupting blood, and fired his pistol in the air as if he were starting a race. My father exhaled a loud groan and collapsed.

When I screamed, the bikers all turned and stared at me.

"He lived and died by the cue," Blue Eyes said.

They caught me before I could reach the door and dragged me back. I fought them, tried to keep them from hitting me, but there was no stopping them. There was no getting away.

I saw them, though in some way it wasn't me. I saw each of them as they held me down and used me the way they wanted. The way they grunted over me and knocked me around in the glare of the billiard table lights, the three of the four thugs that still could, there among the carnage in Henry Chin's Poolroom.

There was laughter. Noises rang in my ears. Would they ever stop hitting me? I slipped in and out of consciousness. My head was swimming. It was like being under water. No, I wasn't under water. I was choking on blood, and I had to wake up. I had to wake up.

I knew where I was when I came out of it.

I was on the floor, and it was strangely silent. There was fire, and the dirty yellow smudges that I could see tracing soft arcs through the thick gray smoke were the lights at Henry's, slowly swinging above his tables.

2

"SHE'S SEVENTEEN GOING on thirty," I'd heard my dad tell someone.

"And how do you suppose that happened?" I'd asked him later. "You think being on the road with you, hanging out at pool halls all over Texas had anything to do with it?"

"Get your feathers down, Baby. Maybe I only meant you're better read than most college graduates," he'd said, using that smile.

Life on the road wasn't the kind of romance that made you younger—sleeping in the back seat of a car, brushing your teeth at gas stations. Even with all that, I loved my dad, and I'd dare anyone to try and take him away from me.

Seventeen going on thirty.

What did age have to do with anything, anyway? It was experience that made the difference, if the Devil really was in the details.

During a year and a half on the road with a pool hustler—t-bones when we won and baloney when we lost—I'd learned to keep an eye out for the details. And I'd seen some stuff happen, too.

Never like that night at Henry Chin's Poolroom, though. That night changed my life.

At the hospital in Abilene I was in more pain than I'd ever felt. Sounds hurt. *Cover my ears*, I wanted to say. *Make everyone shut up*, I would've said if I could've gotten my mouth to work.

They stuck me with a needle.

Silent, bursting colors. I'm on the floor and they're dragging me. I'm crawling and they're laughing. They're laughing and kicking me. I wake up and there's fire. Henry's face is dripping blood and his mouth moves without sound. I see my father's lifeless eyes, open, unseeing. When I cry out and try to run, the nurses hold me, and their bodies become misshapen and their arms engulf me, swallow me until I'm too weak to fight, and nothing is being done about my hearing.

When I came out of it many hours later, I found that one of my ears, though bruised and sore, had recovered from the beating. I would suffer diminished hearing in the other. My broken jaw had to be wired and held in place until it could heal.

The wiring, the loss of several teeth, and my lacerated gums made talking impossible. Added to forced silence, I had cracked ribs, a broken nose, and my eyes were battered shut. When I moved, I hurt. Hell, when I blinked, I hurt.

When the puffiness around my eyes subsided, I was allowed to see my bruised and stitched, discolored and swollen face. I didn't ask for a mirror again while I was in the hospital. A surgeon told me to come back and see him about the scars. He said he could erase them.

It wasn't that I'd been so beautiful. No one wants a scarred face. A nurse told me that I could fix my pretty blonde hair over the damaged part of my ear. Boxers called what I had a cauliflower ear. No one said they could do anything about that.

So what. I would just cover it with my pretty hair. The scars that mattered didn't show, anyway.

Everyone had a morbid story to tell that was supposed to help me get past witnessing my dad's murder. The stories were useless. All I had to do was close my eyes to see and hear it all again.

I understood what they were getting at: not letting the experience color everything in my life, not blaming myself because I survived, the things they'd read in books to tell others. It was always about losing my father, though. Nobody ever mentioned me losing myself to a gang of rapists.

Nobody ever mentioned that.

The gang had torn and bruised me during their assault. And through the drugs and through the ringing of my damaged hearing, I still heard things that first night.

"They used something. My God, look," a voice said.

"A stick, maybe," another voice said.

With all that the gang did to me during their depraved attack, they didn't give me any diseases. I heard a nurse from between my ankles. "I don't have *that* to deal with," she said. "Now, if she's just not in a family way."

If I was such a burden to her, why didn't she leave me alone? I wanted everyone to leave me alone. But no such luck.

A slump-shouldered, tough-looking Abilene police detective came to see Henry Chin, who was recovering down the hall. Afterwards they came to see me.

The detective's name was Hansard, and he was cursed with a plain, square face, dull eyes, and a cheap suit. He wasn't married. A wife would have thrown that suit out years ago.

"Her name's Van Dijk?" he asked Henry.

"That her name," Henry said without difficulty

"And her first name?" Detective Hansard asked.

"Kristin," Henry mangled with his Chinese accent.

Who knows what the detective scribbled in his little notebook.

Henry looked over and nodded at me. He had limped down to visit many times over the past week, and we'd agreed he could call me Baby like my dad used to, since Kristin was so hard for him to say.

Detective Hansard smelled like a beer joint at closing time and had a way of curling his lips and shifting his gaze around from below the brim of his disgusting old fedora that failed to inspire my trust. He asked questions about the killings but said nothing about the assault.

At first, I thought it was because the murders were more important or that talking about something sexual made him uneasy.

But I began to get it.

"Why was she there?" he asked. "Wasn't that late for her to be there?"

He believed that a girl my age in a pool hall late at night was just asking for it. I realized that the nurses thought that, too. But Hansard was the guy that brought it into focus. He was the spokesman for the angels of mercy.

Hell, I should've known better than to go and get myself raped. I felt very alone, more alone than I had ever felt in my life.

"I don't wanna give you false hopes," the detective mumbled.

"False hopes?" Henry asked.

"Yeah," he said. "There're a lot of motorcycle gangs out there. They move around, and they move fast."

"You not go after them?"

English may have been his second language, but Henry recognized sidestepping when he heard it.

"They kill son. Kill her father. Bad to her. Look her face," he said.

But Hansard had seen my face when he walked in. He didn't want to look at it again.

"They didn't leave us much to go on, burning the place down and all," he said. He dropped his pencil stub into a limp jacket pocket and closed his greasy little notebook.

"Give you name gang," Henry said.

"Say again," the detective mumbled.

He'd heard Henry just fine. Hell, *I'd* heard Henry just fine.

"The gang name Lost Demons," Henry said more loudly.

"Yeah, we got that, and there're some fire investigators looking into the incident, too. And the insurance company's already been around. Not much left of the bodies, though."

Bodies? My dad and Henry's son weren't bodies, they were human beings murdered by thugs.

Detective Hansard curled his lip at Henry and gazed just past him.

"Yeah, Mister Chin, that was good, you giving us the name of the gang. You think of anything else, you give me a call, huh? We're gonna try and find them, bring them in."

Uh huh. A two-bit pool hall got torched. A Chinese guy, a biker punk, and a pool hustler got murdered. And another Chinese guy and a teenage slut got what they deserved because they were stupid enough to be there.

Detective Hansard was going to send out an all points alert and put men on overtime. Bring those animals in.

I turned my bandaged ear toward him.

Henry did nothing to disguise his anger, either. The instant that Hansard left, he whispered in my good ear, "No police justice. Henry know more ways one skin cat."

3

I WASN'T REALLY thirty. So I had to provide the name and address of a relative before the hospital would discharge me. That was why the Greyhound ticket I was given the day I checked out was to Oklahoma City. That ticket and a form I signed relieved the hospital of any liability when releasing a minor.

Henry picked me up at the curb in front, like we'd planned. I couldn't talk yet, my face was still wired together. I could write notes, though, and Henry could read as well as the next guy.

I got into his old pickup truck, and we headed off to his place, a half section of Texas prairie out northwest of Sweetwater.

"Long drive," Henry said.

I shrugged. So what.

Many miles later, we left the highway and followed a single telephone line that scalloped between skinny poles out into some flat, dry brush acreage dotted with mesquite and creased by arroyos.

"Homestead," Henry said.

I looked around. It wasn't the end of the world, but you could see it from there. Henry told me the county originally graded the rutted dirt road that led to his place to go to an oil well site several miles past him.

"Wildcat man drill after war. Never pay off," he said.

"Only people make mistake come down this road."

Henry had a way with words.

"Where aunt live?" he asked.

I showed him my ticket to Oklahoma City.

"You not go there?"

He saw no in my eyes.

"You stay here long as like, Baby Girl."

Good. I knew that I would never go stay with Aunt Dora. It was enough that I knew I was soiled goods. I didn't need her reminding me that no decent man would ever have me.

Henry looked concerned.

He put his finger to his lips and said, "Henry Chinaman and you young white girl. This Texas, you know."

Hell yes, I knew. And I didn't care if he came from Mars. I owed Henry Chin my life.

I tried picturing it, since at five-seven I was taller than Henry, and at one twenty-five, I weighed as much as he did. How he managed to drag me from the fire, put me in his truck, and get me to the hospital was a mystery.

He did those things with a fractured skull, cracked ribs, a bullet lodged in his thigh, and who knew what else?

That first day at his place, he said, "Build *hacienda* for Will. Now Baby Girl live in long as want."

Henry's homestead was a shallow pond, a stand of large pecan trees with limbs loaded with paper shells, and a scattering of even larger cottonwoods that served as a windbreak and shade for his tile-roofed adobe buildings: a thick-walled main house, a woodworking shop, a big, barn-like garage, and the little *hacienda* that was set back away from the main house.

The landscaping was a cement birdbath, a stretch of corral fencing, and a string of windblown, gnarled jacaranda trees out by the county road.

Months later I would climb the windmill that stuck up over a square cement tank of water and stare out at even more prairie and tiny, distant oil derricks. I knew out there somewhere was the edge of the earth.

Out at Henry's there was a winter silence that happened after the motor in the shop kicked off, the electricity shut down, and the breeze quit making the windmill squeak and the trees rattle. That silence was deafening. I'd sweat through it every night.

When sleep did come, it was fitful, and with my good ear toward the distant county road. And when I woke with a start at some nightmare hour hearing the frantic squeal of coyotes or the low hoot of hunting owls, it was a relief in comparison to listening for things that I was afraid I wouldn't hear until it was too late.

I reached a nervous truce with myself during those first few weeks at Henry's. I struggled for the belief that I was safe, though I never stopped listening for the horrors that can come for you out of the darkness.

Death showed up unannounced. I had seen that for myself. After the dust settled you were among the living, or you were *shit outta luck*, as a girlfriend of mine used to say. I wondered if I'd ever see her again.

I slept for days that turned into weeks, getting up to suck meals through a straw before easing my throbbing head, sore ribs, and aching pelvis back to bed, where I relived the brutal laughing faces and relentless hard fists in my nightmares.

I asked about the time passing.

Henry tugged at his old straw hat and said, "You have appointment somewhere? You sleep. Sometime you wake up. We talk."

The days passed. I saw his limp disappear and watched the bandages come away from his wounds. He carried angry scars from the pistol-whipping. I felt sorry for him.

When I thought about my scars, I felt sorry for me, too. I feared how I would look someday when the bones were set, the bruising was healed, and all the surgery was history.

Those days when I woke to take the pills that eased my pain, I heard Henry in his shop, his tools humming. I believe that what sleep did for me, work did for him. Together, without hurrying, we got our strength back for living.

The first trips I made away from Henry's were after Christmas in late December.

"We go Abilene. Meet plastic surgeon," Henry told me. "Next month, we go Lubbock. Meet dental surgeon. Soon Baby Girl know all surgeons in Texas."

Henry also found me a woman doctor in Lubbock for the other stuff, an older woman with thick glasses, and a prudish manner. Her office was as quiet as a gallows, but less cheerful.

My medical visits ran a close second in level of pain to being beaten. After a few visits to the doctors, I hated my attackers even more for putting me through all that. Getting my nose to resemble the way it once looked, holding still and keeping silent with my feet in stirrups, and unwiring my jaw were the high points. It was all downhill after that.

Henry claimed that I should be happy with the plastic surgery that was used to remove the facial scarring.

"I'm happy," I said. "I'm thrilled with little pink lines here and there all over my face."

"Make face more interesting," Henry said and slapped his knee and laughed.

So much for feeling sorry for myself. We checked our post box in Lubbock, and I had a reply to my letter to Aunt Dora.

"She said an insurance man paid her a visit. He was asking questions about the fire."

"Why he bother aunt?" Henry asked.

"He was looking for me. She doesn't say why. She's embarrassed about not knowing where I am."

"Good thing she not know," Henry said. "It secret where Baby Girl stay."

Henry was right. She didn't need to know where I was. I

didn't want to talk to anyone, anyway. I was still weeks and a lot of dental work away from comfortable speech.

"Heal body," Henry said. "Make face new. Think about future."

He was right. I *did* have some decisions to make about the direction of my life.

And riding back from Lubbock the day Henry told me to think about the future, I began dreaming about shooting pool. That was an odd thing for me to think about, I suppose. I guess all that time on the road with my dad had gotten the game into my blood. It was strange in one regard and good in another.

At least I was thinking about something other than that night.

"Bad, yes. Maybe could be worse," Henry said, referring to the night of the fire.

That was probably true, but unless I could be who I was before the attack, it was a stretch for me to get philosophical. However, Henry was being more specific than I realized.

"We survive, so we witness, too," Henry said. "Gang think witness make trouble. We lay low."

"Lay low?"

"Charlie Chan say on radio."

"Uh huh. So if the gang finds out we're alive—"

"Not good. We lay low."

"Jesus, Henry. We have to hide from those bastards? What a way to live."

"Hide okay long as not give up."

Henry had gotten us pistols.

"Put under pillow."

"I don't know about guns, Henry."

"Point, pull trigger," he said. "Not hard learn that."

"I'm not sure about having a loaded gun around."

"Not around all time. Only in bed."

"Oh, only in bed. That's different. You just want me to sleep with it."

"Sure thing. Learn point and shoot, too."

Henry was saying I wasn't safe there. I was just hiding out. So, sleeping with a stinky piece of oily metal didn't seem as far-fetched an idea as it first appeared.

He showed me the basics of how to hold and shoot a Colt .38, and I took it to bed with me that very night.

Before going to sleep, I thought of Henry saying he had done his best to protect Will. He knew my dad had done his best to protect me, too. And in the end it wasn't enough, was it?

"Now, get a good night's rest," I told myself.

4

February 1953

ONE MORNING IN early February with the sky slate-gray and the air smelling of rain, Henry said he wanted to take me someplace.

"Show where father rest," Henry said.

We drove over to Sweetwater and visited some modest granite stones that were assembled beneath a line of old oaks beside a tiny wood frame church. It was where Henry's wife, Lilly, was buried. It was where he buried Will and my dad, too.

My dad being planted so close to a house of the Lord was a churlish twist of fate. Grow up, I told myself, Dad's beyond worrying about that.

While Henry arranged stalks of pussy willow that he'd brought, I stared at Dad's headstone, wondering at not having any feelings. *Marvin Van Dijk*, it said in crisp Gothic lettering. *1913-1952*. I hadn't cried at my mom's funeral, and I didn't cry that day at my dad's gravesite.

My mom told me once, "Don't make tears like an actress. You'll cry when you're supposed to."

I wondered when that would be.

As I stood there, the sounds of that horrible night, the brutal laughter, the gunfire came back to me as it so often did. I saw my Dad's lifeless eyes staring across the bloody floor at Henry's Poolroom, and I knew that might be the strongest picture that I ever had of him. I cursed my memory for that.

The cold made my face ache. Henry appeared at my side and said, "Rain soon. We go."

As we drove away, I tried to add it up. My father was a pool hustler with literary tastes and a new Cadillac. He died in a pool hall fight and damned near took me with him. Maybe he was with Mom now, or maybe he would just always be in that patch of ground back there. Either way, he'd for sure left me for the last time.

"I don't want to come here again for a while," I said.

"Don't have to," Henry replied and pretended not to notice when I looked back.

The dust from our truck had obscured the little white church and its yard, leaving only a tangle of dark oak limbs reaching upward through the billowing grit.

Reaching for what?

I didn't look back again.

Later that afternoon, after the rain stopped, I was snooping around and found Dad's Cadillac in Henry's garage. The window the thug had broken had been fixed; it was clean and waxed and had that fine layer of dust that everything in West Texas seemed to have.

My heart rate picked up as I moved around it, looking in. When I opened the door and leaned in, the scent of my dad raised the hairs on my neck.

I almost finished high school in that car—did finish more books than most people read in a lifetime. I slept plenty of nights in there, wrapped in a blanket while Dad drove.

I'd wake up in different places, not knowing if it would be somewhere we'd been before, or somewhere new. I was grumpy sometimes, but overall I liked the adventure of travel. I'd lift up mornings and peer out to see where we were. Once, without meaning to, we parked the night in a roadside graveyard.

Sometimes in little towns Dad would park us in front of a hotel or a restaurant, and I'd get out ahead of him. I'd have breakfast by myself and read the morning paper like an old geezer.

"By your own self this morning, dear?" waitresses would ask.

"Yes, Ma'am."

"Where're your folks, honey?"

I was sixteen when Mom died.

Dad sold everything we owned and bought that new Cadillac: bright red with a white top. He gave me the choice of moving to Oklahoma City and living with Mom's older sister, or going on the road with him. He said he'd send me an allowance if I chose Aunt Dora.

"You're kissing me off, aren't you? Getting rid of me. I'm just a kid you can handle with postcards from anywhere you chalk a cue."

"I love you more than I've ever loved anything in my life."

"That won't get you out of this one," I told him.

"I understand you're angry and upset, Baby. But I'm not gonna tell you what to do about this. Your mother wasn't supposed to die before you were grown." He sighed. "She did, though, and here we are. You know? Here we are."

"Uh huh," I said.

"Do you wanna be with Dora in the suburbs? Dresses and dances, ball games and pep rallies, boys and cars?"

"Church three times a week."

"Okay, that, too. And maybe that's better than hanging out in smoky, dull-ass pool halls watching me hustle a tax-free living."

"Why do you do it, Dad?"

"So I can travel around, see this country, listen to jazz,

read a book when I want to. When I was in a foxhole being shot at, that's what I decided I was gonna do. And you know, Baby, I like doing it. Someone told me the sole difference between a rut and the grave is the depth."

"That's got to be a Burma Shave sign."

"Or maybe it's gospel," he said.

Like he knew gospel.

"Sooner than you think, you're gonna be making your own life," he said.

I couldn't tell if he was trying to sell me something or sell himself something, and in the end it didn't matter. I made my decision, and less than a day later we were on the road.

My dad—

I could see him in my mind's eye, his Scandinavian features, his platinum hair cut short, his reading glasses down on his nose, his lanky body turned sideways, leaning against the driver's door, an existentialist French paperback in his hand.

"Listen to this," he would say before reading aloud some flawlessly turned phrase.

His jazz LPs and player would be in the trunk, along with god only knew how many books and a lot of my personal stuff. I missed his music. The things in the car would help make Henry's *hacienda* into my home.

I slid my hand over the taillight fin as I walked around to the back to open the trunk.

A shape pulled my eyes away. Nearby, there was a tarp covering something. I caught my breath and carefully removed the canvas.

It was a Harley. I held my breath for real when I saw the emblem on it.

Lost Demons.

My heart slammed against my ribs. I felt clammy all over. My nerves began itching. I backed up and sat against the Caddy fender until I got it. The one Will killed. Sure. The biker who tried to hold his guts in. They couldn't take his motorcycle with them, and somehow Henry had ended up with it.

I stared at the machine until my heart settled down; my breathing came back to normal. The next thing was to get myself over to the woodshop.

"Brought home evidence," Henry told me. "Neighbor across road push away from fire. He good man. Push away you father car, too. Keep safe. Police never ask. No one think to ask. Motorcycle belong man murder Will. Now mine."

"What do you mean, evidence?"

"Got license. You see? Find things. Lead to others," Henry said.

My heart jumped.

"What things? What're you talking about?"

"We go in house. Talk how find more evidence."

He turned off his machines, and we went inside to sit at the kitchen table and talk.

Henry said he didn't understand why the police weren't going to take action. But they weren't, and he wasn't willing to accept that. He wanted to find the murderers, even if the police didn't.

I said, "You think I don't want those bastards caught? I do. Let's face it, though, it's not like you know anything about how to find murderers, Henry."

"You sleep for long time. I go Fort Worth, hire man Chinese friend know. He Eyes."

"Eyes? You mean private eye? An investigator?"

"Like Sam Spade on radio. Take license number, find name, address. He watch for others. Eye Man see where killers go."

My skin began to crawl.

"You know where they are. The guys that—"

"Murder family?" Henry finished for me.

"Yeah," I said.

"Know little now. Know more later."

"He watches all the time? This Sam Spade of yours?"

"All time," he confirmed.

"My god. That must cost a fortune."

"No, be surprised how little. My Will, you father worth much more."

"So, what do you do with the information?" I asked him. "Tell that worthless slug Detective Hansard so he can wipe his butt with it?"

"You bad mouth for young girl."

I did have a bad mouth, didn't I?

Hell, I thought of my attackers every day. I saw their faces, heard their voices. I knew them by the names I'd given them: Scarecrow, Mechanic, Blue Eyes, and Bear. I could imitate the way they moved. I practiced in whispers what I'd say to them, do to them, if they were in the dirt at my feet, helpless.

Henry had put it on the table. He had done something, hired someone to get names, addresses. He said he wanted to do more than that. He knew he had no police skills and no talent for defending himself.

"Others learn. Why not Henry learn?"

He said that if he didn't make an effort to bring the gang to justice for what they had done to us, it would never happen.

"We always sorry and killers go free," he said.

"For sure that Detective Hansard's never going to do anything," I threw in.

"Fish or cut bait," he told me.

I must have appeared surprised.

"Hear Jack Benny say that. You hungry? Fix chops, open can cream corn. Eat supper early. We talk more."

Henry was right. Maybe it was time to fish or cut bait.

"Start roll ball with Eye," he said.

"If I got a chance to put them in jail or hurt them, I would. But I don't know how to fight back. How the hell do you do that?"

Henry saw how agitated I'd become.

"You find out things sometimes, talk on phone. That all Baby Girl do."

Uh huh. He reminded me of my dad trying to sell me one of his bill-of-goods.

Henry said some of the self-defense skills that he wanted to learn were skills that he felt would help me with my confidence. So, as long as he was studying, why shouldn't I study, too?

Where was that going?

"Learn protect self. Sleep better nights."

Henry went on as if I had agreed.

"We learn things. Find out things," he said.

He slid a skillet onto the stove.

"Men make careers out of knowing these things, Henry. How're we supposed to make that happen?"

My jaw was starting to ache from all the talking.

"Like make anything happen, Baby Girl. Start with stick of wood—work, work. Soon have house."

I wanted to believe him, but his idea seemed far-fetched. He put a pile of carrots and a paring knife on the table.

"Peel carrots, drink Dr Pepper, unless face hurt too much."

As we prepared supper, Henry told me about the thirty thousand dollar policy that Will had taken out on their little billiard parlor. He said a man from the insurance company had come to the house and settled the matter with him during those first weeks while I was sleeping.

He put his finger to his lips.

"Insurance man ask about Baby Girl. 'Where girl from pool hall?' Insurance man ask. 'What girl?' Henry ask back. 'What girl in pool hall?'"

"You suppose he was the same insurance man who spoke to Aunt Dora?"

"Maybe. But why? Money already paid," he said.

"That is strange, isn't it? The money's been paid, and they're still looking for me."

"He say he need answer about fire. Maybe that why go see you aunt." He shrugged to change the subject. "Important thing money in bank now. Insurance money help find killers."

"I have insurance money, too, Henry. My Mom's *and* my Dad's."

"That money for future. You keep. Use fire insurance money find killers."

Henry wanted to track down the murderers. That was clear.

"I fix that gang so you sleep okay. We both sleep after fix gang."

I thought I knew what he meant by *fix,* and *fix* was fine with me. But it seemed a long way from where we were right then.

"Good plan make good job. We move when know how. No matter how long take. Maybe not long. You see."

I said, "All right. I'll help with the search. I'll do the things you've been talking about because I want those bastards caught and punished."

"You study self-defense?" he asked.

What was I supposed to do? Disappoint the man who saved my life?

"Sure. I'll do that," I said.

Instead of an expression of encouragement or satisfaction, or whatever it was that I was expecting, Henry's face crinkled into a grimace. Was he going to cry?

Holy Christ!

Some ferocious, deep-seated thing within him came to the surface and stared out at me. I wanted to back away. I couldn't. I was seated, frozen at the table.

Henry Chin was exposing his burning hatred like a monster that was hidden within him. There was something volatile in there, something that I had never seen before. And just as that other Henry had come, he was gone, and the Henry I knew was back.

He went on as if it had never happened. "We make list, add, subtract. Time pass in good way, we learn so much. We show we very much alive. Some people maybe sorry we so much alive."

Maybe some people would be.

One thing was sure clear to me. My life was about to change again.

5

I SAW HENRY through the window, hurrying out to the *hacienda* to get me. I met him at the door.

"Phone call," he said. "Long distance."

Harlan has finally returned my call, I thought as I hustled into the parlor of the main house. The telephone set on one of Henry's beautiful walnut side tables, one of the pieces of Mission style living room furniture he'd built in his shop next door.

"Where've you been?" I said as soon I picked up the receiver.

"Back east on business, Kristin. I'm sorry I haven't been in touch."

"I miss you," I said.

"I understand," Harlan replied.

I could hear the hurt in his voice.

"Henry told me everything a while back. I'm almost finished here. I won't be too much longer."

"When?"

"Next month."

"Come sooner. I need to talk to you about something," I said.

"What?" he asked.

"I've been thinking about shooting pool."

"Shooting pool," he repeated, his voice noncommittal.

"Yeah. I want you to give me some instruction."

"How do you mean?"

"I want to learn to shoot well enough to earn my living at it," I said.

"That's quite a commitment."

He wasn't sure it was a good idea. I could hear it in his voice.

"You know I'm not bad with a stick. I think I could learn to be real good if you'd work with me."

"Hey, I don't wanna discourage you."

"I'm not full grown yet."

"Besides that, shooting pool's a man's game. Hell, you of all people know what pool halls are like. They're no place for girls."

I toughened my voice.

"I'm past that. Hell, Harlan, you're the last person I thought would be stuffy about this. What difference does it make what I am if I shoot like a pro?"

"Like a pro," he repeated.

He sounded like Henry learning new phrases. I could hear the wheels starting to turn in that con man's head.

"Hmmm. You could be right," he said.

"You'll think about it?"

"Won't hurt to think about it. I do recall you being pretty darn good when we were shooting around. I saw you beat your dad more'n once."

"Not very often, but I have a good eye. You know I do. I miss the life, Harlan. I'd like to get back into it."

"You would, huh? Let me talk to Henry," he said.

"Get over here soon," I told him.

I handed the phone to Henry, and left the house.

I was shivering by the time I got back to the *hacienda* where I had a fire burning. I got into bed, pulled the covers up, and watched the flickering firelight on the ceiling. I'd planted the seed, now we'd see what grew.

I kept hearing Harlan's voice as I thought about my dad.

We had been way the hell over in El Paso, the single time I was ever in that city. At Fred Carson's. Nine tables. Framed pictures of national parks on the walls.

I'd been to see that handsome Gary Cooper in *High Noon*. When I got back, Dad was still at it with the stocky cowboy he was shooting with when I left. A big-boned guy on his way to fifty in a black sweat-stained Stetson, a weathered face, wistful, pale gray eyes.

"I work a spread over south of Salt Flat," I heard him tell my dad.

He walked, talked, and dressed like a working cowboy and it didn't matter. Dad wasn't buying it. So, of course, I was suspicious of him, too.

After a few more games, he and my dad put away their cues, and we went over to a place called Bishop's to eat. At supper, we learned that Harlan wasn't a cowboy at all. He was a traveling salesman for Coca-Cola.

My dad laughed. "You're a salesman pretending to be a cowpoke."

"That's no worse than you pretending to be a salesman," Harlan said.

"I guess not," my dad allowed. "After it's all said and done, we're just pool hustlers doing what we do."

Harlan had been a pilot during the war, and now he flew a Piper Cub.

"I put her down wherever I want. All I need's a flat patch of land or a stretch of macadam," he told us.

"How do you find time for billiards?" my dad asked. "With your sales job for the beverage company?"

Harlan winked at me.

"He means pool and pop. Your dad likes high-falutin' words."

To my dad, he said, "I make time. Just like you do. I make time." •

They struck a deal over lamb chops that night.

They agreed to show up places and hustle games as a team. They had it figured out how they could score big. I became the navigator, since Dad and I had to be at certain locations on a schedule to meet up with Harlan. I also did a lot of the driving.

Those were fun times. We made a couple of bucks, and Harlan, the con man, kind of became my uncle. Watching him operate taught me a lot of things about how people believed what they wanted to believe.

And here I was. I wanted to learn to shoot pool, and Henry wanted me to learn self-defense. I decided to do both because I was beginning to see things stretching out ahead of me. I was learning that life's little twists of fate could be like opportunities that I might not get twice.

There was a breeze up the day Sarge came to call, hazy sun and nippy. So the pup he had with him didn't mind being held and stayed calm when he was pushed into my arms.

"His name's Jim and he's yours. No discussion," Sarge said.

We were standing out by the shop, all of us dressed for the weather. I was in my cowboy boots, long johns beneath my Levi's, a work shirt over a turtleneck, a black sheepskin jacket, and an old black wool stocking cap of Will's that I found and learned to love.

Sarge was a construction foreman and looked like one. Khaki pants, work shirt, plaid jacket. Strong jaw, suntanned face, thinning sun-bleached hair. He had lean muscles from hard work, and he moved like...sort of on his toes, like he could be quick if he needed to be.

Before he parachuted into France on D-Day, he'd been an Army close-quarters combat instructor. He must've been in his thirties somewhere.

He said, "I thought you'd sleep better if you had a dog. He's no bigger than a minute right now, but he'll get there."

Jim was an eight-week-old fluffy pile of fur with sweet breath. I held him close and could feel his rapid little heart beat in the palm of my hand.

After the puppy transfer was settled, Sarge said, "How do your ribs feel?"

"Much better," I told him.

"Hurt when you take a deep breath?"

"Not much anymore."

"Can you put your hands over your head?"

"I still feel it a little when I do that," I said.

The way he looked at me made me feel like a bug being examined.

"Your other wounds. Hurt when you walk?"

He must know everything.

"I'm pretty much over that," I told him.

"How far out to the wildcat hole, Henry?"

"Three mile."

Sarge locked his green eyes on me until I spoke up.

"You want me to walk to the oil well?"

"Think you can?"

"That too far," Henry said.

"Maybe," Sarge said. "Won't know till she tries it."

He stared at me again without speaking, until I realized that it was his way.

"I'll walk out there," I said.

"That's the idea. You don't have to go all the way, just as far as you can. Then come on back in. Go mornings and again later. Swing your arms. You know. When you can get to the old well and back, call me."

"You show us?" Henry asked Sarge. Without waiting for an answer, Henry said to me, "He show us."

Sarge looked me up and down before he asked, "You're how old?"

"I'll be eighteen in July."

"You're tall enough. You play any sports?"

"Used to. Basketball. Volleyball. Swimming."

To Henry, he said, "We'll put some muscle on'er, she'll do fine. Of course she has to get'er ribs back first."

He asked Henry to put up a shaded area so that when we got started we could work outside without being in the weather. Henry said he would.

"And maybe an old square of carpet if it's a big one."

"Buy special," Henry assured him.

We crunched over to Sarge's truck through the fresh gravel that Henry dumped each year in anticipation of the wet weather. Sarge gave us some Army pamphlets that had drawings showing different moves and strategies.

Henry reminded him not to tell anyone what we were doing.

"Oh, I agree to that. Who needs to know I'm teaching—." He paused. "What're we calling it? Self-defense?"

That was the first time I saw Sarge smile.

"Nobody business what Baby Girl and Henry do," Henry pointed out.

"How does that jaw feel?" Sarge said as we stood by his truck.

I didn't realize until after they were there that my fingertips had gone to the scars.

"Still some dental work to finish up. It's pretty much healed," I said.

He pulled himself in behind the wheel, slammed the door, and spoke to Henry out the window as if I weren't there.

"She doesn't seem to be a whiner."

Henry shook his head. "She never whine. She seventeen go on thirty."

That made my heart turn over.

"Good," Sarge said to Henry. To me he said, "Don't spoil that mutt."

I shifted Jim's weight and squeezed him tighter to me. "What kind of dog is he?" I asked.

"German shepherd," Sarge said. "He's got some growing up to do."

Sarge was the first of my teachers. He showed up twice a week to instruct me in fight strategy and body movement and what he called *close work,* the use of various concealed hand weapons.

In that cool, dispassionate way of his, he summed up what we were doing by saying,

"Sooner or later you'll be on the front line. That's when you want your actions to be automatic so you can keep your head clear and not waste moves. You'll get rid of the amateurs and reckless dopes pretty quick. The ones who know what they're doing, they're the ones you're keeping your head clear for. See what I mean? It's just a job, Little Miss, and whoever does the best job gets to go home. Going home. That's the incentive."

Sarge was the only person I'd ever met who referred to killing people as a job.

A month or so after starting with Sarge, I told Henry that I wanted to learn how to shoot, too. It was about numbers. I knew what it was like to be outnumbered. Pistols would be my backup if things started going south.

"Baby Girl have pistol. Point. Shoot."

"No, Henry. I want to learn the right way to do it. Do you know someone?"

"Henry know man back from Korea. He like vulture."

"What do you mean by that?"

"Albert smell blood like vulture. Kill people easy for Albert."

That put a chill up my back.

"I want to meet him," I said.

Less than a week later, Albert showed up.

It was the first day in quite a while it hadn't rained; water stood in puddles, the sky was clear, the air was cool. Jim was still just a puppy, of course, but he was a German shepherd, so he told me someone was coming.

I dog-eared my book and got outside to watch a new Lincoln sedan leave the county road and drive the quarter mile to where I waited. Red mud had streaked the tires and fender skirts of the low-slung, shiny black car.

The young man driving was alone. As he parked, I saw that he was Mexican, or at least at the time I thought he was.

He rolled down his window and spoke to me. His accent told me Spanish was his first language. "That's a big dog you got there."

My puppy was sitting at my feet.

I said. "May I help you?"

"My name is Albert Sun Man Ramirez. Henry here?"

"He told me you were coming. He's not back from town yet."

"When I get out, will the dog attack me?"

"Not unless I tell him to."

Albert opened the door and turned in the seat so he was facing out. Reaching back, he brought crutches up from where he kept them behind his seat. Putting them down in front of him, he pushed them into the gravel.

His movements weren't fast just smooth and deliberate. He was up and moving toward me before I saw that he was missing half of his left leg.

He flicked the door shut behind him almost without my noticing since most of my attention was on his flying motion, his long, loosely-cut dark brown leather coat, and the turquoise jewelry he wore everywhere.

Seeing the man's swinging movements and the flapping coat unnerved Jim who moved behind my legs.

Albert ground his one, hand-tooled, snakeskin boot into the gravel in front of me, and came to an erect stop with his crutches clamped under his arms, angled back out of his way. He looked me in the eye. We were the same height. I could smell whisky on his breath.

"You like my car? It's a V8. One hundred fifty-four horses under that hood, man. I could drive through the gates of hell with that car."

I glanced over, but brought my eyes back to him.

"Here. Take my keys."

I took his keys.

"I'll take those back."

I gave them back and wondered what that was about.

"So, what do you know about me?" he asked.

"Henry told me you're a Korean War veteran and that you're his friend."

"Okay, yeah, that's true, but what do you know about me now. Here. From meeting me just now?"

"I don't know what you mean."

"I'm missing a leg. Did you notice that?"

"Of course."

"I have *cojones*, did you notice that?"

I was a bug again, being examined.

"Okay, I get it. Your eyes are dark and don't tell me anything. You have a nice smile, but it's a tool you use. Your teeth are too white, too perfect. I think they're Government Issue."

"Anything else?"

"You've been drinking."

"I like you already, Little Sister. You see things and you can talk. Tell me this, which of my hands gave you my keys?"

I had to think, but he had no patience for that and answered his own question.

"My left, and you took them with your right. What does that tell you?"

"You're left-handed and I'm right-handed?"

"So, you know which hand goes for my pistol," he said.

"Why would I think you have a pistol?"

"In Texas everybody's got a pistol."

"Even so, why would you go for it?"

"Why not? Who's to say what's going to happen? People kill people in pool halls for not very big reasons. Don't you think?"

I was surprised at how indifferently he spoke of the deaths of my father and Henry's son. I could feel a pressure begin at my temples.

"Watch this," he said, and smooth as a jazz riff filled both his hands with guns.

He gave me a breath or two to grasp my situation. My heart was beating so hard I was certain that he could tell.

"Are you scared?"

"Yes."

"Because a man with pistols is a dangerous man?"

"Yes."

"Get over being scared, Little Sister. You're going to be the one with pistols from now on."

Albert Sun Man Ramirez was slender, almost delicate, with flawless light brown skin any woman would sell her soul for. He had a gleaming ducktail haircut, narrow shoulders, very fast hands. Maybe twenty-two. High forehead, straight narrow nose, girl-pretty mouth.

Who would have thought by looking at him that he was an efficient and remorseless killer? The Marine Corps gave him medals.

"Marines like Albert. War okay for him, except lose leg," Henry said.

Albert was angered by what happened to Henry and me, and the fierce loyalty that he felt toward his friends and the friends of his family was enough to bring him out to the homestead weekly for over six months.

He was the second of my teachers. He also taught Henry. He taught us everything there was to know about pistols.

"With pistols you have to see it before it starts," Albert told me in that excitable way he had of saying and doing everything.

"Like chess, Little Sister. He does that, you do this. Look everywhere at everything. When you're facing several men with weapons, always shoot first. Especially shoot first if they think you won't. Shoot the ones who look fast, then the others, and count your shots. Drop empty pistols, grab loaded ones, and when you start, don't stop until you've killed everything that moves. Don't stop for anything. And always, always know where you're going when it's over, and go there. Be on your way out the door while the hot cartridges are still bouncing around."

"I'm not going to go around killing people," I explained to Albert.

"That's what you say, Little Sister. That's what you say."

6

March 1953

A WEEK OR so after meeting Albert, Henry asked me to go over to Fort Worth with him to hear Otis Millett's first report. Otis was the private investigator Henry had hired.

A fierce wind came up on our way. Furious sheets of icy rain swept across us parallel to the slick road, making driving at times close to impossible.

It made the trip longer than usual with Henry leaning over the steering wheel, holding his face in a grimace, squinting through the windshield. But it didn't keep him from telling stories about Otis that he had heard from his Chinese friends.

"Eye Dallas cop one time. Big man. Muscles. Nose broken. Have big past include throw wife's lover on second story. Break window."

"He threw his wife's lover out a window?"

"Not kill. Lover land on drug store—"

"He landed on an awning?"

"Break leg. Not break neck."

Henry said that Otis destroyed the love nest, dragged his naked wife down to the street, and offered her to strangers until the police arrived and rescued her.

"Wife name Dixie," Henry told me. "She bleach hair."

The way I understood Henry's English, heavy drinking and further bad behavior led to Otis losing his job on the force. After a few years, he went on the wagon, settled down, obtained his license, and began confirming men's suspicions about their philandering wives.

"Cheating women Otis specialty," he said

"It's his *raison d'être*," I informed Henry, just as my Dad would have done.

"Eye keep mouth shut," Henry told me.

"He uses discretion," I suggested.

"That bring jobs to Eye."

The Millett Agency was an office/apartment that Otis kept upstairs from a Chinese restaurant in a nondescript brick building in a blue-collar section of the city. Otis often had his supper downstairs, and was there the night a couple of armed robbers tried to knock the place over.

Henry said that Otis took their shotgun away from them, beat them silly with it, and dumped them beside the road, far out of town.

"That's better'n a jail term in my books," Otis had told Henry. "They wake up somewhere out halfway to Waco, naked as jaybirds with nothing to their names besides head-aches, a mess of their fingers broken, and most of their teeth missing. They'll think twice about going back where that happened to them."

Henry told me that after Otis foiled that armed robbery *gratis* and without involving the police, the Chinese commu-nity took notice and began turning business his way. That was how Henry came to learn of him and how he became our *eye* in Fort Worth.

It was after six in the evening when we parked in the unpaved lot in back of Otis' building. We entered the back door of the restaurant, with the kitchen staff staring at us, and tracked mud up the worn wood back stairs and through the dingy upstairs hall.

Otis met us at his office door. At the time, I just thought

he'd heard us coming up the stairs. I was to learn that Otis had his tricks.

"Oughta park in front when it's pissing like this," he said.

Otis hung our dripping raincoats and Henry's soaked straw hat on hooks by the door and told us to make ourselves comfortable.

"There's a fresh deck of Luckies on the desk," he said.

Neither Henry nor I smoked cigarettes, but Henry had a pipe most evenings after supper. He'd stand out by the windmill, have his smoke, and stare toward the highway like he expected a late night visitor.

The lights in the private investigator's large, dull office were on early due to the weather. But I thought it was just gloomy in there, anyway. The one big window that might have allowed a little outside light was covered by dusty Venetian blinds. The place smelled of stale cigarettes, burnt coffee, and a myriad of other unidentifiable odors.

The hum and rattle of an antique electric fan on a tall stand came from the corner over past the desk. If the fan was supposed to help with the odors, it wasn't working.

The huge old cluttered desk with cigarette burns along the edges and the tired brown leather sofa and matching club chair should have been given to charity. Henry and I chose the straight-back chairs with the small table and filthy ashtray between them.

After we were seated, I noticed I could see into an adjoining room that looked equally as dreary. I saw the corner of a bed. And, reflected in a full-length mirror, I could see an open door on the other side of the room.

The life of a private eye appeared neither profitable nor exciting, and certainly not romantic.

"I work most nights," he said from where he was making coffee in a small area that had a disgusting sink, a refrigerator I'd have to be paid to open, and a small table with an electric hotplate.

Over his shoulder, he told us, "I don't get in till sunup. I reckon this is about as early I take appointments."

He looked as if he'd been in his clothes all day.

He was a fashion statement in thick-soled brown shoes and brown suit pants pulled up underneath his firm belly by a wide leather belt sporting a large and gaudy silver buckle. His limp white shirt had the collar open and the sleeves rolled into a mess half way up his big hairy forearms. Unbuttoned vest. Loosened tie with a dark flower pattern. Brown suspenders.

I'd read somewhere that a belt *and* suspenders indicated pessimism. We'd see. In our worn Levi's and muddy boots, Henry and I looked ready for a prayer meeting in comparison to Otis.

"Here's what I know," he told us as he turned his back on his boiling coffee, stuck a cigarette in his mouth, snapped a match with his thumbnail, and lit up.

"I find an address for Mr. Procter. That's Lamar Procter, the criminal whose motorcycle you ended up with. The address is easy to come by. Don't mean squat. He ain't lived in that rat-infested claptrap for years."

He kept talking as he moved over and took a squeaky seat behind his desk.

"So I ask around. Get another location. Ask around. Go to some other places. Waste a few days asking around. I run into a guy at a bike shop that knew him. He says the bikers Procter rides with ain't been around for a while. Always on the road, he says. I say it's an insurance matter. There's some money coming to him. That should open it up some maybe. Still nothing yet."

He squeaked back in his chair and blew a stream of smoke at the ceiling. His shoulder holster with the butt of a big automatic bulging out of it was hung on the corner of his chair. The heavy thing swung around as he rocked forward to study us a moment before going on.

"This ain't gonna happen like going to the store for something, Hank. These guys ain't interested in being found.

That's why it's good you're in for the long haul."

"We long haul," Henry confirmed.

"And how're you doing?" he asked me.

"How do you mean, Mister Millett?" I responded.

"Otis. I hate formalities."

"Otis it is."

"What I meant was, you got pushed around, I understand."

I guess everybody's got his own picture of how that went down. Otis was giving me such a once over I had to think that seeing me in person was helping him fill in some blanks. He could try all he wanted. He'd never know what it was like.

"That's behind me," I said.

Hell, let's say it wasn't behind me, would I tell *him*? Henry trusted him. I barely knew him. It was quiet in his office except for the old standing fan, which made me wonder why he even needed a fan the way he flapped his mouth. I wasn't certain I even liked Henry's Sam Spade guy.

"Thanks for asking," I added in a pleasant voice.

"Good manners put people at ease," my mom always said. I always took at ease to mean off their guard.

Otis dragged a little spiral notebook from his pocket. Must be a police staple. It was the same kind used by Hansard, the detective in the hospital. While Otis thumbed a few pages, going over his notes, I glanced at his coffee boiling away. He started up again.

"Yep. I talk to a muscle man with a tattoo of Pudgy Stockton on his shoulder. He thinks this Procter guy's dead. He hears he died in a fire over Abilene way. Big step, Hank."

"Big step," Henry repeated.

"I'm in the wrong pew with this muscle-bound altar boy, but I'm in the right church because he knows about it. So, I seem surprised. Dead? At his age? Who would've thought? Now I'm looking for a relative to give the money to, right? You with me here, Hank? A friend who knows a relative even. Somebody who says he's a brother is gonna creep out of the woodwork, see. We'll learn some shit. Excuse me, Missy."

"Not a problem," I told him.

"Good. I think we should all be ourselves here," he said.

"I do, too," I said, putting a touch of sincerity in my voice.

Otis went over and cut off the heat below his coffee.

"Brother want insurance money?" Henry asked.

"Sure. Somebody's gonna get greedy and try'n make some stupid play or other, and that dickwad's gonna know more about what happened over Abilene way than he should. See? That's my theory. Little by little. Step by step. Coffee, Hank?"

"No coffee," Henry said.

"I'll try a cup," I said, which was a mistake I would never repeat.

Driving home, I asked Henry about something Otis had mentioned as we were leaving.

'I'm still working on what happened to the file,' he'd said. "What file was he talking about?"

"File police misplace," Henry said.

"Our case?"

"Eye investigate. Not right put report someplace not find. Murders. Fire. Baby Girl hurt. Not right."

It was easy to believe that Detective Hansard was just purely dumb and lazy, but losing a report? That seemed extreme, even for him. I agreed with Henry. There was something *not right* about a murder report being misplaced. In fact, it was damned mysterious.

After meeting Otis, I began thinking we were going to find out things. I felt as if he could find an explanation for the police lacking interest in our case. Or, if it was more than just indifference—say, *negligent on purpose*—he could find out about that, too.

So, dumb and lazy maybe, but I'd wait for Otis to look into it before I settled for that.

The weather got nicer, and the ground was pretty much dried up by the time Harlan buzzed us. He flew low over the homestead without any warning, jarring our nerves, and making Jim bark. He set his little plane down out past the tree line, out where Henry had used the tractor and chains to drag away the mesquite.

A swooping flotilla of ill-tempered crows jeered at him as he walked in with that black Stetson of his pulled down low, a cowpoke heading for the bunkhouse. He carried a soft overnight bag and his cue case.

We sat around the kitchen table. Harlan with a beer. Henry with tea. Me with a Dr Pepper and puppy Jim on the floor with a bone. Henry told about that night, but I wasn't yet ready to talk about it.

Harlan moved from outrage to despair as he listened. And, when Henry explained his intention to locate the killers, Harlan was anxious to help.

"Just let me know how," he said.

"Gang shoot pool," Henry said.

"So you think they might could show up someplace I go."

"Maybe. You watch."

"Sure, I can do that. I'll watch for them," Harlan said to Henry.

To me, he said, "All right then, let's talk about you learning billiards, as your dad would say."

"We fix place in garage," Henry said.

"So you two just went ahead and decided I'd do it, huh?"

I said, "I'm hoping you will, Uncle Harlan."

He arched his brows and gave Henry a look.

"You hear that? *Uncle* Harlan. She just might have enough con in her to make the grade. We'll see."

"I don't want to be treated like a charity case. I'll work hard," I told him.

"Okay, I'll go for that. You have to know I wouldn't waste my time if I didn't think you had some natural talent."

"Now you're conning me, right?"

"No, Kristin, I'm not. Your dad had his days. I think you can be a whole lot better."

I didn't know what to say. No one had ever encouraged me before.

Harlan said, "What's the matter? Changed your mind?"

"Absolutely not. I'm ready to get started."

"That's good. I'm sure Henry'd like to see you do something besides read books and listen to jazz all day; maybe this'll get you started earning a little cash. Start pulling your weight around here."

"Then it's settled? You'll teach me?"

When Harlan and I shook hands, Henry laughed and slapped his knee.

A couple of weeks before that, Henry had his cabinet installation crew come by to help him move a rebuilt Brunswick table he had stored in the big garage.

Albert's dad was Henry's foreman, and I got to meet him for the first time. He and Albert looked a lot alike. The dad was stockier.

Anyway, the men pushed some things around and created a space for the table. They got it level and hooked up proper lighting above it and *voila*, as a Cajun waitress I knew in Beaumont used to say.

I snapped on the lights.

"This garage always have a hardwood floor?" Harlan asked.

"Henry put it in around the table so we'd have a good practice space."

"Oh, yeah. Nice set up," he commented.

We removed the table cover, folded it, and placed it aside.

"New felt," Harlan said.

"New bumpers. New everywhere," Henry said.

Harlan ran his hand over the fresh felt and gave the cushions a pull with two fingers. "It'll play different. Older tables won't play this crisp."

He gave me the eye, jutted his jaw, and toughened his voice.

"Now, let's understand something here, Kristin. Just because you show promise doesn't mean you can shoot all that good yet."

"I'll have to practice."

"You'll be practicing, all right. I'm thinking four or five hours a day, six days a week. If that doesn't suit you, tell me now. I won't waste your time or mine making like it's all peachy when it's not. We're giving some direction to your life, sure. But I won't have you out there embarrassing yourself or me, either. If you don't cut it, I'm telling you so."

"Fair enough," I said.

"If you practice and pay attention to what you're told, there's no reason you won't do okay," he said.

"I'm a girl. I have to do better than okay."

"Of course. And the other side of it is you don't need to get all antsy. I'm here for a few days this first time to get you through the basics. You need to learn a proper stroke. How to hold a cue. How to approach the table and rack the balls. Stuff like that. You have to start out right. I won't pick up after bad habits. You've got rules to learn and strategy to study, too. It's not all just chalking a cue and clicking balls together."

"Dad said you improved his game."

"Now, you," Harlan said and moved away from the table lights.

That was when he noticed Dad's car.

"Well, there's that Coupe de Ville he loved so much," he said, pushing back his Stetson and swiping at his eyes like

Henry and I might not notice that he was crying. "It's funny, ain't it? He hustled behind that tired-salesman-at-the-end-of-the-day routine, and then he'd go out after that and get into his new Cadillac. This flashy Coupe de Ville and the way he quoted great writers. That's how I'll remember him."

So Harlan, the tough guy con man, was the last of my teachers and turned out to be soft in the middle. That was okay with me. I already had two teachers made of steel.

Harlan told me, "How you handle yourself from the time you walk into a pool room until you leave has damned near as much to do with winning as how good you shoot. Me? I have to pretend I'm not a hustler. You? You want them to know you're there to take their money. It's psychology, see? They don't wanna lose, and they especially don't wanna lose to a filly. You can see that, can't you?"

"Sure," I said.

"But they can't run away, can they? You're young, you're pretty, you've got a fine figure. You won't dress slutty. But blue jeans that fit will look good when you bend over to shoot. If they're staring at your ass, they're not watching the game. This is confusion. The more confused they are, the more you'll win. Pretty soon only the best and the arrogant will be left. And that's who you want."

"Why do I want them?" I asked.

"You know, Kristin. Use your head."

"Because they'll hock everything they own trying to beat me."

"That's my girl," Harlan laughed.

7

BETWEEN STUDY, PRACTICE, and workouts, my days during that first spring at Henry's were active and full.

Henry and I fired our pistols before breakfast almost every day of the week and became good shots faster than I would have thought possible. Our targets were one-square-foot pieces of wood that Henry made by the dozens. They hung thirty feet away from us on a tight wire between two poles.

I never mentioned to Henry that I pictured the faces of my attackers on those wooden targets. I can't help believing that doing so made me a better shot.

After breakfast, Jim and I ran out to the wildcat well and back before I practiced my close quarter moves. Sarge had taught me that no matter how someone comes at me, there's an exact move to take him out.

"You'll learn them all before we're finished," he said.

When I practiced alone, I'd dance around the carpeted space that Henry had fixed behind the garage, talking to myself as I fought invisible thugs. I could've been thought to be insane by those who couldn't hear the music. Ask Nietzsche.

After practicing my moves, I'd bathe in the big tub in the *hacienda*. It was books the rest of the morning and into the early afternoon. Never later than two in the afternoon, I went into the garage, uncovered the table, and shot pool until six or seven in the evening.

I treasured the crisp sounds that occurred within the silence of the garage space, the sharp crack of the balls, the satisfying gulp of the pockets. Those sounds combined with the quiet became an integral part of the experience as I surrendered myself to study and practice, and the hours disappeared.

Jim would snap me out of it when supper was ready.

After we ate, Henry had his one smoke of the day out by the well. Next, he liked his radio. Some evenings I listened with him. Most often, Jim and I would go to the *hacienda*, put on some jazz, and read.

One evening I put my book down, went to my big mirror, and took an appraisal of myself. I was spending a lot of time with and being influenced by men of violence. I was being trained to kill, to kill without conscience.

I was concerned that the months of intense study and practice were leaving a mark on me. I was never a *girly-girl*, and being a *tough girl* had never been a goal of mine, either. The fact was I was becoming as well trained as any young warrior our country sent into battle.

So I looked at myself to see if my appearance, in any way, gave away my training.

"Look vulnerable," Sarge had told me. "Never let them see your confidence."

"Tell lies with your eyes, Little Sister," Albert had said. "Poke out your chest for them to gawk at, give them a smile when they don't expect it, anything so they don't watch your hands."

"Show nothing," Harlan had told me. "A poker face is the best face in a pool hall."

I wake in the middle of the night sometimes and say to myself, "It's just business, Kristin." In my heart I know that using words like business, work, and jobs is Sarge's way of talking about killing.

Albert says, "Stop a man," instead of "kill him."

Henry has his euphemisms, too. "We fix," he says.

"They know what they're teaching you to do," I tell my image.

No one is saying it straight out...and the more I look in the mirror, the more I realize that I'm not saying it, either.

I've become an actress—a dangerous actress—full of deceit and lethal skills.

Late one evening some five months or so into my pool lessons, Harlan, Henry, and I were relaxing in the lawn chairs we kept out near the pond. The bullbats had come and gone as the long summer dusk faded, taking with them their tiny cries, leaving the evening quiet.

The darkness would have been complete had it not been for the glow from the thick canopy of stars. Nights had been pleasant for several weeks owing to the lack of mosquitoes and the abundance of fireflies. Jim's muzzle was luminescent green from snapping the tiny insects.

The men were absorbed in matters beyond our surroundings: Henry was sorting out the Milky Way with his huge Navy surplus binoculars, and Harlan was saying in a soft tone of voice that it was time for me to resurface in the world of billiards.

"You were your daddy's little girl when they last saw you. Now you're grown, returning as a player. Big difference," he said.

"I haven't changed *that* much. People will remember me from before."

"We'll avoid them, then. We'll be careful where we go. You should appear out of nowhere. I want you to be a humdinger of a surprise to a bunch of country Joes who think they can shoot pool."

"I guess I better win sometimes, huh?"

"I hope your tongue's in your cheek," he said.

"Jesus, Harlan. I've spent damn near half the year

practicing every day. I think it's okay to believe I'll win some."

"You'll lose some games, too, till you get used to the attention you're gonna get."

"You're my uncle? That's how we're doing it?"

"It's nobody's business how we're related. Let them wonder. The less folks know about you, the better. You'll be the quiet type. Don't tell people your name. In fact, when they talk to you, just don't answer. I'll call you Baby, like your dad used to. You can be this mystery tomato who shows up looking like an angel and shooting like the devil."

"Mystery tomato good," Henry said.

The idea of being a girl of mystery appealed to me, too. I was confident about the way I looked. I was running six miles a day and in the best physical condition I'd ever been in.

"Make men crazy," Henry said.

On a hot, dry August afternoon a few weeks after my eighteenth birthday and nine months after my dad's death, Harlan and I climbed into his plane with our cue cases and overnight bags and flew off to initiate my career in the pool halls of West Texas.

Harlan told me, "We'll start up in the high plains and move south. If we get you out there every weekend, we'll put a dent in it."

And dent it we did. During those first few weeks, I was introduced in pool halls in every little backwater you can imagine up around Amarillo: Borger, Hereford, White Deer, and a bunch of others.

In Pampa we played in a pool hall called Crystal's whose claim to fame was it survived the big tornado of '47.

I told Harlan, "It should be famous for not having a single level table."

"Level tables or not, the way you're gonna learn how to handle yourself at a man's game in a man's world is to get in there among them," he told me.

He was right about that, and little by little, weekend after weekend, parlor after parlor, I not only learned to win at pool, I began getting my confidence back around strangers. Not as many fellas noticed or commented on my facial scars as I thought would, and those who did seemed satisfied when I told them, "I was in an accident."

The women I met suggested makeup products, but hiding my scars seemed like more trouble than it was worth, since it became clear to me that men were a lot less concerned about them than women were. And also, I could see that they were fading with time, just as the doctor said they would.

"What do you like about these weekends?" Harlan asked me.

"How do you mean?"

"You get in the plane, we fly around to pool halls. You win more than you lose. So what? Do you like the life? Is it the way you remember it?"

I thought about it and told him, "Yeah, I think I do. I like the challenges. I like the extra bucks, the chance to do some shopping. I like staying at motels with swimming pools. I like eating in cafes. In some ways it's like being with Dad again, except I win more than he used to."

"You like winning, don't you?" he asked with that look in his eye.

"Yeah, Uncle Harlan, I do."

"If you had some sincere larceny in you, I'd teach you some grifter tricks and we'd be off'n running. But you have an honest streak in you that I'm not sure you'll ever be able to kick."

My mother taught me honesty. What Harlan taught me was life.

All in all, I enjoyed the break from the day-in day-out routine of the time I spent at Henry's. And I was shooting pool well enough to earn a nickname. The guy that owned Andy's Snooker Palace in Amarillo came up with it without knowing he'd done it.

He complained to Harlan that his *Baby* was a shark.

Harlan put on a grin that I'd never forget.

He said, "Baby Shark. That'll do it."

While Harlan and I—or should I say, Harlan and Baby Shark—were on the road winning at nine ball, Otis was continuing his search and reporting to Henry. So on a Sunday evening in late September when we returned from one of our regular west Texas parlor tours, there was some interesting news for me.

"Otis say Detective Hansard dumb and lazy like we think. But that not why file misplaced."

"No? Why then?" I asked.

"Otis think somebody say make file disappear. That why."

A chill went up my back.

"Who can tell the police to do that?"

"Otis say high up police, maybe judge, maybe politician. He say we lay low more. He find out."

I called Otis.

"Okay, let's get this clear from the jump here. Like I told Hank, I ain't got no more'n the piss I told him already and that's why I ain't told him more. I'm looking into it."

"Then I want to hear what you think. Forget about the piss you don't know," I told him.

"Don't get pushy and maybe I *will* tell you what I think."

He made me endure a half-minute of silence before going on.

"I don't understand why somebody with enough power to detour a murder investigation would have any interest in what happened out there that night at Henry's place. That's what I think."

"Yeah? So?"

"You have any ideas on that?" he asked.

"Me? None," I said.

"Maybe your daddy was into something?"

That made my head buzz. I thought of Harlan and all the tricks he could think up, but I was certain my dad wasn't into anything besides hustling pool.

"Like what, Otis? What're you getting at?"

"I'm just asking could that be it? That's all. I mean your daddy spent a lot of time around hard types, in and out of pool halls all over the place. I'm just wondering if maybe he had something else going, or maybe he just heard something he wasn't supposed to. You know. Something like that, maybe."

"I was on his hip night and day for months. I would've known about it if he'd been *into something*, whatever the hell that means. And as far as him hearing something, well, Christ, Otis, I don't know. I'll tell you this, though. I don't like you asking crap like that."

"I guess not, the way you got your claws out," he growled.

"What do you expect?"

"You ain't trying to tell me how to do my job, are you?"

"Oh, don't start that. You know what I mean."

"There's a connection there some place," he said. "I guess even you see that, don'cha?"

If he'd been there, I'd have stuck my finger in his eye. I kept quiet.

"Sure, you and Hank want to know. So do I. Look, I think this information brings us closer to knowing. Okay? I don't *really* know yet, and you gotta understand something. My muscle over in Abilene only goes as far as a detective named Gustman. He owes me a favor because I saved him from getting took to the cleaners during a smelly divorce. You see what I'm saying here? I got no pull higher than that in Abilene. And Gustman told me to quit asking, if I knew what was good for me."

That woke me up with a start.

"Wait a minute. Did I hear that correctly? This detective friend of yours said you were in danger if you kept asking?"

"I guess we read that the same, Missy. And the problem I got is, I never do know what's good for me. So I'm still asking around."

Maybe I'd have to mellow my opinion of the ol' windbag.

He went on: "And another thing I ain't fond of, is hearing that there's stuff the higher-ups can know, but us *peóns* can't. That's not the way I understand the Constitution. Like I was telling Hank, the way I hear it, this order to butt out comes from nosebleed country. That means it'll stay gossip until some turkey gets drunk and forgets to keep his beak shut."

"I understand," I told him.

"I know some barkeeps where the boys uncork a few, and they know I'm good for a sawbuck if they phone me. So, give me a minute or two."

Otis got his 'minute or two.'

Over eight months passed with just one tiny snippet of information filtering in about the gang. Otis heard from a police contact of his in Corpus Christi who said the gang had been through. "They made some noise and moved on," he said.

So, the better part of a year passed without us locating any of the killers, and all we knew for sure was at one point the gang had been riding along the Gulf Coast. And about who hushed things up or why, we learned nothing.

Marlon Brando's motorcycle movie was all the talk during that time, but I didn't see it. I didn't think I needed to.

It was spring again. The mesquite leafed out across the greening plains surrounding the homestead, and the jacaranda was in bloom.

Jim was weighing in at over a hundred pounds, even if he did still act like a puppy. And Harlan had established Baby Shark as a pool shooter to be reckoned with, just as he said he would.

I had gotten used to the months passing without any significant news about our search, so the expression on Henry's face as he and Jim crossed the field to meet the plane that evening in May was momentarily confusing to me.

"Eye find one," Henry told me as I climbed out of the Piper Cub.

"Which one?" I asked, my mind whirring.

"Scarecrow," Henry said.

8

THE BIKER I'D nicknamed Scarecrow was the guy my dad had put his boot toe into so hard it changed his voice. It had taken Otis over a year to locate this thug, and I was amazed he'd found even one of the four. Texas was their territory, and that big state went forever in all directions.

Harlan always did what he called a modified touch-and-go when he brought me back from our weekends away. This time was no different. He left the prop turning, brought my luggage around, shook Henry's hand, gave me a kiss on my forehead, and climbed back in his plane.

Henry and I waited until our friend was up and gone and we were walking toward the house before we spoke again.

"We go see tonight. Make sure," Henry said.

I suppose I believed it would happen some day. Now I was being told that day had arrived. Also—and it was a big also—Henry was talking about me going with him.

"Tonight? Where?" I asked, my nerves tuning up.

"We meet Otis. He take us place see Scarecrow."

"He's certain that's who it is."

"Baby Girl make certain. Maybe Henry not see that night."

"I'll go," I said.

There was a reason for me to go. Maybe I'd recognize

the man and Henry wouldn't. We couldn't take that chance. I'd go, but that didn't mean I wasn't as nervous as a cat in a room full of rocking chairs as Otis would say.

If I ran into trouble, would I remember all that Sarge and Albert had taught me? My teachers had cut their visits down after the first few months of working with me. It had been a while since I'd seen either of them.

Albert was single and had more free time than Sarge. He drifted by now and again, most often drunk as a skunk. Sarge had a family. I hadn't seen him for several months.

Later that evening, Henry and I met Otis at a truck stop over near Mingus. He was driving an old Chevy two-door junker.

We left our pickup there and rode with him to a nearby roadhouse called Turk's Bar-B-Q. When we pulled into the parking area, Otis asked Henry to wait in the car while he and I went inside.

"No offense, Hank. A chink guy's gonna turn heads. This is a quiet in, quiet out kind of thing."

"Quiet in, quiet out," Henry repeated.

So I went in with Otis, and Henry waited in the car.

We entered through the restaurant; Otis steered me past the toothy hostess and around the corner away from the dining room. The heavy sweet aroma of hickory-smoked barbeque was everywhere.

We went down a dark hall until we came to a place where I could see through some latticework into the noisy, smoky bar. Rex Allen was blaring from the jukebox.

"Tell me if you see him," Otis said.

I looked and realized that the barflies weren't going to notice me. Otis was half a ruler over six feet and big as a house, and he didn't seem concerned.

"You think he's here, don't you," I said.

"You tell me," Otis said.

There were a dozen men and five or six women in the room, talking, smoking, drinking; the bartender was leaning across the bar acting foolish to amuse a hard-featured redhead.

I glanced at the seated customers. Didn't recognize anybody. The ones standing were laughing, talking, moving in and out of the light. It wasn't easy to sort them out.

My heart skipped a beat before it began pounding harder than I would've expected. I had a hard time catching my breath. Otis put his hand on my lower back like he thought I might fall back, or collapse. My knees felt shaky, so maybe he was doing the right thing.

"He's in there?" Otis asked in a whisper.

My mouth was dry.

"I think so."

There were others in leather. But this fella had on a sleeveless Lost Demons jacket. He was tall, gangly. He turned and I saw his spotted face. He was exactly as I remembered him. Exactly. Except this time he wasn't rolling on the floor holding his crotch.

Otis spoke with his mouth near my ear.

"The asshole with the wild hair, right?"

"Yes."

"The guy with all the freckles. Next to the blonde?"

"Yes."

I felt strange, conscious of my breathing.

There was Scarecrow acting as if everything was perfectly all right. He hadn't been involved in murder and rape. Not him. Not Scarecrow. He was standing there swilling beer and laughing as the sounds of that other night filled my head. The vicious laughter. The gunfire.

"That's it then," Otis said and guided me with firm hands back up the hall and out of the roadhouse.

I spoke to Henry when I got into the car and have no memory of what I said. I'd lost my focus. My ears were humming. As Otis drove us back to our truck, I opened my window and put my face in the night air. When I got it together and rolled up the window, Otis was talking, of course.

He was saying, "This was good. I know who I'm watching now. This guy Rusty's the biker you call Scarecrow. That description helped me find him."

"What you do now?" Henry asked.

"I follow him, Hank. One *cucaracha* means more *cucarachas.*"

"More *cucarachas,*" Henry said.

"Or maybe it don't. This guy? Scarecrow? It's like working cattle, ain't it, Hank? You just cut one outta the herd while the others ain't looking."

I smiled when Otis laughed and wondered if it was time to make jokes.

"As far as having a sit down with him goes, that'll happen when it's supposed to. My guess is a few days. So get your plans together. Be ready when I call."

"Fish or cut bait," Henry said, his face as serious as I'd ever seen it.

The morning after I saw Scarecrow, I gave Sarge a call and told him about freezing up at the roadhouse. He came over that day.

As we began again under the big shade tarp out behind the garage, Sarge said he was pleased that after six months my movements were still so crisp.

"It figures when you add it up," he said. "You've easily had twenty times the training the average G.I. gets in his few weeks of basic."

I'd been faithful about practicing alone. But having Sarge there was different. I knew that in order to win even a few of our practice encounters, I had to concentrate. Sarge never *let* me win. So when I did take him it was sweet.

"Focus," he'd say.

"Sharp. Quick. Quick," he demanded.

"Snap back, don't draw back. Show some muscle," he insisted.

I appreciated that he was unforgiving of my mistakes. I wanted to be as good as I could be. I never wanted to fear anyone again.

"You can never let anything stop you. I paused once in Germany and almost paid for it with my life," he said and took off his shirt.

In all the time we'd trained together, he'd never done that.

"It was near the end of the war," he said, showing me the mess the battlefield surgeon had made across his stomach and lower back.

I thought I had scars.

He told me the Nazis were throwing young kids into the front lines. He'd heard about the children, but hadn't seen any until they were taking a little town street by street and he'd taken cover in a doorway.

He said, "There was nowhere else to go but inside. When I shouldered the door open, I found myself in a small room with three German soldiers."

They were as surprised as he was, he said, and they all began shooting. He got two of them, and when he spun around to face the third soldier, he saw that he was just a kid.

"He was maybe twelve, thirteen. A kid in a uniform that was too big for him. And the time it took me to grasp all that was the time he needed to shoot me. I shot him, too. And killed him. I was the better marksman as it turned out, still, he got me."

"Because you paused," I said.

"That's right and he put me in the hospital. We were one less soldier in the war because I paused. Your situation at the rib joint and mine in Germany weren't exactly the same, but they have similarities. We were both surprised by our reactions, and we both survived. Saving graces. Don't you see? I'll never pause again and you'll never panic again because it's just business, Little Miss. It's the business of staying alive."

Sarge fascinated me. I was eighteen and alone on a hot

West Texas afternoon with a strong and confident shirtless man, damp with sweat, taut with muscle, who moved in a kind of primal dance as he renewed for me the finer points of his lethal art.

I learned again—and this time forever—his beautifully executed moves that guided cuts, thrusts, and lifesaving parries with no wasted motion. In. Out. Distractions. Hidden actions. Death strikes and many types of withdrawal to reset for the persistent adversary.

He must have seen the adoring look on my face because that day he told me something that he had never bothered to mention before.

He said, "Don't ever kid yourself, Little Miss. A knife fight is ugly. It's bloody and violent. Even if you win, you'll probably get hurt, too. If you must fight, get it over with as fast as you can."

I was grateful for those few weeks of what Sarge called my post-graduate study. Those final lessons with him in May and June could not have been better timed. Henry got the call from Otis in mid-June telling him he had zeroed in on a time and place for the meeting with Scarecrow. That was June 19, 1954.

I remembered the date so precisely because it was our first *Trial by Fire Night*. Albert had come by, and we were all outside. Henry was cooking steaks over charcoal.

"How come your vicious mongrel didn't come to the car and threaten me?" Albert wanted to know.

I said, "He's inside recovering. He had a big fight a few nights ago."

"What happened?" Albert asked.

This was Henry's tale, and he waved his long spatula as he told it.

"Our Jim normal dog. You know, growl at you."

Saying that made Henry laugh, since it was true that Jim always growled at Albert.

"Jim normal dog. Chase grasshopper. Skunk. Tease snake. He bring home prairie dog once, twice week. Even got armadillo one time and all time chase rabbit. Never catch. One night this week, Jim chase coyote. I see, moon full. Not big coyote. Have long legs though. He make Jim good run."

I reminded Albert that Jim wasn't even two years old. "I know he weighs over a hundred pounds, but still, he's not mature yet."

"Puppy part make trouble for Jim. He chase coyote too far. Another coyote wait in dark. Jim bigger, but they two. They mean business."

"And he'd run pretty far," I said.

"Coyotes think easy supper. Jim fight for life. He got scars now. Leg stiff in winter some time, you bet. Two dead in arroyo. I find next day. All over flies.

"I was over in Odessa with Harlan. I missed the whole thing," I said.

"Jim sleep two days, wake up. Eat like horse. Learn never chase coyotes again," Henry said.

"The coyotes learned a harder lesson," Albert said.

"It must have been horrible for Jim. So far from home, outnumbered," I said, and Albert made a face at me.

"*Pobre mamacita.* He knows how strong he is now," Albert assured me in that *macho* voice he sometimes used.

"We figured it marked the end of his puppyhood," I said.

"Rite of passage," Henry said just to impress me. "Jim get steak for supper."

"We're going to celebrate it every year," I told Albert. "I hope you'll join us."

"As long as I'm alive and out of jail, Little Sister. As long as I'm alive and out of jail."

Two .45s appeared out of nowhere, and Albert fired into the night, both big pistols blazing, hot cartridges flying, until the magazines were empty and our ears were ringing. This was a guy who knew how to celebrate.

I heard the phone ringing while Henry was inside getting more beer.

A call at that hour had to be the call we'd been waiting

for, and I knew when he came out looking somber that something was up. He told Albert and me that Otis had found a time and place for the 'sit down' with Scarecrow and wanted to meet with us the next night to discuss it.

The time had come.

Henry was going to face the first of the gang. It had been a long wait, and his plan was finally in motion.

Albert was electrified by the news, and rational conversation became difficult. Henry and I exchanged a look that said we would talk later. Albert was up and swinging himself about with an alarming dexterity that concerned me until I realized he was simply pacing. He was pacing as any high-strung nervous person might.

His pacing was—I don't know—brilliant to see as he maneuvered himself on his crutches, out a few yards and back. Out a few yards and back. My god, he was flying. He was drunk, of course. He had swung himself out away from the house and into the darkness several times during the evening to "piss in the freedom of the night," he'd told us.

"It's a man's privilege to do so," he'd explained.

I guessed it must be. I had long ago noted Henry's habit of doing the same thing over near the windmill after he finished his pipe and before he went in the house to listen to the radio.

However, Albert wasn't up to relieve himself. He was up to do mayhem. As he paced, he would let fire vindictive threats in bursts of Spanish.

"Esos ojepes. Culeros!"

I'd never seen him like that, though I knew he had it in him, that deeply rooted anger. For the first time since I'd met him, I dredged up a little pity for his enemies.

He challenged Henry: "Let's go tonight and shoot some holes in that piece of shit. We'll make that *pendejo* pay for what he did. I don't care how many there are. We'll kill them all."

"We plan too long. No mistakes now," Henry said.

I could see that Albert's enthusiasm worried him.

"We do right way," Henry said. "Not wrong way. No matter how much feel hate."

Henry was right, of course, and eventually Albert cooled down and agreed that picking the time and place made sense. He insisted on being there and offered some convincing reasons why it would be a good idea to have extra firepower.

So, Henry gave in to his request with the understanding that it was not Albert's operation.

"This my revenge," Henry said.

"Nobody's arguing with that, *Maestro*. I'll be there to back you up. That's all."

It made sense to have help. I was certain that the single reason Scarecrow hadn't taken part in the murders and rape was because Dad's kick had put him out of action. It was reasonable to believe that he was just as vicious and treacherous as the men he ran with.

"You come, too, Little Sister. You ask the questions. We'll get the answers," Albert said.

That was a surprise, and it caused me to pause. The idea of being face-to-face with Scarecrow wasn't easy to digest, but I warmed to the idea. What was all my training about if I couldn't go along just to hear some men talk?

"I'll back you up, too," I told Henry.

"Baby Girl not have to go," Henry told Albert in a soft voice without looking at me.

Albert readjusted his sticks and spoke directly to me.

"You need to go, Little Sister. You know you do."

I locked eyes with Albert and said, "How can I face my enemies if I can't face my fears? That's what you're saying, isn't it?"

"Are you a vulture?" Albert asked, lowering his voice as he leaned toward me.

"I'll go," I told Henry.

Henry looked at me with concern in his eyes.

"Do you smell blood?" Albert asked me in a drunken whisper. "Do you smell blood, Little Sister?"

9

June 1954

NEAR SUNSET THE next evening, Henry and I met Otis at his place in Fort Worth. He was in rolled-up shirtsleeves and loose tie. He appeared held together by straps with his suspenders and gun holster crisscrossing each other over his thick chest.

"Now I know we're in the same hymn book. Now let's see if we're singing the same song before we get this prayer meeting started," Otis said to us through a cloud of smoke from behind his big desk.

"Sing same song as Otis," Henry said.

"Good. Well, let's just see here. This Rusty Neugent, the felon you call Scarecrow, was at the pool hall the night your loved ones was murdered. And you wanna have a sit down with him regarding the whereabouts of the others in his gang. Am I on key here?"

"We talk to Scarecrow," Henry confirmed.

"Because we can go to my detective friend, point this criminal out, and get him arrested. We can go that way."

No one spoke. Otis continued.

"Until we know who's slowing things up and why, of course, we don't know how much luck we'd have getting your outlaw behind bars."

Why did he mention it then?

"We talk to Scarecrow. Find others," Henry confirmed again.

"Okay, then, because I mean, if it's just a matter of bush-whacking the evil turd, I could name a few places a person could get that done."

"No, just talk," Henry confirmed yet again.

"So, it's nothing more'n a sit down. You want him to give up the others, and that calls for a quiet talk?"

"Jesus, Otis. How many times does he have to say it? Put a sock in it. You're such a windbag."

Both men swiveled their heads around and stared at me. The solitary sound in the room was the rattle of the old fan. I guessed Otis never turned that fan off. Probably ran night and day, just like he did.

"Maybe I'm a windbag and maybe I ain't," he said. "But some things need to be talked over."

"Be patient," Henry told me.

"Thank you, Hank," Otis said.

Me, I was wondering why something that had already taken over a year needed so much blather. Otis took his time crushing out his cigarette before starting in again.

"All right then. If it's just a sit down, why not his home? I ask myself. So I let him lead me out east of here to a weed-covered scrap of dirt I wouldn't slop Razorbacks on. Where's he taking me? I wondered, until I see he's living in a dump of a trailer house that's got three nasty-tempered junkyard dogs attached to it by long chains. Hell, it might as well be a mansion behind a high gate because them mutts is three too many problems, no matter which way you shovel it."

'Shovel it' was an apt phrase. It was damn near impossible for that man to get to the point.

"Where else, I ask myself, can this fella be found alone where Hank can have an uninterrupted sit down with him without getting his ass bit or his head blown off?"

"Where?" Henry asked.

"Be patient," I said to Henry.

There was another one of those pauses before Otis grumbled, "It's just natural for you to be cantankerous, ain't it?"

I assumed his complaint to be rhetorical and remained silent as they both stared at me.

Otis sighed before he picked it up again. "So after trailing him around for a good while now and watching his shenanigans, I narrowed it down to a place. It ain't what I'd call the ideal spot, but it's sweet in some ways."

"Where?" Henry asked again and shot me a look.

"Over by the stockyards, Hank. You'll see it tonight and make up your mind."

We left our truck out back of his place, and Otis drove us over in a dented up Buick to a section of warehouses near the stockyards. The few businesses still open were closing down.

Otis knew his way around, and after a couple of turns, he parked us in a dark spot up the way from Helen's Bay Side, a honky-tonk set back on its lot in a cavernous brick warehouse.

The entrance to the nightspot was through a wide-open, double-width roll-up door. The huge entrance made it easy for the bikers and their women to stroll outside and sit on their bikes while they drank their beers. Even at that early hour there were two dozen or so motorcycles parked in front.

Conversation mixed with jukebox music drifted to us.

Otis said, "I've tried to park us so we ain't got a problem."

"What problem," Henry asked.

"Look here, Hank, there'll be lights coming up behind us from time to time, see. When they do, just keep down so we're not three silhouettes on a stakeout."

Henry and I scrunched down, leaving just enough of our heads up to see out the car windows. I was in the back peering between the two men.

"That's the idea; and once we're set, let's stay that way. Motion attracts attention, and attention ain't something we're looking for. Now here's what I know," he said in a voice that dropped to a level a bit low for my flawed hearing.

I got my good ear closer to Otis as he began talking.

"A tough dame named Helen Mercer owns the Bay Side. She bought it with her husband's insurance money after he took a bayonet on some sandy piece of paradise in the South Pacific."

"This biker place?" Henry asked.

"It sure is, Hank. It's a rough and tumble biker honky-tonk. And Helen Mercer don't care how rough it gets, as long as the boys pay for what they break and don't mistreat her female barkeeps. And I can tell you, them barkeeps is a piece of work."

"Scarecrow go there?" Henry whispered while Otis was taking a breath.

"Wanna get to it, do you, Hank? I don't blame you. It's been a spell, ain't it?

Four big bikes rumbled up from behind us, their lights sweeping through our car as they growled past on their way to Helen's Bay Side. The event took split seconds, but it felt longer.

"Does this place seem a little crowded?" I asked in a quiet voice.

"Now, let's don't be getting that cart out there too far in front of the horse, Missy."

He was still pissed about me calling him windy back at the office.

"I'll watch that," I told him and yanked out a full pinch of short hairs from the back of his neck.

"Goddamn it!"

"Now, we're even."

"Don't be doing shit like that," he snarled over his shoulder.

"Don't school-girl me," I replied in a pleasant voice.

He twisted his big frame around and gave me a tough face. Our noses were inches apart.

"You looking to get slapped silly?" he said.

"You looking to get snatched bald-headed?" I said.

He huffed and twisted back around.

"She's a pisser, Hank."

"Treat with respect, no trouble."

That got Henry a hard stare before the big man pinned me in the rearview.

"This ain't finished, you little maverick."

"Save it for someone who gives a shit," I said back to the mirror.

That twisted him around so we were nose-to-nose again.

"Have to have the last word, huh? You one a them?"

"Can't say, pal. How about you?"

He exhaled a groan as he turned back, this time settling in behind the wheel, rubbing his neck, and staring out the front window.

"Maybe you tell plan now, Otis. And quit move so much, somebody see."

That got Henry another hard glance. So, Henry shot me a hard glance proving shit runs downhill. Everyone was quiet for a minute while Otis wrangled his pride.

I had nothing against Otis. But I hadn't spent the past year and a half learning how to take crap off people. When he cleared his throat, I figured we at least had a truce.

"Okay, no more history. Here's the deal. This guy Rusty calls one of them bartenders his lady friend. She's a bottle blonde from New Orleans with a French name no Texan can say proper, so she goes by Peggy. She's got a sheet. Prostitution, assault, lewd behavior, hell, more malarkey than you can imagine, and she ain't thirty yet. Her and Rusty're lovebirds. He shows up the nights she works and keeps her company till closing time and after."

He glanced in the mirror and added, "It ain't crowded then."

He wanted more hair yanked out. That was easy to see.

"Good to hear," I said and smiled.

"Helen ain't open on Mondays, seeing as how she restocks and cleans on that day. She opens again on Tuesday night. And since Tuesdays are butt slow, she goes home early and lets her bartender close up. Only night of the week she does that. The weekend deposit goes in Monday morning, see, so she ain't losing much if one of her ladies decides to go shopping with a slow night's receipts."

"So you're saying Tuesday night," I put in to move things along.

"I reckon I am. Peggy closes that night."

"If Peggy there, Scarecrow there," Henry said.

"That's the number, Hank. Lover boy has, without screwing up even one time, followed his hard dick into Helen's Bay Side every Tuesday night for the past four weeks. And there're usually some others with him who wear the same colors. The deadbeats are drinking free for a few hours every Tuesday night after closing. Now, I have some ideas about how to get in and out of there."

Otis started the car.

"I wanna show you a couple of things out back of this place and call it a night. You can come around in daylight and jaw things over till you're blue in the face if you want. It don't stay dark but twenty minutes this time of year, and I gotta be someplace before sunup. I got other clients besides you."

Otis showed us how to get to the back of the building, which was not a simple route. He showed us where the Bay Side's back door was, which was not an obvious location. And finally he showed us where the phone line came down to the building, which anyone could have figured out.

While driving us back to the office, he explained why it was necessary for Henry to exit the back way and why it was essential that his visit be timed precisely.

"Hank, you know these gorillas ain't solid citizens. There's no telling what might happen when you corner this knucklehead."

"Gorillas and knuckleheads," Henry said.

"You've got it, Hank. That's why it's important for you to know other ways in and out of the place. Like I said, this location ain't ideal, but I couldn't find any place better. And just keep in mind, unless you wanna spend the night at Helen's Bay Side, you gotta watch the time."

"You may be worth your money, after all," I allowed.

"And I reckon I might could use a haircut," he conceded.

Henry laughed and that caused Otis to laugh. I laughed, too, and that's how we patched up our differences. Otis told Henry later that he figured our little fuss was just me having a case of nerves.

Maybe so. Although I think he got the message, whether he wanted to admit it or not. I wasn't going to put up with him talking down to me.

Over the next few days, Albert remained sober, came by Henry's every day and contributed with intelligence to Henry's plan. Well, Otis' plan with modifications.

The three of us drove together to see the streets in daylight that we would need to know at night, checked out and discussed to Henry's satisfaction the layout of the building, and became familiar with its entrance and exits.

I was feeling confident that things would go right.

By Monday we were ready and by Tuesday, the time was passing like a snail moving through cough syrup. Henry and I were too nervous to have a normal day and ended up cleaning and oiling our weapons twice.

Tiring of the silence that hung between us, we decided to see if we could get a little rest. My mind was racing about, not out of control, but I wasn't calm and collected, either. Taking some time alone, and trying to relax seemed like the way to go.

Jim knew something was up and was on extra alert. He scrambled to his feet when I stood and stayed close on our walks to and from the *hacienda*. He was delighted to take a nap with me when he realized that was what we were doing and heaved a big sigh as he stretched out on his rug near the bed.

I was forever trying to fall asleep that afternoon. I thought about Henry, how he hungered for revenge. I thought about that night, how my dad had died. How Henry's brave Will had killed that thug and been killed himself.

I thought of the brutal beatings that Henry and I had suffered and the vicious indifference of those animals. I saw their faces again. Heard their voices again, their vulgar comments, their laughter, their repulsive sounds as they attacked me.

Henry woke me when it was time to go.

The trip into Fort Worth was without incident. We arrived on schedule at the agreed-upon spot up the street from the bar. Albert was there and waiting. It was graveyard quiet.

One of his duck-tailed associates got out of his car and came toward us, moving in that insolent way they had of walking. Those gangsters were known for being unpredictable.

Henry moved closer to me and the *pachuco* got in, bringing the scent of Pomade, booze, and the sweet aroma of the 'roll-your-owns' they smoked. Never speaking. Never uttering a sound. He drove us the rest of the way, stopping seconds later in front of the Bay Side.

I opened my door and got out.

As Henry stepped out behind me, I heard the door of Albert's car close. The scrape of the steel tap on the toe of Albert's boot as it left the brick street created a predictable tempo that measured his progress as he swung himself over to join us.

And as heavy as the odor of the stockyards was on the night air, it didn't mask the smell of whiskey on Albert's breath. It was too dark to see his face clearly.

True to our plan, Henry's truck stayed where it was, and Albert's car was driven away.

The three of us started across the parking area. We

directed ourselves toward the walk-through door that was used when the truck door was closed. The sounds we made as we crossed the almost empty lot were the syncopated scratches of Albert's tap falling between the squeak of his rubber-capped crutches.

There were two bikes parked there.

Good. Two bikes was manageable.

As we drew near the door, we began hearing voices. Loud, exuberant voices. Drinkers talking over each other. Strangely, the jukebox was silent.

Albert pounded on the door harder than I thought was necessary. It grew quiet inside. We waited and he started to pound again. I caught his arm.

I smiled and said, "That's enough."

I was close enough to see that he was drunk. We were too far along to change our plan. I could only hope that he'd control himself.

A man's voice came from inside.

"Who is it?"

I released Albert's arm. He moved aside.

"I need to use your phone," I called out, pitching my voice higher than normal.

There was no reply.

My heart was slamming around. I heard a muddle of voices.

"I need to use a phone," I called out again. "May I use your phone?"

Another pause.

The lock was thrown and the door opened a crack. I looked up at a face I recognized. He had been with Scarecrow at the roadhouse. Tall. Young. His cheeks were flushed from drinking. He looked around. He didn't see Albert and Henry, who were off to the side.

I served up a girlish laugh of embarrassment and used my helpless voice. "I feel so silly. I'm sorta lost. Could I use your phone?"

The door opened more as he turned his attention to the

interior. He was muscular as well as tall and wore an olive green undershirt.

"It's a girl wants to use the phone. She's lost."

Laughter erupted from within. The man at the door laughed, too. When I saw his eyes coming back to me, I backhanded him hard across the mouth with my .38. I put my shoulder to the door and pushed past him before he could recover.

Behind me, I heard the door slam full back, metal against metal. I heard Henry ordering the big guy around as I advanced into the cavernous interior. Behind my legs, I held a .38 automatic in each hand, both cocked and locked.

I'm committed now.

I realized that I was holding my breath.

Breathe. Focus.

A woman and a man were at the bar on the far side of the room. They were sitting on red leather padded, chrome-legged stools. They saw me approaching and continued to talk. They were not yet aware that anything out of the ordinary was happening. In a dozen more steps, they would be the same distance from me as the targets on our pistol range.

As I drew closer, I could see that it was Scarecrow. I saw his attention go beyond me to the altercation at the door.

His attention came back to me.

He realized how quickly I was advancing, and his moves became significant. He twisted on his tall seat and extended a leg to put a foot on the floor for balance. His body motion had him going for his weapon next.

Without breaking my stride, I brought my hands up, arms extended, pistols ahead of me. I thumbed off the safeties and made his chest my target. The door slammed behind me, and the lock clanked into place.

Scarecrow put it together. Once he understood what was happening, his hands came up palms forward. He was smarter than I would've given him credit for.

I angled to my right to keep a clear field of fire as I felt Albert soar past on my left. He came to an abrupt stop near the ash blonde in the blue jeans and skimpy top. She was staring at Albert, her scarlet mouth agape.

Scarecrow had a foot on the floor and he was still seated on the stool next to her. Albert was on their flank, perhaps a little closer than he should've been. I'd stopped ten feet or so out in front of them, my pistols steady.

Scarecrow's freckles were easy to see at that distance.

We were on plan.

Peggy snapped out of it and raised her voice at Albert. Her tone as brassy and shrill as a Beaumont hooker yowling from her cell window to her pimp on the street below. *"Tu sais a qui t'as affaire, espece de salaud?"* she screeched.

Albert moved in and slugged her so hard it sent her toppling off her bar stool to the concrete floor. She landed on her back in an unconscious heap with her mouth still open and one firm breast defiantly free of her denim halter.

Scarecrow reacted.

"Don't do it, Rusty."

Hearing his name startled Scarecrow. He threw a quick glance at me and stayed where he was. But he couldn't ignore what Albert had done to his Peggy.

"You'll pay for that," he said.

Leave it alone, Albert.

Henry arrived with a pistol in one hand and a curled length of clothesline in the other.

"This one clean," he said. He deposited the big guy at the bar, dropped the cord, and hurried off to open the back door.

Big Guy's mouth was gashed and bleeding where I'd hit him, and I don't think he was even annoyed. He was drunker than I realized and seemed amused by what was happening. He spoke too loudly.

"Girls, cripples, slant-eyed gooks. Is the fucking circus in town?"

Albert's eyes were red, and the crooked smile on his face made him resemble a mental patient. *"Pinchey cabron,"* he said, squinting hard at Big Guy.

Scarecrow said, "If you're here to rob the place, what're you hurting people for? Take what you want and go."

Big Guy moved toward Scarecrow.

"Get away from him," Albert said.

"Fuck you, Sticks," Big Guy said and gave us a bloody smile as he stepped in next to Scarecrow.

Albert produced one of the .45 automatics he kept beneath his full coat.

"We just want to talk to you, Rusty," I said, trying to get things on track.

Big Guy pulled a small revolver from behind Scarecrow's back. I saw it coming out and moved to my right. Albert saw it coming out and shot the big man in the groin.

The noise from Albert's large caliber weapon was deafening, and the punch from it folded the Big Guy over like Rocky Marciano had landed one below his belt. He bounced back hard off the bar and straight down to his knees.

The wild shot that he squeezed off as he fell sparked the cement near my feet and stung my face and neck, arms and hands with tiny hot residue. My ears rang from the double assault, my heart was pounding, and my stomach felt sick, but I kept Scarecrow covered.

I was determined to hold it together.

The crotch and thighs of Big Guy's blue jeans darkened with blood at an alarming speed. He collapsed from his knees to the floor, rolling onto his side, groaning. He still held the pistol.

"I don't shoot too good. I aimed for his beady little eyes," Albert said.

Scarecrow said, "You're gonna be sorry for that, too, you fucking greaser."

"I'm not a greaser, you dumb fuck. I'm a half-breed Comanche," Albert said and took the groaning biker out of his misery with a clean shot to the head.

"What the fuck!" Scarecrow bleated, jerking back from the splattering blood and brain matter that hit us all.

The loud blast was like an unknown force had driven

into me. My face felt frozen in a grimace. A pilot reacting to G-forces. For a sharp instant, I wasn't certain of my footing. Albert's voice cut through to me.

"Now I want *you* to pull a gun on me," Albert was telling Scarecrow.

I spoke up at once, my voice distant and hollow through my ringing ears. "Take the pistol you have in front there, Rusty. Take it with two fingers and put it on the bar. Push it away."

He was confused, but he did as I told him. During that pause, I noticed the burning in my nose. The acrid scent of gunpowder was beginning to rival the stench of stale beer.

We were off plan.

Henry called out from the back as he re-entered the room, "I hear shots."

"We're okay," I called back to Henry.

"Ten minutes," Henry replied as he came toward us.

Not soon enough for me.

"Do you know me?" I shouted.

Scarecrow gave me a blank stare.

"You and your friends killed two men, raped a girl, and burned down a pool hall. You got kicked in the nuts that night."

His face flushed. I'd made contact. He glanced down at what was left of Big Guy and back to me. One of his eyes pulled shut to a slit and his mouth began moving.

"My friends? I mean, maybe they ain't my friends."

"You were with them."

"I didn't kill nobody. I didn't rape nobody. I didn't set no fires."

"I saw you there," I told him.

"Oh, yeah?"

"Yeah, you fucking *pendejo*. My little sister saw you there."

Albert had his pistol out and he wanted to use it some more.

I moved a step toward Scarecrow, bringing his attention

back to me. His half-closed eye began a perceptible twitch as he looked past me and watched Henry squat down to check on the unconscious bartender.

"I think you know who I am," I said, using that patient tone of voice reserved for drunks.

"I mean, shit," he stammered. His booze-addled mind was grasping for strategy. "Okay, I was there, but I didn't do none of the things you're pissed off about. I was riding with those guys, yeah. But I—I didn't do none of that shit you're saying. Maybe them other guys. It was a while back. I mean, you been carrying this, ain't cha? I can tell. It's been festering in you bad. But I don't run with them guys no more. I ain't seen them forever. I'm changed."

I said, "I know what you did and didn't do, Rusty. It's the others I want, not you."

"Me and Peg's getting married," Scarecrow told me. "We're moving to Oregon. I'm not who you want. I had a fight that night, yeah. Come out on the wrong side, too. But this shit you're pissed off about, that's not my doing. Not murder. Not rape."

Henry came over holding his pistol at his side. He stopped beside me.

"Eight minutes," Henry said.

Scarecrow's body stiffened, and his eye twitch got worse.

"You're going to help us find them, Rusty." I said.

"I remember face," Henry said under his breath.

What was he getting at?

He stepped closer to Scarecrow, moving me more to my right. There was a wordless pause of a second or two. It seemed longer; and during that timelessness, I realized the ringing had stopped in my ears, and I heard the agitated chirp and flap of sparrows—scores of sparrows high in the rafters of that vast room.

"This man murder Will," Henry said, and drew and cocked a second pistol.

"I didn't murder nobody. He don't know what he's saying," Scarecrow said.

"See spots on face. You shoot my Will," Henry said and raised his pistols.

"He's wrong," the biker insisted to me over Henry's shoulder.

"Henry," I said.

"He's wrong," Scarecrow pleaded, his eyes going mad-dog crazy.

He dived for his pistol on the bar, and Henry shot him point blank.

Those first two bullets killed his son's murderer as dead as he was ever going to be, destroying his heart as they tore through his body. The impact of those hits slammed Scarecrow back into the bar, scattering beer bottles and ashtrays and spilling Peggy's green liqueur.

Henry kept shooting the biker even as gravity began its pull. The barrage of bullets caused the body to jerk about as it slipped down behind the falling stools. He continued shooting Scarecrow's lifeless body until it came to rest on the floor tangled in the brass foot rail.

He kept shooting the body until his weapons were out of bullets.

"You killed him, Henry," Albert confirmed and swung himself around to finish off Peggy.

"Don't do it," I said.

Albert's bloodshot eyes swept from me to Henry and back to me before he holstered his big automatic and swung away.

"We go," Henry said with a certain urgency.

As I followed the two men into the back and out of that immense space, I thought of the laughter at Henry Chin's Poolroom the night they killed my father, because the last sound I heard at Helen's Bay Side was the chittering lament and flutter of the frightened sparrows in the rafters.

As we stepped out of the building, into the warm night

air, the man assigned to the task took an ax to the electrical service line. All the lights went out. The phone line had been cut earlier, before the back door was opened, and Albert's men began lugging out cases of booze.

Stealing liquor had never been part of the plan. Boys will be boys, I was learning.

"We go. We go," Henry called out.

We rushed across the service road, stepping gingerly as we made our way over the uneven surfaces of gravel, steel, and ties that made up the several sets of railroad tracks that ran behind the warehouses.

"Here come train!" Henry shouted.

And two minutes later, the mighty Santa Fe diesel that thrice-weekly serviced the stockyards with its mile-long string of odoriferous cattle cars thundered past at the plodding, relentless speed of ten miles an hour and slowing.

When it came to a stop and began the grinding back and forth process of disengaging a section here and a section there, it would cause a three and a half hour, middle-of-the-night, bell-clanging blockade at eight city roads including the two streets providing access to Helen's Bay Side.

No matter when Peggy woke up in that pitch black, corpse-littered cavern of death, she had no phone, and she wasn't leaving the area until the train moved.

We had ample time to disperse, drive home, and burn our blood-splattered clothes. Plenty of time before Helen Mercer got a call from the Fort Worth police to meet them at her place of business to discuss robbery, two murders, and an assault.

Just another slow Tuesday night at Helen's Bay Side.

10

"THAT WASN'T OUR plan," I said to Henry when we were in the dark cab of his truck on the highway, heading west.

"Think on feet," Henry said, keeping his eyes straight ahead.

"You could say that, I guess."

It had been a simple plan: Henry, Albert, and I would go in and take Scarecrow hostage. We'd tie up, gag, and leave behind anyone who was there with him—no phone, no way out. The motorcycles had been chained to the back of Henry's truck, dragged a few blocks away and abandoned at the curb as junk.

"We knew it could go bad if someone from their side got stupid," I said.

"Albert say big man pull gun," Henry said.

"That's how it happened, and Scarecrow went for his, too."

"He killed my son."

"I always thought Will killed the man who shot him," I said.

"I think that, too. They beat me. Shoot me. I wake up. All fire, smoke. You under table. I know face. No mistake. Never forget. Scarecrow man murder my Will. I kill man with spots on face. I kill man murder my son."

Revenge is a kind of wild justice, Bacon said, but I don't think he approved of it.

I watched Henry and tried to imagine the thoughts behind that stern face. Fifty years ago he began his life as a carpenter's apprentice in China. I wondered if he could ever have believed that his destiny would have led him to commit murder in Texas.

"Our plan good plan," Henry said.

"Was it? I'm not so sure," I said.

After we secured the Bay Side, we were going to take Scarecrow to a secluded spot and make him tell us how to find the others. After that, we were going to leave him tied up and naked on the streets of some God-fearing little Texas backwater with his guns nearby.

Finding him like that and a peek at his arrest record would have gotten him a Sullivan charge and put him in jail.

"What Sullivan charge?" Henry had asked Otis.

"There ain't one of them in Texas exactly. What I mean is if a felon like Scarecrow gets caught with guns, it don't go easy on him."

The weapons that Henry and I carried into the Bay Side were to be used for protection and to make people see things our way. Uh huh.

The best laid plans.

We killed the man who killed Will, and maybe that was the way it had to be. I don't know. It had all been out of control. We ended up with no leads to the other killers, and getting leads was the purpose of the exercise. No matter how I tried to slice it, we were left with a jagged edge. We'd made a mess of it.

"I'm tired," I said to Henry.

In fact, I felt nauseous.

"You sleep now. Jim glad see you later, you bet."

I don't know what I thought revenge was going to be like. Though now I knew for sure it wasn't pretty. And I became convinced of another thing, too. Life was never fair, no matter what side of the fence you stood on. Big Guy had never done anything to any of us. He was just drunk and at the wrong place at the wrong time. Wearing Scarecrow's colors was his misfortune, misjudging another drunk's sincerity his mistake.

I didn't doubt that we had done the world a favor by exterminating some vermin, but hadn't I crossed some line in their direction when I became an accomplice to murder?

Hell, I was fretting too soon about what I'd become. If revenge was to be my path, I was simply a quarter of the way to what I was going to be.

"Our plan wasn't good, Henry. I see it now—now that it's too late."

Henry argued that there was nobility in revenge, and I knew from my reading that there was abundant historical precedent to justify his point of view. Though that wasn't my point.

"I'm not saying that what we *did* was wrong, Henry. I'm saying we didn't think things through. We didn't plan well enough."

"Things went wrong," Henry agreed.

I said, "Yeah, they did. And we left Peggy, the barkeep, behind because we weren't willing to slaughter an innocent woman, no matter how poorly she chose her lovers. So, that's a witness on their side. From our side, line them up: Otis, Albert, and two duck-tailed liquor thieves whose names we don't even know."

"Albert know names."

"Yeah, and the police, too, no doubt. Six in all, counting the two of us. Seven actually. Peggy has to be tossed into the count."

"She sleep all time."

"True, and she'd been drinking. So, who knows what she'll be able to put together? Still, there are seven who know at least something about what happened at that honky-tonk tonight. Even if we never tell Sarge and Harlan, they'll find out some day, so that makes some more. Taking out an ad in the paper might have involved fewer threats to our freedom."

"Ad bad idea," Henry advised me.

I was suffering from that ice water plunge of afterthought that comes after the deed is done and you know it was all a mistake.

After training for over a year, I could shoot accurately, duck, weave, and slice with the best of them, and even win at nine-ball. But I was a rank amateur in the game of vengeance. And I came to realize something else that night. It was not just Henry's dream of vengeance. It was mine as well.

I'd read that women usually did one of two things after being abused. They either found another abuser because they felt they weren't worthy of anyone else. Or they tried to find someone to protect them. It was the exceptional woman who decided to learn to protect herself.

Over the hammering wind, I said, "Henry, I pledge to you that if we're lucky enough not to be dragged off to prison and executed for what we did tonight, I'll perfect *all* my skills before approaching another member of that gang. Because I want the rest of them. No mistakes. I want them."

"I pledge, too. No mistakes. I want, too," he said.

I was admitting that night what I'd been afraid to voice until then. I wanted those savage murderers dead at my feet more than I had ever wanted anything in my life. I wanted the rest of them dead: Mechanic, Bear, and most of all, Blue Eyes.

It was then that I saw the future.

I knew that to remain free—and stay alive long enough to see through to the end what I was feeling that night—it would have to be no witnesses. No accomplices. Just revenge.

A mile or so down the highway, I touched Henry's arm. He took a look at my face and pulled over so I could get out and throw up.

The next morning I sat up in bed with such a start that Jim hurried to his feet thinking there were barbarians at the gates.

My heart was pounding. My pillow was damp. I sat where I was and squinted at Jim who had his hackles up. The poor dog was not yet steady on his feet. I tried not to think, but was unsuccessful. What had I done?

I got up and approached the mirror.

I saw a girl there in a man's t-shirt with a sweaty scrunched up face. Wrinkled forehead. Matted hair. I would be nineteen in less than a month. How could the girl in the glass look so old and used up? I stared at her in silence, my head aching.

I could also see Jim's reflection, his bandaged leg and the places here and there in his thick coat that had been shaved so Henry could stitch his wounds. Jim had had a true trial by fire. I had been an accomplice to a drunken response to insult and a hotheaded act of revenge.

Was that fair? Big Guy had pulled a pistol on Albert. How long would I have waited before doing something about Big Guy?

Albert told me, "I have no doubts about you, Little Sister."

Standing there near the deafening roar of the train, he'd shouted, "Be proud. Tonight you're one step closer to taking back your dignity."

Albert was clear on our position. A father and son murdered. A daughter assaulted, beaten, left for dead. That called for time-honored bloodshed to regain respect for the families, and to reclaim the daughter's honor. Simple. Straightforward.

"We'll kill them together here, Little Sister. I'll kill them again in Hell."

Now I understood what Albert had known all along. Reason would never play a part in this. It was kill or be killed. Or, walk away and live with it.

Of course, there was the wild card. Why had the police been pulled off the case? I was asking Otis about that often enough to piss him off.

"Quit calling me about that, Missy. I'm working on it, Goddamn it."

Jim emitted a tiny squeak of discomfort as he stretched and yawned and stepped over to the door. I could stand in front of the mirror philosophizing and wallowing in conjecture if I wished, but the dog needed to pee.

That snapped me out it. I remembered my pledge from the night before and knew in my heart that I meant every word of it. I wasn't walking away from anything. I opened the door for Jim, took a couple of aspirins, and started drawing a bath.

The HONKY-TONK MASSACRE pushed the McCarthy hearings out of the headlines for a few days. Last year, *Three Dead in Pool Hall Fire* had gotten two paragraphs on page eight.

After the police leaked that what happened at Helen's Bay Side was a rumble between outlaw motorcycle gangs, the papers played it up. After the papers played it up, there were more shootings involving nervous bikers, confirming that the police knew what they were talking about.

This set off the newspapers for another round with headlines screaming MORE HONKY-TONK WAR, outraging an already frightened city that feared its citizens would be caught in gangland crossfire.

Otis said that public ire increased the arrests of bikers citywide and diluted the investigation of the original Bay Side killings.

That was good for us, he pointed out, folding up that day's issue of the Dallas Star-News Journal and tossing it on top of the mess on his desk. "The reaction's a two-edged sword," he said. "On the one hand, the department is shoving bikers through their system faster'n grass goes through geese, and that's getting me names through my connections. Now the other side of that is motorcycles are leaving town, and the ones who're left are jittery as hens with a rooster loose."

Otis had a sip of his nasty coffee and stared at us. Trying

to think up more barnyard references, no doubt. No sound in the large room except for the rattle of his fan.

"It was always surgery we talked about if it came to rough stuff."

"Surgery?" I threw back at him, not caring for his tone of voice.

"Yes, ma'am."

I could see he was winding up, so I held my tongue.

"A little sit down was what it was supposed to be, a sit down that might could turn nasty. Okay? I believe I got that confirmed."

I continued to hold my tongue.

"We talked about it might get nasty, but if it did, always surgery. Never blunt instruments. I swear I don't recall a thing about Mexican gangs or shooting up bodies like Swiss cheese."

"Circumstances alter cases," Henry said. He'd practiced that answer before we left home.

"Well, you know, Hank, I guess they must."

Otis sat back on the edge of his desk and took a deep breath.

"It could be that working so close to the stockyards was a bad influence, but dad gummit what I did for you was the same as pulling a trigger in the eyes of the law. Excuse my French, but I don't like my tits this near the wringer. You following me here?"

Henry nodded, though I wasn't certain he had a total grasp of tits and wringers.

I said, "Okay. We shouldn't have put you in danger. But what's with all this surgery talk? You knew it could go bad."

"Maybe so, but you get what I'm saying."

"Oh, yeah. I get it." And I did, too. He didn't like where the killings had left him, any better than I liked where they'd left me.

He said, "In the State of Texas it's a valid defense to say they needed killing. I'll give you that. But the *unreasonable use of deadly force* and a thing the law calls *mutual combat*. Well, that's where it's gonna break down."

He stared past me during one of those long pauses that were beginning to annoy me.

"You got one piece of luck. The boys downtown ain't fessed up to it yet, but they got nothing. Peggy's their one witness, and she can't talk because her jaw ain't working so good since somebody loosened half her teeth."

No one had more empathy for her than I did.

"And being as how she's just an illiterate bayou trollop—and dumber'n a mule on top of that—the notes she scribbles look like supper checks from the Mandarin Palace downstairs. No offense intended, Hank."

"No offense, Otis."

Otis sipped his awful brew and stared at us again for a while. Henry and I sat like I recall sitting in the Principal's office, wanting it over with, just waiting to leave.

"And you know, we ain't got much either, since the dead can't talk," Otis said.

He was baiting me. I kept quiet.

"I'd hunker down if I was you, Hank."

"Hunker down good idea," Henry said.

"I'll see what these collars turn up and get back to you. That's all we got for now."

Good. I wanted to get out of there. But Otis wasn't quite finished.

"It was like something from the Bible, all them motorcycles leaving the city at one time."

I couldn't let that one go.

"Which Bible's that, Otis?"

"I mean the floods and all, the locusts. You ran them bikers to ground pretty good, you know."

"We know," I said, hoping he was finished with biblical references.

"You can't just rope a calf anyway you see fit, though. There're rules."

"Jesus, Otis. Put a cork in it. It got out of hand, things happened. We didn't go in there to make that kind of mess. We know better now."

I guess that was what he wanted to hear. He nodded.

"I hope so. Like I say, I'll see what the collars shake out. Till then, keep it low."

"Keep it low," Henry repeated, and we stood up to announce we were leaving.

We'd started for the door before I remembered to ask about the dogs.

"What dogs?" Otis asked.

"The three you told us about out at Scarecrow's trailer house," I said.

"What about them?"

"Can you call someone so they don't starve to death or something?"

Otis wiped a hand down his face to let me know he saw irony in my request.

"You will then?" I wanted a commitment.

"I will," he said.

"Thanks," I replied pleasantly.

Otis looked past me to Henry who was waiting by the open door.

"Okay, Hank. I'll do my best here."

"Best good thing," Henry said.

"I'll give you a jangle the first I hear of something, but I wouldn't hold my breath."

He'd explode if he held his breath, the bag of wind. But Henry and I took his advice and headed for the homestead to start hunkering down.

We talked on the way home.

"When newspaper story go away, police go away," Henry said.

"After all the time we've spent being careful, how could we have lost it so big the first time out of the chute?"

First time out of the chute? Had I said that?

"That sound like Otis," Henry noted.

Moving it along, I said, "We can't worry about something that somebody might say or do some day."

"Can't predict," Henry said.

"Exactly. I think we have to hope for the best and prepare for the worst."

"Who say that?"

"I did."

"Good idea anyway."

"Look, Henry, what if the guys in the gang try to get us where we live?"

"We need make homestead strong maybe. Better doors and windows."

"And, if we need to, come up with ways to keep it from appearing that we've done things."

"How you mean?"

"I don't know. But if someone looks in advance, like we did at Helen's Bay Side, we don't want them to see our defenses."

That was when Henry's homestead started becoming a fortified zone of sorts.

We established primary and secondary positions and fallback contingencies. Henry loved the military language. Putting the verbiage aside, what we did was dig some holes and trenches, plant some shrubs to conceal iron and cement barriers, string and bury some strong steel cable, and cache some weapons and ammo in different places around the property.

The last thing we did was rig some hiding places for sawed-off shotguns in our vehicles.

Along about mid-summer, a few weeks after we'd been over for our dressing-down, Otis invited us back. He said he thought he'd found another one of our guys.

When we got there, he asked me to wait in the hall until Henry looked at some pictures. "I don't want you two influencing each other, see."

So I waited outside, and after a few minutes, Otis had me

come in and look at a half dozen mug shots he had spread out on his desk. Henry stood to the side, a canary halfway down his throat.

"That one. That's Bear," I said.

"Hank picked him, too."

Otis pushed a butt in his mouth, tipped his chair back, and threw a foot up on the desk before he lit up. He'd never done that before, so I figured it was because he was feeling proud of himself.

"Bear was the one who pulled me from the car and forced me back inside the pool hall that night," I told Otis.

"Is that a fact," he said.

"You know where he is? Who he is?" I asked.

"Yep. His name's Roy Birns, he's a parole violator, and he's on his way back to jail."

Henry and I showed our disappointment.

"How long go jail?" Henry asked.

"It would've been six months, Hank, but he said something stupid to the judge, and it turned into nine months before they could drag his sorry ass out of the courtroom."

"Man," I said. "Nine months? It'll be—damn it—next March before he's out."

"Don't fret, Missy. Think of the upside," Otis said.

"Tell upside," Henry said.

"We know where he's at," Otis explained.

The disaster at the Bay Side had stirred up one lead, even if we did have to wait the better part of a year before we could follow up. Otis said it was like having money in the bank. And, while he was on the subject, he tapped Henry an extra fee for the pictures.

"I had to grease a couple a guys down at headquarters to get this stuff," he explained.

He didn't need to make excuses to us. Otis did his job, and adding it up, he wasn't going to retire on what he was taking in from our case.

I made money on my tours with Harlan. I helped Henry with the costs. That's how I knew the arrangement, and all in all, Otis was being fair with us. When he said he'd keep digging around for the others and try to find out who quashed our case, we knew he would. He was long-winded and could bore a person to tears, but he was honest and hated bad guys with a passion.

So Otis went back to hunting for Mechanic and Blue Eyes. Roy "Bear" Birns went to Huntsville to serve his time, and Henry and I went back to work on our fortifications.

A couple of months later, when Henry and I were finished, we inspected our work and agreed that we had done a good job.

I had found solace in being at Henry's side through the summer and learning many of his skills. The long days and the steady physical challenge had put me in even better condition. My stomach was flat and firm. I had a deep tan. I was clear-eyed with healthy, sun-bleached hair down to my shoulders that I kept pulled back in a ponytail.

I was beginning to like what I saw in the mirror. My scars had faded, and my figure was definitely less girlish. I was wearing a light gloss on my lips and had learned to put on my eyes from how-to articles in glamour magazines. After hours and hours of practice I was feeling confident with mascara. Or, to put it another way: I had learned that with mascara, a little goes a long way.

For the first time since moving to Henry's, I felt the urge to go shopping for something besides Levi's, socks, and t-shirts. I was tired of looking like Annie Oakley.

I was feeling restless, and I knew it was more than just being bored. I wasn't certain what I wanted to do. I just had a longing to do something besides shoot pool, read books, listen to jazz, and train at my close-quarter combat skills. I needed a change of pace, fresh faces.

I wanted to get away from Henry's for a while. I called Harlan's office in Austin and left a message.

Trips away with him weren't what I'd call exciting, but

they were fun. Flying with him to pool halls all over west Texas at least presented a variety of personalities. Harlan would call ahead, the parlors got the word out, and cowboys showed up from everywhere to try and beat me.

"Baby Shark creates a party atmosphere," Harlan told me. "I'm thinking the parlors should start paying us a percentage of increased revenues just for showing our faces. I know for sure their Coke sales go up."

The women at those places never misunderstood that Harlan was like an uncle to me. But the young men were unclear about things; they always suspected there was more to it and asked a lot of what I think they believed were innocent questions.

Cute guys the right age showed up now and again. If they behaved themselves, I'd dump a game or two so I could get to know them better. Harlan was okay with that, since it was good if I didn't win all the time. That was pretty much all the girl-boy practice I ever got, and the chances of seeing any of those guys again were slim to none.

So much for romance on the road.

Who was I kidding, anyway? How was I supposed to have a normal life? Any guy who ever found out what happened to me would never be able to look me in the eye without thinking about it. Not so many years ago, I would've been called Soiled Dove instead of Baby Shark.

Harlan returned my call.

He was over in Austin busy with a new sales campaign and said it would be a while before he could take some time off to shoot pool. He asked if I was practicing.

"I am, Harlan, but I need to get out of here for a while. I'm going stir crazy."

"Of course, you are. I understand that. Let's see. I won't be free to take you out again for—damn. I don't know—six, maybe eight weeks."

"It'll be after Halloween by then," I said, fighting to keep the disappointment out of my voice.

"I'm afraid so. Listen, Kristin, this should cheer you up.

A Dallas newspaper reporter tracked me down. He wants to do a story about Baby Shark. I told him I barely know you. I told him I just run into you here and there. Haven't seen you for months. He offered me good money to help find you. The newspapers think you're hot stuff."

"Real exciting," I said.

"I'm sorry, Kristin."

"I know. Thanks, anyway."

"You gonna be okay?"

"I'll figure something out," I told him.

I tried keeping myself busy with my regular schedule of practice and study. It didn't work. Everything had become boring. When I thought about the Scarecrow killings or the vicious thugs that Otis was trying to find, I became angry or depressed.

I called Otis so often that he finally blew up. "Didn't I tell you I'd let you know? You do not have to keep calling me every fifteen minutes. I'll call you, Goddamn it."

One day along about then, I spent an entire afternoon slouched in a lawn chair, watching crows peck seeds from our dried sunflowers. I needed to get away. The Cadillac was mine, of course, and I could take it out any time I wanted. The problem with that was it was too recognizable to those who knew my dad.

That's when I got the idea to ride the motorcycle.

Although Henry thought I was crazy at first, he warmed to it when I said I'd quit being so moody. So he got the machine licensed, repainted, made some adjustments to make it fit me better, and got a grease monkey friend of his to come by to get it running right.

I was anxious to begin riding it. Though I knew I had to start at the very beginning and learn the two most difficult things for someone my size: the technique of kick-starting it and the ability to pick up the heavy machine when it fell over.

Henry and I rigged a method for me to lift cement blocks, using my legs more than my back. We increased the poundage little by little, until I had the strength to handle the Harley.

Kick-starting the motorcycle took some work, too. Learning to stiffen my leg and throw my total weight down on the starter was an action that I did over and over again until I got it.

Then it was out and back to the wildcat well until I was in control of it. When I got over the fear of handling the brute, I found that I liked knowing how to ride a Harley. I spilled a time or two. I wasn't hurt badly, though, and the bike survived. So what.

"Where you ride?" Henry always wanted to know once I started taking it out.

"Over to Sweetwater and back," I usually told him. But I rode around to other small towns, too. Folks stared, of course. They'd never seen a girl driving a motorcycle.

Hell, *I'd* never seen a girl driving a motorcycle.

11

October 1954

SAN ANGELO WAS seventy-five miles or so south of Henry's. Not a great distance, but it would be the farthest from home that I had been on my bike.

When I told Henry I was going there, he asked me to bring back a cobbler from Wilma's Café. We'd made a point of staying away from Wilma's when we were in San Angelo since we didn't want anyone who knew me with my dad to put Henry and me together.

Wilma's Café was across from Charley's Pool Hall. It was handy and had a decent menu so Dad and I used to eat there when we were in town. Julio, a rotund Mexican cook in his sixties, and a rangy forty-year-old named Wilma owned the café. Wilma used to put her hands in my hair, pull it this way and that and talk about hairstyles as she made bedroom eyes at my dad. I wondered if she would remember me.

It was just after noon when I parked my bike in front of the café, stuffed my stocking cap in my jacket pocket, and went in to join the twenty or so customers.

Another twenty and it would've been standing room only. I remembered the smell, like Grandma's kitchen. I glanced around. Plenty of Halloween decorations. No Wilma. A waitress I didn't know was taking an order on the other side of the room. The jukebox was playing something by Nat King Cole.

I took a stool at the counter and waited.

Wilma saw me as she straight-armed the swinging doors and lunged sideways from the kitchen, three plates full of steaming food on her trailing arm.

"You're a sight for sore eyes," she said as she passed.

So much for her not remembering me.

Three or four giant strides and she was across the room. Her pale yellow uniform, a size too small as usual, strained against her full curves as she sashayed around tables and chairs. Her thick auburn hair was caught up in a yellow cotton yarn snood that kept it from swinging loose about her wide shoulders.

She had a Rosie the Riveter kind of look.

I saw Charley and his sidekick Eddie in a booth near the fogged windows. They were finishing their lunch. Charley was a stout, old, white-haired guy with bad skin and a red face. The pool hall across the street had been his for more than twenty years.

Eddie, an ageless little bald-headed guy with a sunken chest, high arching eyebrows, and darting eyes, shined shoes and sped about doing the housekeeping for Charley.

Wilma came back, chewing gum as usual, and leaned a firm hip against the oilcloth-covered counter. She jammed one hand in her coin-heavy apron pocket, jiggled the change there, and ignored the customers trying to get her attention.

She spoke to me in a low-pitched, confidential tone. Her large brown eyes peek-a-booed from below her shaggy bangs.

"What's it been, honey? Gotta be two years at least."

"Something like that," I said.

She had a long face, a wide mouth, even white teeth, and a pretty smile. She could've done lipstick ads.

"I heard about your daddy. In Abilene, was it?"

"Near there," I told her.

"I looked, but I never saw anything much about it. There was a fire?"

"That was the night, yeah."

"I heard there was a fire. Sorry, honey, and you know I sincerely mean it."

"I know, Wilma."

"He was a handsome man, your daddy."

"Uh huh."

"And gave you that platinum hair."

When she brought her hand from her pocket, I saw it coming and had to hold myself from moving away. And, like old times, she ran her fingers through my hair. Her expression changed when she saw my ear.

"Oh, honey, what happened?"

I reached up and brought my hair back in place.

"Nothing, Wilma. A little accident," I said and smiled.

She returned her hand to her change pocket.

"You okay?"

She recognized the results of a beating. Her eyes told me so.

"It was a while ago," I said.

She searched my face. I saw her eyes moisten.

"Not your daddy."

"No. Definitely not."

Her face relaxed, she gave me a brave grin, and popped her gum.

"He bragged on you, your daddy. He said you read the same grown up books he did."

She shifted her weight and gave the room a once over, smiling and nodding at the customers who wanted service. But she held her ground. Her reaction to me was the first time I ever felt as if I knew something about her beyond her cafe. I guessed that she'd had some sad parts to her life, too.

"You're all grown up now, ain't cha? What brings you to town?"

"Just took a ride over to say hello."

"Well, ain't you the sweetest thing. Where you living now?"

"Out west of Abilene."

"You don't say. Out Sweetwater way?"

"Near there. How've you been? You married yet?"

"Ain't one man can keep me happy, honey. How about you? You look trim and fit and all full of tricks yourself."

I felt my face flush, and she pushed my shoulder with her fingertips.

"Just teasing. Take off your jacket. Lemme get you some split peas with weenies. It's better'n it sounds. Julio's still the cook here, so it's got kickass little peppers in it."

"Good," I said.

"You gonna peek in across the street for old time's sake?"

"Thought I might."

Wilma turned some heads as she shifted a well-defined hip away from the counter. She snapped a nickel down near my hand.

"Play Nat Cole again, will you, honey? Gives the place a little class."

She popped her gum and moved away.

After lunch, I left my Harley where it was, carried my jacket, and walked over to Charley's.

It was curious how I felt. I had entered many pool halls by that point in my life. Never alone, though. That was just enough of a difference to jack my nerves up a notch.

It was dark inside. It took a moment for my vision to adjust.

Charley was hiked up in a tall chair near the register reading the paper by a gooseneck lamp, a ratty dead cigar butt in his mouth. Eddie was in among the tables sweeping the floor. Some kid had a pinball machine clanging.

"You old enough to be in here?" Charley asked, his face in the sports page.

He'd done his looking while my eyes were adjusting.

"I'm old enough."

"Don't cause no trouble," he said, keeping his face where it was.

I placed a dollar on the counter near him. "Is buying a table for a couple of hours what you call trouble?"

His paper collapsed. He snatched the horrid scrap of tobacco from his mouth and brought his eyes to mine. "Who you with?"

His squint was supposed to scare me. It didn't.

"I'm alone," I told him.

"What d'you want with a table?"

"You think a girl can't shoot pool?"

"Don't you sass me or you can get out and stay out."

He stared at me long enough to make his point, put the awful thing back in his mouth, and took my dollar from the counter.

He went back to his newspaper before he said, "I don't want nobody having words over you. Is that clear enough?"

"Clear enough," I said and moved into the room.

There were seven tables, each under its own circle of light. The two enshrouded in clouds of smoke were in use. The young guys at those tables all watched as I tried to find a decent cue and laughed among themselves about how it was a chore for me. Even the kid on the pinball machine came over to join the fun.

I changed tables until I found one that was level enough not to have a mind of its own. That was even more amusing to them. They didn't care that I knew they were making fun of me. I was in their territory.

There were five of them, all wearing worn out blue jeans, boots, wool shirts. One of them had on a sweat-stained cowboy hat. He was the old timer in the bunch—maybe twenty.

I dropped in two on the break and heard them go silent. A few minutes later, after I'd run the rest of the table without missing a shot, one of them wandered over.

He said, "Where'd'you learn ta shoot like gat?"

I lifted my eyes long enough to see he had a kid's face, brown hair, shifty eyes, and a pallor that said he wasn't out of Charley's too much.

"You ain't from around here, are ya?" he asked.

I ignored him and began racking the balls. His friends laughed at him until he retreated. They kicked it around and another came over. He spoke so quietly I had to turn my head to hear him.

"You wanna game or you just wanna shoot around by yourself?"

I tightened the group and put the rack aside before taking a gander at the fresh volunteer. He was the guy in the cowboy hat. He was leaning against the table holding his cue vertically, toying with a chalk. He looked right at me with a steady gaze. He probably had sisters. Girls weren't a problem for him.

"You want a game?" I asked him in a voice as quiet as his.

"Will you cry if I beat you?"

He was still speaking so the others wouldn't hear.

"Will *you* cry if I beat you?" I replied.

He smiled and sort of tipped his head. "Can't say. Never shot pool with a girl."

"Maybe I'm the wrong girl for you to start on. I wouldn't want your friends to see you cry."

I liked his laugh. It was quiet and real.

"Go ahead and break. I'll get my handkerchief out," he said.

The others meandered over when they saw that we were going to play, so I left him a spread he could work with. He'd been a gentleman. His friends were quiet until he scratched and it became my turn.

"She's gonna whup your ass," they said. Laughing. Punching each other. Growing loud.

I stopped, stepped back from the table, and stared at them until they settled down. "Tell you what, guys. I'm paying ten dollars to anyone who can beat me. Okay? And if I win, you pay me a buck. Fair enough?"

I saw Charley with his paper lowered, listening.

"We break," one of them insisted.

"If you're quiet, you break. If you're noisy, I break. You in?"

It worked. They got quiet, and I got busy. In less than two

hours, I'd beaten them all twice and a couple of them more than that. I split my winnings with Charley up by the register under a sign that said: *Absolutely No Gambling*. I bought Cokes for the boys and a pack of Juicy Fruit.

"You're welcome back," Charley told me as he lit up a new stogie.

I smiled and spoke to him with respect.

"Thanks, Charley. See you in a couple of days."

I slipped on my jacket as I crossed the street. The ride home was going to be cold. At the café what I had left of my winnings covered the peach cobbler for Henry as well as a nice tip for Wilma.

"That's too much," she said.

"Take it," I said. "I won it off some boys across the street."

She glanced out the window at Charley's. "How's that? You beat some boys playing pool games?"

I nodded yes and she eyed me as I held the money out.

"Your daddy teach you how?"

"Yeah, he did," I lied, and remembered the Juicy Fruit. "Oh, I got you some gum."

She took the gum and the money.

"You remembered my brand. When're we seeing you again?"

"Soon. I already miss Julio's cooking."

She popped her gum and widened her eyes.

"Wilma?"

"Yeah?"

"I need a favor, and I know I can trust you."

"You sure can. What is it?"

I said, "There are things I don't want people to know about me. It's important, or I wouldn't ask it."

"What things, honey?"

"Charley and Eddie don't remember me with my Dad. You do, and I'm glad you do. But I don't want anybody else to know who I am."

"Well, I'll swan. Why's that?"

"There was a bad thing that happened, Wilma. One of these days, I'll tell you about it. Until I do, I just want a life of my own. One not connected with my Dad. Nobody else knows me around here. So, if you don't say anything—"

Wilma moved to take me in her arms. I stepped in and took her hands in mine instead.

"Your secret's safe with me, and you know I sincerely mean it," she said.

She came outside and watched while I strapped down the cobbler. As I pulled on my stocking cap and put on my sunglasses, I noticed Eddie and the boys across the street standing around. Maybe they wanted to watch their money leave town.

I kicked over my bike and gave Wilma a smile goodbye. Knowing they were all watching, I gunned that Harley for effect as I roared away.

Once the wind was in my face, I thought about my first day out of the nest.

"It's never the same going back someplace," my dad told me once. He must've been talking about long absences, since that was what he knew most about.

Still, even with that warning, I wasn't prepared for what happened several days later when I rode back into San Angelo.

12

IT HAD BEEN a normal morning. Target practice with Henry. My run out to the old well and back with Jim. The hour and a half of strike and response moves that Sarge demanded. A couple of hours at the table practicing lags and breaks. I wasn't going to be so generous about breaks in the future, and boning up on my technique didn't seem like a bad idea.

Henry was already gone when I was ready to go. Jim saw me off, barking and running beside me out to the gate. I knew that after I was down the road and out of sight, he would trot back to his place near the cellar door and become the watchdog he was bred to be.

That second ride down to San Angelo was nippier than the first. I arrived at Wilma's several degrees shy of an icicle.

It was after the noon rush, so I shivered my way into an almost empty diner. I sat at the counter as close to the warm kitchen as I could get, knowing by then that I had picked the wrong time of the year to start riding a motorcycle.

Just in case I'd missed that revelation, Wilma mentioned it. "Are you outta your mind? You're gonna make yourself sick riding that thing on a day like this. Can't cha borrow someone's car or something?"

I motioned for hot chocolate. While I was getting feeling back in my hands and face, she asked me if I was Baby Shark. I didn't show that I'd been caught off guard.

"Who's asking that?" I got out through my cold lips.

"Someone told the boys they'd been suckered. You know Charley can be crookeder than a dog's back leg, so there's some out there saying he asked you in to make a little extra for hisself."

"Charley doesn't know who I am, Wilma."

She winked at me. "He doesn't know who you really are. But are you the pool player they're talking about?"

I nodded yes, and she popped her gum.

"Maybe two days ago that old fart didn't know you from Adam's off ox. Don't open your purse on that one today, Miss Baby Shark."

Wilma and I looked up together when Eddie arrived. He stepped in, closed the door gently behind him, and sidled over next to us, his baggy khaki pants flapping around his skinny ankles. His eyes careened around the room and settled on me.

"Charley wants to know if you're shooting pool today."

"He does, does he?" Wilma wanted to know, giving her gum some hard chewing.

Eddie's eyes lurched her way a time or two before coming back to me. I didn't answer him. Finally, he said, "Same arrangement as last time's fine with him. 'Cept you don't gotta pay greens fees."

I still didn't say anything. Wilma couldn't stand the silence and sniffed. "He oughta give her a better arrangement. She's picked your business up, ain't she?"

Eddie's eyes zigzagged around and he shrugged his bony shoulders. "He's willing to talk."

I let him blink and glance a while before saying, "Tell Charley I'll be over."

He nodded his head like a string was pulling it, backed away, and hustled out the door.

Wilma lowered her voice. "I ain't been in that dreary, smelly place since your daddy used to shoot there. Now, today, I'm feeling the urge. Are you as good as they say?"

"I'd ignore gossip, Wilma."

"Well? Are you?"

"Against some big shot player from Chicago, who's to say? But here in San Angelo—"

I grinned, and Wilma rewarded me with one of her marvelous smiles and a little push with her fingertips.

"Let me make you a tuna melt. Charley can just wait," she said and snapped her gum.

The pool hall was busy when I walked in but went quiet when everyone turned my way. I'd seen guys respond that way before, guys anxious to test my skill.

Eddie got to me first. But Charley came over smiling, which was a strange thing to see.

"I didn't know you was Baby Shark," Charley murmured through his teeth, trying to keep his conversation with me confidential.

I didn't say anything, so he went on.

"You are Baby Shark, ain't cha?"

Charley didn't play long shots.

"That's what they call me," I told him.

Eddie, who was hanging on every word, lit up like he'd been plugged in.

"You have a full house," I said.

"Word gets around," Eddie said, and looked a little sheepish.

"You feel like playing?" Charley asked.

I looked past him at the hushed room of players standing around like guys in a duck blind at daybreak. Maybe two dozen all together. The place had a different smell to it with that many men there, most of them smoking, drinking beer.

"I'll use the same table as before," I said, giving over my outer layers of clothing to Eddie.

"Which was that?" Charley asked.

"She played five last time," Eddie chimed in.

"Five, it is," Charley mumbled, giving Eddie a frown.

"And if you want fifty percent, Charley, you tell these guys we're playing by the rules. If there's a bad hit or a foul, I'll step back, you'll call it. You handle the money. You keep the place quiet. I don't talk when I play, and I don't like noise."

Charley nodded his head all the time I was talking.

"What's the bet?" he asked.

"Twenty dollars."

He puckered and blew air.

"We'll lag for break every time. That keeps the sniveling down later on because I'll only play even up."

"You mean no handicaps," Charley confirmed.

"That's right. If I lose an inning, you pay immediately, and all future bets go to twenty-five."

"Ouch. You sure about that?"

I shrugged. "I can take my business somewhere else."

"No, no. I didn't say that. It's just we got some good players here today."

"I'm why they're here, Charley."

As I turned away, I saw Eddie beaming. He liked the way I talked to his boss.

I kept a poker face as I walked over to the table where I planned to play. They got out of my way, the guys who all wanted to beat me. It was as if they'd lose their luck if they got too close. I'd seen it before. Like I was an untouchable China doll or something.

Harlan said it was just another form of superstition. "Everyone you beat helps you beat the next one. They're not just pool players, they're also gamblers. Never forget that."

Eddie scooted over to rack the balls while I got out a stick. Henry had made my cues, as well as my hardwood case. The case was a birthday present. When Albert first saw it, he couldn't keep his hands off of it, turning it this way and that, feeling the polished surface with his fingertips.

"Henry's going to make my coffin, man," Albert had informed me.

Harlan said that it was important for my opponents to see how valuable my case and cues were. "You don't pay for that stuff by losing," he said.

I placed the beautiful, lightweight box on the corner of the table where the silent men could watch me open it and choose a cue. Eddie was careful when he took my case away. I had another look at my competition as I put my stick together and chalked it.

I recognized a face here and there and nodded. Guys from other places coming back for more. They liked being recognized. A couple of the kids from the other day were in the crowd looking pleased with themselves. They'd done some advertising. It was too bad the stakes got too rich for them.

"Buy those boys Cokes on me," I told Eddie under my breath.

Charley got it started. He made sure everyone understood the rules and the bet. There was some grumbling about the bet being too steep and some borrowing began. The serious players were ready.

I played almost seven hours that day at Charley's and lost a pair. It was toward the end of the session. The guy who took those two games was a skinny little runt in rundown boots. He won the lags and ran the table on me twice.

He had a self-important swagger, a bad case of BO, greasy hair, and a hideous little snigger. Guys just naturally wanted to whip his ass as soon as they saw him.

Nevertheless, he could shoot pool. He had a sharp eye and a decent stroke when he didn't hurry. His flaw was being too casual with the cue ball. Charley paid him off.

After he stuffed his winnings in his baggy blue jeans, I took him five games straight. I was glad when he threw his hands up in surrender, mostly because of his rancid odor. But also because it had been a long day, and I needed a bathroom break.

"I don't know how you held it so long," Wilma said.

We were in the Ladies Room at her café. We'd run across

the street because I needed to go so badly. She was at the mirror and I was behind the stall door.

"They'd have to put a gun to my head to make me pee over there," I told her.

"It was nice how the men clapped for you at the end. Must make you feel like a movie star or something."

"Not really," I said.

"You made Charley a lot a money today, honey. Did he ask you back?"

"Uh huh."

"Maybe you shouldn't go."

"What do you mean?"

Wilma waited until I'd washed my hands and we were leaving the restroom before she answered me. "I'm worried about you riding that motorcycle home in this cold and it being dark and all. You're welcome to stay at my place tonight, if you don't mind cats. You can get on home tomorrow."

"That's nice of you, Wilma. I would except I need to get back."

"Maybe there's another way to do it," a male voice offered.

Wilma and I were both surprised to find a tall man standing in the middle of the dark restaurant. He turned so that what little light there was illuminated his face. He was maybe late twenties, dressed like a rancher.

We stopped at the end of the counter, keeping our distance. I was carrying several hundred dollars, and a lot of people knew it. Adrenaline was flowing as I moved a step away from Wilma and did a quick weapons check. I was ready.

"I've seen you before," Wilma said.

"I suppose so," he replied and took off his Stetson, exposing a head full of dark curls.

He was younger than I'd first thought.

"I've eaten with you a time or two. Name's Al Mackenzie. Folks call me Mac. Didn't mean to startle you."

"We're open for breakfast and lunch, Mac. Unless there was something else you wanted."

"I guess I was thinking pretty much the same thing you were about a night like this. It's getting colder and coming up rain."

"What about it?" Wilma asked.

He'd kept his eyes on her during that exchange, but brought his gaze back to me. He was hands-down good looking and had a friendly face. Especially when he smiled. I told my heart to mind its business and reminded myself that friendly is how a con game starts.

"I was over here dropping off a yearling," he said, looking at Wilma again.

"Uh huh," she said.

"I ranch up near Weatherford, so I've got an empty trailer."

He had an agreeable voice, and I could tell he'd paid attention at school.

"Yeah? So?" she wanted to know.

He brought his eyes back to me.

"I could trailer up your flathead-K, get it outta the rain," he said.

I didn't understand what he was getting at.

"The guys across the way say you ride in from up Abilene way."

I didn't say anything.

"That's on my way home," he said.

"That dog don't hunt," Wilma pointed out. "Not if you ranch in Weatherford."

Mac smiled and shrugged, keeping his eyes on me. "I'm just offering you and your Harley a ride. That's all."

"Well, why didn't you say so instead of scaring us to death," Wilma said.

"Sorry, ma'am."

She popped her gum and switched on the lights.

"Lock the door, Mac. And make sure the sign says *closed* before any more of you cowboys try sneaking in here."

"Yes, ma'am."

To me, she said, "Teach me to lock a door behind myself." She turned back to Mac and said, "You should know before Kristin decides what to do about going home, she's having supper."

That was news to me.

"Sit back in the corner there so people can't see from outside. I ain't gonna feed the whole town. Just Kristin and you, if you're hungry."

Wilma was full of surprises.

"No thanks, ma'am. That's too much trouble," he said as he moved to check the sign and lock the door.

"No trouble," she said.

"Coffee'd be nice though," he said.

Now we're locked in with him, I thought, watching the strong, confident way he moved. I could understand Wilma's friendliness. She dealt with customers day in and day out. Maybe it made her a good judge of character, too.

Or maybe it didn't.

It would've been easier to maintain a watchful eye when I met Mac if I hadn't been so tired and if he hadn't been quite so handsome, quite so tall. I knew that line from one of my dad's jazz albums. Some bluesy gal singer with a husky voice who was falling in love. Quite so handsome, quite so tall.

That was in my head, melody and all, while Mac and I had a private supper in the back corner booth at Wilma's Café on a rainy autumn night in San Angelo, Texas.

As it turned out, he was as hungry as I was.

As we washed down mesquite-grilled t-bones, grilled potatoes, spinach with bacon and hard-boiled egg, and buttermilk biscuits with hot coffee, I got to know him. Or at the least I learned that he was polite and had good table manners. He wasn't a chiseler, either. He insisted on buying our suppers, even though Wilma wanted us to be her guests.

I tried to help her clear the dishes. She wouldn't hear of it.

"You stay where you are and settle what you're doing about getting home with that noisy thing you drive," she said, and gave me a secret wink that got my heart revved up.

After she walked away, Mac said, "You don't say much, do you?"

We both knew it wasn't a question. I shook my head anyway. He talked a little more about his family's ranch and the cutting horses he loved. He was repeating himself, and we both knew that, too.

He lowered his voice when he said how glad he was about seeing me at work across the street. I didn't remember seeing him at Charley's. I was under the table light most of the time, of course, and there was a crowd. Still, with his looks, he would've been hard to miss—unless he hadn't wanted to be seen.

"Is 'at work' the proper way to put it?" he asked.

"At work's okay," I told him, uncertain until I spoke that I was going to have a voice.

The guy was having an effect on me. He leaned forward, driving my heart up my throat, and said, "Mostly, I'm glad I got a chance to meet you. You know, have supper with you, talk to you."

He sort of ran out of steam and got a little flustered. He shook his head and laughed at himself. "I'm not doing this so good."

I didn't want him to stop. I liked the way his voice made me feel. "Doing what?"

"You know. Tell you how happy I am that we met."

"You said that okay."

"Yeah, but now you'll be afraid to let me drive you home."

"No, she won't," Wilma said from where she leaned on a table near us.

Mac and I looked up.

Wilma said, "Because I'm riding chaperone. And after we drop Kristin off, you're bringing me back. See what you got yourself into, Sir Galahad?"

The delight I heard in his laugh was the first real hook he got into me.

Wilma woke me up when we got to Sweetwater, and I insisted on unloading my bike at a filling station that stayed open late. It was still sprinkling rain. I assured Mac the rain was not an issue and that I would see myself home from there.

When we had my motorcycle out of his trailer and that was settled, I said, "You called my bike a flathead-K. How do you know about Harleys?"

He grinned. "I rode a Hydra Glide the summer before I started college. They're fun, aren't they?"

"Cold, this time of year," I said, and we laughed.

We said goodbye, and I watched him climb back into his truck.

I wasn't comfortable with the hug that Wilma insisted on, but as long as she was up close, I reminded her with a finger to my lips that we were keeping a secret.

"Honey, I always let men do all the talking. Makes them feel special."

She looked around and made a face.

"You all right here?"

"I'm fine. Don't worry about me," I told her.

Before she could give me another hug, I herded her back into the big pickup. It would be after midnight before Mac made it home to Weatherford.

After they were gone, I slipped the man at the station a couple of bucks to keep my bike inside his garage overnight and telephoned Henry to come get me. I waited outside under some tin roofing that stuck out over the pumps.

I stood there very much like a statue, bundled up in my winter clothing. Not paying attention to the occasional car spraying by on the highway and not listening to the static of the drizzle on the tin above me. I was doing one thing: thinking about Mac. I couldn't get him off my mind any more than I could make my heart behave.

I knew that I was afraid of affection and I knew why, but it didn't keep me from wondering if I would see him again when I returned to San Angelo.

It cost almost all that I won at Charley's to have the Cadillac painted blue. Albert assured me, though, that where he took it they removed all the chrome and did it right. It looked as if it had been done right. The surface of the car was like liquid, the blue so dark it was almost black.

"That's six coats of hand-rubbed lacquer, man. You can swim in that paint job," Albert told me the day he brought it back from Mexico.

He had the interior painted the same blue and changed the white and red upholstery to black tuck-and-roll leather. He also had the whitewalls reversed so the tires were black and had a few other things done that he called 'customizing.'

Anyway, it came back a different car. It was no longer what Albert called a Detroit Popsicle. It was now a dark blue Cadillac Coupe de Ville that one of Albert's friends might drive.

"This car will disappear on a moonless night, Little Sister," he promised me.

And perhaps that wasn't a bad thing.

Getting to San Angelo in my car was warmer and more comfortable than riding my bike. I hadn't spoken to Wilma since the night she and Mac delivered me to Sweetwater. The truth was, I sort of missed her. I hadn't had a girlfriend since I was sixteen and had left school to go on the road with my dad.

It was mid-afternoon and Wilma's was closed. The door was still open, however, and music was playing. The café was empty except for some people I could see moving around in the kitchen. Wilma was sitting in a booth with her head back and her eyes closed.

She hadn't heard me come in because she and Kitty Wells were singing *"It Wasn't God Who Made Honky-Tonk Angels"* at the tops of their lungs.

I stood by the counter until they were finished and she opened her eyes.

"She don't sing that one ounce better'n I do," she said, and laughed at herself as she got to her feet.

She got me a Grapette, made herself some mint tea, and we sat down across from each other in the back booth where Mac and I'd had supper the other night.

She told me that he'd come in looking for me every day for that first week I was gone. My stomach reacted, and my head spun a little. Where was I going with those reactions?

"Considering how he was driving down here from Weatherford and it drizzled all that week, I'd say you got that young man breathing kinda hard," she said.

She gave me a smile as big as I'd ever seen her deliver.

"Now this past week or so, he's been in—let's see. Maybe two or three times."

She made a sad face that made me smile.

"Don't know if he just had to get back to work or if it's belated pride."

She laughed and then grew serious.

"What do you have to say for yourself? You gonna get into it with this boy?"

"I don't know, Wilma. I'm not sure what I should do."

"You like him, don'cha?"

"I guess that's what I'm feeling. I just don't know him very well."

"He talked to me that night we drove you home, and he's talked to me some waiting around here to see if you was showing up. Sounds like he comes from a good family. He knows a lot about horses, and his ranch sounds big."

"It wasn't like he was trying to brag. Do you think?" I asked her.

"Nah, he's not a blowhard. Easy to like. I think he's been around some, though. You know, maybe traveled with his horses and whatnot."

"He's been to college."

"Maybe that's it," Wilma said.

"You didn't tell him anything about me, did you?"

She waggled a finger and scolded me with a look. I smiled to reassure her.

"Not even your last name did he get. Kristin and Baby Shark is all he knows. And you live somewhere up near Sweetwater. You can bet he's been back to that oil station, though. He was looking pretty desperate. Do they know you there?"

I shook my head no and glanced toward the door.

"You going over to Charley's today?"

I shook my head no again.

"I didn't think so. The blouse you're wearing is way too nice to waste on them. Is it new?"

I felt my face flush. It was a blue that I knew brought my eyes out.

"Got it special for him, did'ja?" Wilma put her hand over mine and left it there as she talked. "I know you lost your mama a few years back, your daddy told me that."

I nodded yes.

"And then you lost your daddy. How old're you now? Nineteen?"

I nodded yes again.

"Still, you ain't had much to do with the male of the species, have you?"

"Not to talk about," I said and that was the truth.

Wilma patted my hand.

"You ain't never been a tail-swisher, that's for sure. You gotta get started some place and Mac seems nice enough. You want me to call him?"

"You have his number?"

"Honey, he forced it on me that first day he was here sniffing around. But I told him I wouldn't call unless it was okay with you."

What was painting the car about and listening to all that sultry Chris Connor? Why did I go shopping three days in a row? What were those long, day dreamy hot baths about? Sure, I wanted to see him. But I couldn't say it. I laughed at myself. If he were attacking me with a knife, I'd know what to do.

"I'm calling that boy. Unless you tell me not to," Wilma said.

I looked up when the breeze from the opening door fluttered the paper pumpkins.

He removed his Stetson just inside the door, and I watched his profile appear from behind the hat as he brought it down. My heart caught not from recognition, but from the newness of his appearance, all that I did *not* recall about him. I wasn't even a little bit sure of myself.

When he found me, I watched his eyes grow alert. He smiled, and my heart began to somersault. I had to get a hold of myself.

Easier said than done.

I didn't know what I would say. I just knew I was happy to see him coming toward me. To be with me. To join me in our booth at Wilma's, where I did find things to say, and we talked and talked and talked.

I got to know his face and how he smiled and what made him laugh and how his hazel eyes changed colors. I'd think that I should be careful, not say too much. But my concern was turning into something that I had to remind myself to think about. Between learning the fresh smell of him, how beautiful and strong his hands were, how he wore no rings.

"I have ropes going through my hands. Gloves on and off all day. I don't wear a wristwatch, either," he explained.

He showed me the old silver pocket watch he carried.

It had been his grandpa's. It had a brownish picture in the cover of his grandma when she was near my age.

"Maybe I'll take it out some day. When I have a picture to put in its place," he said.

Wilma was beside herself from the moment Mac arrived. Her face was alternately serious and full of purpose or gay and flushed with delight. She behaved admirably.

The café was closed, and her kitchen crew had finished cleaning. The afternoon turned into evening and she made us supper before disappearing. She left us alone with the nightlights on and platter after platter of romantic Nat King Cole coming from the jukebox.

We never left the back booth. The day simply happened around us as Mac and I got to know each other. I'd never had a conversation that lasted so long.

When I told him that, he said, "You went from being the quietest girl I ever met to the talkiest."

My face hurt from smiling.

"However," he said and paused before going on.

"However?"

"With all the talk, somehow I still don't think I know you. I mean, I've learned some things about you, but I don't think I know who you are yet," he said.

"It's gotten dark since we've been here," I pointed out to him.

He looked around.

"Everyone's gone," I said.

"They are gone, aren't they?"

When he brought out his watch, I took it from him and looked again at the picture of his grandma.

"Don't ever take her picture out. Family's more important than you know," I said.

Something changed in his face. I couldn't read what it was.

"Wilma told me you lost your mom when you were young," he said.

"We don't have to talk about that."

I was wary of the change I saw in him. But he wanted to talk about it, and I found myself brushing up close to things in my past. Things in my present. Things that I could never reveal.

"So your dad left you again after coming home from the war?"

"Yeah, but when Mom got too sick to work any more, he showed up again. They make jokes about husbands who go to the store for a loaf of bread and never come back. Dad's deal was a little different. We always knew where he was. And when I was on the road with him—those last months I was with him—I call that time 'my exquisite instant' from a poem he liked."

"You read poetry?" Mac asked me.

"I read everything. My dad started that habit. I cherish books and reading because of him. There were times when I was with him that we would drive to somewhere pretty in the morning and just read our books until it was dark. And we would consider that a day well spent. I was never more certain of his love than on days like that."

"I'm sorry about you losing your dad."

"I'm sorry about that, too," I told him.

We said our *first* goodbye while we were still inside the café. Outside, he held my hand briefly and we said our *second* goodbye.

We promised to meet in two days.

Mac drove off toward the road to Weatherford, and I drove off toward Sweetwater.

During the drive home, I relived our first goodbye over and over in my mind. The way he stopped me with a hand on my shoulder when we stood up beside the booth, back out of sight from the curious who might have passed the front windows. How he turned me to face him. I knew he was going to kiss me, and I wanted him to.

I was more frightened than I believed I would be. It was all I could do to keep from pulling away. I was sure that he could feel my heart fluttering when he brought me close, held me in his arms. I knew that how I was breathing and trembling was a dead giveaway about how I felt. But I didn't care, because I wanted him to kiss me.

I wanted him to hold me to him just the way he did. His kiss became more than I could understand and lasted longer than I ever could have imagined it would. I didn't want that first kiss to end, but of course it had to. When he held me away and looked into my eyes, I wanted him to kiss me again.

But I was glad he didn't. I had something to look forward to.

I'd dropped my guard. It was too soon to trust again.

My head told me that, but those fears didn't keep me from daydreaming all the way home about his eyes and how he'd held me in his arms.

However, when I saw one of Otis' cars parked near the house, I snapped out of it in a hurry. Henry and Jim came out to meet me.

"Bear out early. Someone pull string," Henry told me.

13

"I DON'T GET it," I said to Otis.

We were sitting around Henry's kitchen table, the place where my life's decisions were being made those days. Otis had a hot cup of Henry's coffee in front of him.

"How can he be out so soon?" I asked.

"Missy, when the right papers show up and they've got the right signatures, wardens do what they're told."

"Who could care about scum like Bear?" I wanted to know.

"I think what you're asking is who with the power to cut his sentence in half could care about scum like Bear. That's your question, ain't it?"

I got goosebumps.

"I know that was *my* question," Otis added.

I said, "Whoever stopped the police investigation at Henry's place—"

"Same whoever let Bear go," Henry finished for me, his voice excited.

"It's about the gang, isn't it, Otis? That's the connection," I said.

"Someone protect gang," Henry tossed in.

"Ain't you two the crackerjacks?"

"Where's Bear? Do you know where he is?" I asked.

Otis had waited for that question so he could give me one of his pauses and a smug look. I screwed my patience down tight and saw it through.

Finally, he said, "I do, as a matter of fact. I know exactly where he's parking his bike these nights, and I'm thinking if I keep a good tail on him, we're going to find us the rest of them."

That was what we'd been waiting for. Why wasn't I glad? Henry was thrilled and showed it, smiling, getting up, pouring more coffee for Otis.

Otis studied his cup and said, "You know, Hank, you oughta let that coffee perc a while longer. Give it a chance to reach a kind of inky color. Get a little body. I'm not saying it's weak, exactly."

"Let boil for Otis," Henry said.

I heard Otis and Henry discussing coffee, but I wasn't listening to them. I had something on my mind. I didn't want to think about murder and rape. I wanted to think about the future, about Mac, about seeing him again.

I also knew that I had to finish what Henry and I had started. I couldn't get all mushy and forget what had been done to me, my father, and Will. I had to remember the promises I'd made after the Scarecrow meeting.

"It'll never be over as long as there's any possibility that gang can find Henry and me," I said, and the men looked over.

"Yeah?" Otis asked.

"Maybe we need to speak to Bear. Have a private conversation," I said.

That got the men's attention.

"Let's give that a minute or two. Maybe he takes us to the others and we got us a package deal." Otis said.

"Your last minute or two took damn near a year," I said.

Henry nodded his head in agreement, and we stared at Otis.

"Let's don't get all riled up, the two of you. If I ain't turned up his friends right soon, we'll figure a way to get a quiet talk with him. Does that suit you?"

"Perfect," I said.

"Perfect," Henry echoed.

"And we're saying quiet talk, now, ain't we?"

"Don't start, Otis," I said, and he smiled.

The next day passed in a haze. The day after, when I told Henry that I was going to San Angelo again and wouldn't be home until late, he eyed my new blue jeans and new sweater and looked troubled.

"You meet man?"

I got a twitchy feeling all over.

"Yes," I replied.

"What name?"

"Al Mackenzie."

"How old?"

"Twenty-six. He's a rancher. He breeds and trains cutting horses."

"He live San Angelo?"

"No, Henry. He lives in Weatherford. He doesn't know much about me, of course. And nothing about you or where we live. I'm meeting him at Wilma's in San Angelo."

"What do?"

"What do we do?"

"What do take all day?"

That was Henry's last question, although he didn't know that when he asked it. I smiled and inquired if I could bring him anything.

"A cobbler from Wilma's?" I offered.

"No cobbler," Henry said, continuing to look apprehensive.

There was a pause during which neither of us wanted to turn away.

Henry said, in a voice as warm as I had ever heard him use, "You careful out there. Henry love so much."

It was as if my breath had been drawn from me. His

statement was so unexpected. I stepped over and took him in my arms, and he put his arms around me. It was so awkward it had to be genuine. It had taken us years to express our feelings like that. We were amateurs when it came to the moves.

"My God, Henry. I love you, too," I said.

Jim, who had never seen such a thing, nosed between us and wagged with satisfaction after forcing us apart with his big body.

"Don't worry. Mac's a nice guy. Today we might go over to Weatherford to see some of his horses at work. That's why I may be late getting home."

Henry's straw hat was tilted from our embrace, so I straightened it for him before saying goodbye. He was still looking uneasy when I left to go meet Mac.

The sky was pale blue and more fair than it had been in days with a few wispy clouds scattered about off to the west. It was going to be a splendid day, cool and bright. A perfect day to visit a horse ranch.

Wilma's was bustling with the noon crowd.

The first time she passed me, she said, "I wanna hear everything."

She passed twice more with smiles and winks before she had time to stop at the counter. "He called. He's gonna be a little late," she said. She arched her eyebrows and smiled. "You ain't leaving till he gets here, are you?"

She pushed my shoulder with her fingertips before charging off through the swinging doors into the kitchen.

"You want something to eat?" she asked me on her next trip by.

I shook my head. I was too nervous.

Mac wasn't very late at all, and we didn't stay long at the café. Wilma barged out the front door to wave goodbye as I climbed up and into his big new pickup.

"How'd you get to know Wilma so well?" Mac asked as we drove away.

"She's a friend of the family."

That took care of that.

"You ready to see my little marmalade and white stallion work some cattle?"

"He's your two-year-old, right?"

"You've got a good memory. So, what makes a good cutting horse?"

"Are you quizzing me?" I asked him.

We were both smiling about as big as we could.

"Well?" he said.

"Bloodline," I said.

"You're right, that's essential. What else?"

"You said temperament was important."

"Yeah? And?"

I laughed.

"You don't remember everything I said?" he asked, smiling at me.

"I'm afraid not," I said.

"Don't worry. You'll have it under your hat by the end of the day," he said, and snapped his head around to look out his side window.

There was a lot of honking coming from someone driving beside us.

"What the hell?" Mac said.

I lifted up and looked out too. Because of the angle, I couldn't see the driver any better than Mac. However, I recognized the old pickup truck.

"He wants us to stop," Mac said.

"Let's see what he wants," I said, my heart racing.

Mac pulled his big truck over to the shoulder and stopped. The smaller pickup stopped in front of us. Before Mac could say anything, I jumped out, ran up, and opened Henry's door on the passenger side.

"You okay? What's going on?" I asked.

"Follow to see."

"Yeah?" I said, annoyed that he would follow me.

"That Mac in truck?"

"Yes, Henry. That's Mac. What do you want?"

"Mac insurance man."

"Insurance man?"

I was lost.

"Insurance man," Henry repeated.

I got it. "The man who came to see you. The fire insurance guy."

"You know Mac insurance man?"

"No, Henry. I didn't know that."

"I think he same man go see you aunt, too. He look for you long time, I think."

"Oh, God," I whispered.

I can't explain the sharp edge of dread that sliced through me. A jolt of adrenaline flooded my system to complicate matters even further. I caught my breath and glanced back at a man I no longer knew.

I'd been conned, and I didn't like the feeling.

"Get in. We go now," Henry said.

"My things," I said.

I knew from all my practice in front of the mirror that I was offering a calm face as I returned to Mac's truck. I opened the door. Reached in. Pulled away my purse and jacket. Mac was surprised and curious. His eyes told me that he hadn't put it together—yet.

"Gotta go," I said in a voice that gave away nothing.

"Hey!" he called after me as I slammed the door of his truck.

I returned to Henry's pickup, got in, and we pulled away. We drove to the next intersection, made a turn, and doubled back through town without seeing Mac again.

"You're sure about this?" I pressed Henry.

"Henry know face. Same man."

"He conned me, Henry." My anger was making me admit aloud what I had already told myself. "Why, Henry? Why didn't he just tell me when he met me?"

"First time follow Baby Girl. Henry never follow before."

He knew that he'd offended me.

"I understand. You were worried."

"Al Mackenzie insurance man."

"If you say so, Henry. You know, I don't get it. Why did he have to lie?"

Why did the son of a bitch have to romance me? If he knew who I was, he knew other things about me. He knew about that night at Henry's. The murders. The rape. I didn't like my next thoughts. None of them were pretty.

Henry drove me back to my car and followed me. We wasted no time getting on the road home. Thank God, hormones weren't leading Henry around.

Mac had humiliated me, and I couldn't come up with a reasonable explanation for why he needed to do that. Thinking of him in connection to that night at Henry's Poolroom gave me the creeps. His motivation had to be sinister. Or, why not just tell the truth?

Albert and Sarge influenced my next feelings. I wanted to hurt the man.

After we got to the homestead and were seated at our kitchen table, Henry and I talked more about Al Mackenzie. We tried our best to figure his angle and it never made any sense. One thing that we concluded was that he had done some research to find Aunt Dora's address.

"You aunt not hide like you. Find easy."

"Not that easy. She's my mother's sister. We don't have the same last name."

"Hospital maybe," Henry said.

"Maybe. It took him a while to find me. He stuck with it, and that's a long hunt. Don't you think, Henry? A couple of years?"

"Maybe Mac like Otis. Insurance eye."

"An investigator? Sure, makes sense. Still, what was there about that night that makes me so important to find?"

"Maybe you see things, know things he want know."

"Still, why would a fire insurance investigator have to lie to me?" I asked, but Henry was thinking about something else.

"What Mac plan once you alone?"

My stomach wanted to sour. I told myself to snap out of it. He wasn't going to have any control over me. None.

"He said we were going to watch one of his cutting horses at work. Of course he's a liar, so I don't know what his plans were."

Henry shrugged. "Maybe watch horse. How know?"

How know, indeed. God! I'd just walked into it. The bringing my motorcycle home. The sweet talk. The kissing.

Henry's question hit the nail right on the head. What were his plans for me once he had me alone?

I wanted to scream. I felt so violated by his dishonesty and so embarrassed by my naiveté. And because of his unknown intentions, there was sincere apprehension mingling around in there, too. As Henry put it so well: how know what his plans were for me?

There was another thing I was having trouble with. If he knew that Kristin Van Dijk was Baby Shark, how long had he known that?

"Insurance man know homestead," Henry mentioned as a matter of fact.

Of course he did. He'd been there two years ago when I was holed up in the *hacienda*, recovering.

"I'm so sorry, Henry. I've put us on the defensive. He may have known who I was, but he didn't know where I was until today."

"Maybe Al Mackenzie bad man. Maybe not."

"We have to assume he means us harm. We don't have a choice, do we?"

"No choice," Henry agreed.

Henry rose up and began pacing about the kitchen, something I'd never seen him do.

"You pay attention now, Baby Girl. Henry talk. Things need say for two years maybe. Now maybe good time. You listen."

I had no idea what Henry was about to say. I'd never seen him quite so intense. I was uncertain if I could take any more surprises that day. Henry went on to say that he had a confession to make, something he needed to get off his chest.

"Chinese say to win battle warrior need thick face and black heart. You know saying?"

"No. What does it mean?"

"Thick face mean not matter what people say. Believe in self. Black heart mean show no concern for others. Do everything, anything to win."

"Why are you telling me this?"

"Because Henry has thick face and black heart. I feel shame for way I treat Baby Girl."

The language didn't come easy for Henry as he took me back two years to our first conversations concerning what we should do about the gang that attacked us. Should we run and hide or work for justice?

He told me he hadn't been honest about his reasons for encouraging me to study with Sarge. It wasn't just for my self-defense. Sarge was to make me useful to Henry in his plans to find the gang and make them pay for what they had done. He'd been desperate. He'd wanted revenge, and he was sensitive to how minorities were treated in Texas.

"Henry foreign. Police not care. No one care."

And I was already primed, so to speak, since the police and public didn't seem to care any more about me than they did Henry. Yet, by virtue of being a white American, I could still gain access. Henry felt he needed me. He needed me for access and for killing if it came to that.

"Baby Girl young, quick. Good student. Not right make decision for you. Not tell truth."

Henry was pretty clever. I guess I should've been pissed off since I was being told I was a robot taught to kill. Although I had become more than that to Henry. It wasn't figured into his hurried equation that we would become family. I got up and went over to the stove.

"Want some tea?"

"Good idea," Henry said and got out his cup.

I started the water going.

I found myself being more concerned about protecting him than worrying about two-year-old motives. I was watching myself during this, of course, and realized how well I had been taught to hide my feelings. That was part of it. The other part was Henry and I were all the family we had.

"You not Baby Girl anymore. You grow up now. Best thing for you go away. San Francisco nice place. I know friends there. You safe there. Make a new life away from trouble."

"You're sending me away?"

"I love like daughter. Life in San Francisco better. No danger there. I feel shame put in danger."

Henry was suffering, it was clear. To make up for what he had done, his solution was to send me away. I had to tell him something that would make things right for him. I decided to lie.

"You need to understand something, Henry, I already knew all this."

His face scrunched up with sincere surprise.

"You knew?" he said under this breath.

"Sure. I figured it out a long time ago. And I don't feel as used as you might think. In fact, I'm okay with what I've learned about taking care of myself. I wanted never to be afraid again. You arranged for Sarge to help with that. And don't forget, Albert was my idea."

Henry was right not to trust me since I wasn't being honest. I mean I had always noticed his interest in my progress as I was learning the arts of war, but I had never dreamed that there was a larger plan behind him encouraging my studies.

He said, "You think over."

"Nah, I don't need to do that. As you pointed out, I'm grown now, and I'll tell you something, Henry. It seems a long time ago, but I meant the promises I made the night you sent Scarecrow to hell."

"You tell truth?"

Now I was telling the truth.

"Absolutely. I've had some bad nights and lots of second

thoughts about what happened at Helen's Bay Side, and I've come to grips with it. I mean those promises more now than ever."

"Can you forgive me?" he asked.

"For what, Henry? Rescuing me from a burning building? Providing me a home? Nursing me back to health? Giving me purpose?"

Henry's relief shifted to concern.

"Insurance man hurt Baby Girl?"

"Just my feelings, my friend. Just my feelings."

As we had our tea and Dr Pepper, I took the opportunity to tell Henry how thankful I was for all that he had done for me. Providing me home and family. He said that was what I had done for him, too.

"We're starting fresh," I said.

"Suitcase not so heavy now."

"You mean baggage."

"Baggage," he repeated, but I think that one slipped past him.

"We sound like a damn soap opera."

Henry laughed and slapped his knee.

"Lorenzo Jones," he said.

We settled down and discussed Mac some more. We felt certain that he represented a danger to us. What danger though? We searched for a motive. What did Mac want? We knew that it was attached to that night, but we couldn't figure it out.

The fact was my life would never be my own in West Texas or San Francisco or anywhere else until those responsible for my assault and the murders were brought to some kind of justice.

"If police not help, choice simple. Run or fight." Henry had said.

"I don't know what your game is," I said in an even voice. Mac kept his eyes on mine.

"I never want to see you again," I said.
My words seemed to hurt him.
"I don't get a chance to explain?" he asked.
"Explain what? That you're a liar?"
"Kristin—"
I couldn't bear to hear him say my name.
"Leave me alone," I cried out.

Jim woke me. I must have called out in my sleep.

How could I be in a sweat? It was a cold, gray winter morning. I looked at the clock. In another hour it would be sunrise and time for target practice.

I had something to do before that.

14

November 1954

I CHOPPED OFF my hair that morning before target practice. Henry saw that I had and didn't mention it.

The next day, after I'd cooled down, I went to see Ivy, the beautician lady over in Dallas, the one that overcharged me the last time I got a haircut, and it looked so good.

Ivy was a stick of a thing and prim as a librarian in many ways, but she had a sailor's laugh and ran her little shop with a firm hand.

"You've made my job harder," she lectured my image in the mirror.

"Sorry," I muttered and stared down a pair of old biddies that were trying to eavesdrop.

Ivy and I had discussed my swollen ear the last time I was there, so it wasn't an issue. I noticed that she turned me in the chair so that no one else saw it. That would've made me like her, even if there hadn't been other reasons.

"I don't care how mad you get at him, next time don't take it out on your hair," she snarled.

"Yes, ma'am," I said.

I was just another broken-hearted piece of fluff who'd been dumped by her boyfriend. If I ever saw Mac again, he was going to be one sorry insurance man. In fact, I was beginning to consider looking him up.

Trapped there in Ivy's beauty parlor, being forced to think about Mac again, I further embarrassed myself by realizing that I had been fooled and trapped by *the mechanics of desire*. That was the subject of an article in a recent Cosmopolitan. I'd sneered and turned the page. Then I turned back and read every word.

We'd see who was the better mechanic.

Not anxious to go home, I spent the rest of the day in Dallas.

I considered seeing Grace Kelly in a Hitchcock movie then decided against it. It looked scary, and I didn't think I needed that. So I did some shopping and sat around a café, after having something to eat. I nursed a Dr Pepper and stared out the window at people walking by. A lot of them looked happy enough; plenty of them looked sad, too.

It was getting late by the time I returned home. After Jim quit barking, I heard the phone ringing. Henry wasn't home, so I caught it. It was Otis.

He said, "If you recall, I told you if that guy Bear didn't give up some of his friends right soon, I'd find a place for you to have a quiet talk with him."

"I recall," I said.

"Okay. Why don't you and Hank meet me later on tonight and let's see how it goes? No promises, but I think I have a good spot. Can you find your way to Weatherford?"

I gritted my teeth and said, "I know where that is."

The directions that Otis provided took me over to the edge of Weatherford, to a dark commercial area of grain storage houses where big rigs loaded and unloaded bales of hay and bags of feed through the night.

On a side street near there I found what I was looking for: a piss-poor excuse of a pool parlor called The Riverbank. It was one of two businesses open at that hour on a long street of boarded-up old homes and storage buildings that poked up like rotten teeth between weed-infested vacant lots.

A half dozen or so flatbed truck trailers were scattered

along the dark street, appearing abandoned, perched on their spindly front legs and sullen rear tires.

Without streetlights, it took some searching to spot the dark gray primer-coated '50 Mercury two-door. It was one of Otis' *invisible* cars he used on surveillance. It was snuggled back in the shadow of a trailer down past the poolroom.

I put my car around the corner where it pretty much vanished beneath the sagging limbs of a neglected stand of trees that was advancing on the pot-holed road. It was half-past two in the morning and chilly. I noticed a breeze coming up as I got out and walked over to join Otis.

He dragged his fedora and camera closer to him as I got in.

"Cut your hair," he said.

"Yeah."

"Short."

"Uh huh."

"Where's Hank?"

"I came on ahead. He'll be here," I lied.

"Coffee?"

"You make it?"

"Fresh brewed at the office."

"No, thanks."

Hank Williams was singing *Cold, Cold Heart* at such a low volume I didn't hear him until after I was settled. Otis turned him off. I wished that it had been warm enough to have the windows down, because Otis pretty much lived in his cars.

I asked if our boy was still in there.

"Yep. Our recently released Roy Birns is in there, and he ain't alone."

"I can see that. Any idea who's with him?"

"Nope."

The chrome on the big rig cab and the two bikes parked outside the place reflected the light from the naked bulb that hung by its cord over the front door. The breeze was giving the bulb a little swing, making the chrome sparkle.

That was an odd contrast, since the pool hall building was an unpainted, ramshackle two-story wood-frame firetrap.

It made my skin crawl to think of it that way. It looked to be about the same size as Henry's place, too, except it had an upstairs. Maybe the owner lived up there. The windows were dark.

Down at the other end of the long block, a two-tone DeSoto pulled in and parked beside a couple of pickups that sat in a wash of dim light that came from the foggy front windows of a café.

I'd looked over at the greasy spoon when I drove by. It wasn't more than a counter, a jukebox, and a red and white neon sign that blinked 'Jax Beer' now and again when it felt like it.

They probably had good coffee.

"When's Hank getting here?" Otis asked.

"Pretty soon, I'd imagine," I said.

"I'm a mite tetchy, I know. I got some things to do, and the dark don't last forever."

"You and the vampires, Otis."

"He was right behind you, was he?"

"He'll be here any minute," I assured him, but that wasn't the truth.

Henry knew nothing about this meeting. I had fixed Jim his supper, changed clothes, and left before Henry got home. The note that I put on the kitchen table said I'd be late and not to wait up for me. I'd killed time in Abilene until it was late enough to meet Otis.

This was something I needed to do alone.

"Where's that *pachuco* friend of yours? He'd come in handy about now."

"Albert's on a drunk."

Otis sighed.

"I know that story," he said with resignation.

"Still think of having a drink, do you?"

"Ah, it's not like I'm an alcoholic. That ain't the case. I drank hard for a while to ease some pain I was feeling, that's all. And I'm told I ain't a nice drunk. So, once I stopped, I just sort of got out of the habit."

We were quiet for a while just thinking our thoughts and watching the occasional truck pass down at the far end of the road near the café.

"The best cutting horses in the state are out this away," he told me.

"I know," I said, feeling it in the pit of my stomach.

We were quiet again. Otis breathed heavily. I noticed it in close quarters like that. He could've lost a few pounds and been better off for it.

"That Mackenzie fella ever bring you over here?"

My heart skipped a beat.

"How do you know about him?" I asked, my voice steady.

Otis treated that rhetorically.

"Hank said he could of been nicer to you."

"He was okay to me. So?"

"So, what?"

"What did you find out about him?"

"Well, he ain't no insurance man."

My heart rolled over.

"What is he then?" I asked.

"He's a horse trader pretty much full time. Best of all, his daddy is one helluva rich rancher named Logan Belmont."

I recognized the name. Everyone knew the Belmont Bar-X was one of the biggest cattle ranches in the state. Make that the world.

"Why does he use the name Mackenzie?"

"Rich as he is, to keep people back off him, more'n likely. It's his mother's maiden name. Your buddy's real name is Alexander Mackenzie Belmont. I can't tell you yet why he was pretending to be something he's not. Except when folks do that, it usually means they're up to no good. That's true with me."

"Why say he's an insurance man if he's not?" I asked, but before he could answer, I went on. "Hell, Otis, he brought

Henry his insurance check. How could he do that?"

"I wondered about that, too, Missy. The only thing I've come up with so far is it has something to do with old man Belmont being one of the owners of the insurance company."

"An owner?"

"Oh, sure."

"I still don't get it. What's going on?"

"Hell, I don't know yet neither. Insurance is just one of the things old man Belmont has going and nowhere near the biggest. Oil's his biggest game. Cattle after that. Things like insurance companies, lumber, horses, heavy equipment, and newspapers. They're all mostly like hobbies, I think."

I said, "Logan Belmont could make a murder investigation go away, couldn't he?"

"You know, Missy, I had that very thought my own self, and I'm looking into it because how could all this be accidental? This Belmont boy just shows up, gets you all hot and bothered—"

"I resent that, Otis."

"You're right. You're right. Anyway, he shows up, makes advances in order to get close to you. Okay with that?"

I kept quiet.

"And we don't know why yet," he added.

"Why would the Belmonts have any interest in what happened at Henry's Poolroom? I mean if it's about fire insurance, fine. Whatever that could mean. Why hush up murders? We're back to protecting the biker gang, aren't we?"

"There're more hams on a hog than you think there are sometimes. Like I say, I'm looking into it. In the meantime, it would be a good idea if you stayed away from that young horse trader until we know the lay of the land."

"That'll be easy to do," I said.

A tumbleweed caught our attention as it rolled out of a vacant lot. We watched in silence as it bounced up the street.

"How old're you now?"

Seventeen definitely going on thirty.

"Twenty next July," I said.

"You're nineteen."

"Have it your way."

"Hmm. You look nineteen all right, but you talk older. You carry yourself like an older girl, too. My grandpa used to say hard decisions make you grow up quick."

I had a reply, but something pulled our attention away. A biker rounded the corner at the far end of the road, rupturing the silence as he rumbled past the café and down to where we were.

Otis got his camera up and clicked off a few shots as the new guy parked his machine near the others and entered The Riverbank. I noticed a flash of red at his throat.

"You recognize him?"

"No," I said.

Otis sighed. "Those shits always have the money for new bikes."

I looked at the motorcycles more closely and thought of something that made my blood run cold.

"Mac."

"What?" Otis wanted to know.

"Mac told me he used to ride a Harley."

"He did, did he?"

"Yeah, a Hydra Glide, he told me."

"I'll just look into that because that's kinda suspicious, ain't it?

"Yeah, it is," I said under my breath, not liking what that might indicate.

"Now, right this minute, let's call this off. Birns and his buddy was plenty. No sense pushing it. Especially now some other fucker shows up."

"Maybe it'll change. One of them leaves, and that brings it back to two."

"Or maybe it's a revival meeting, and these are just the first to arrive."

"You're right," I said because he was.

Otis sighed, glanced at his wristwatch, shifted his bulk, and looked out the car windows in all directions before looking at me.

"Now get this, Missy," he grumbled *sotto voce*, as my dad used to say. "You and Hank's been at this a long spell. Don't get all fire in a hurry. It's gotta be right when you do this stuff, or you'll swing for it. That thing at the honky-tonk last year was kind of like gangs at war and sent everybody pissing on each other. Pure dee luck. Don't get me wrong. I'm all for flushing this scum down the sewer. But be smart. There'll most likely be a phone down there at the café. Can you get a holt of Hank and turn him around?"

"It's too late now. I think I'm here until he shows up."

"Whichever way. Let's just put this in a holding pen for now. We got time, and this punk don't have a clue we're on him. I'm sorry about the long trek over. When Hank shows up, the two of you'll call it a night. Right?"

"Right," I said.

I felt bad about lying to Otis. But I knew he'd never agree to me being there alone, and I was aching to get this thing finished up.

"Thanks for all your help, Otis. You've been a good friend to us."

"I don't like leaving you before Hank gets here," he confessed.

"Let me get to my car before you drive off, okay?"

I gave him a smile, rested my hand on his shoulder, and asked him to let Henry and me know when it looked good again. He said he would.

It seemed colder and quieter as I walked back to where I'd parked.

Otis had just laid a bombshell on me like it was nothing. A twenty-six-year-old rich boy had suckered me. He did it by looking pretty and taking advantage of my loneliness. I felt like even more of a fool. I'd get to the bottom of that guy's game. I promised myself that. In the meantime, I had some business to take care of.

When I blinked my lights, Otis started up and pulled away. I thought for a while about how to handle the situation. The bikers weren't in there alone, and it wasn't going to work with others in the way. So I sat there until I figured out what to do.

When I walked in, everyone looked up.

I didn't appear out of place in cowboy boots, Levi's, and a short, brown leather jacket. Though my fresh cotton shirt the color of jacaranda in bloom set me apart from the cowpokes in The Riverbank. My platinum blonde hair and fair features were differences, too. I'd done my eyes before I left home. I didn't use lipstick. My hair wasn't long enough to be a problem, and I carried my drivers' license in my hip pocket. No purse.

All that I carried that wasn't concealed was my cue case, and even my cue case concealed a couple of lethal items.

I went to a high chair, placed my case across the arms and opened it. I took out a cue, screwed it together, and stepped over to the empty table near the wall. No clicking balls, no conversation, just dead quiet while Baby Shark settled in to do business.

I turned to the room. All eyes were on me.

That included a toothless old man in overalls and long johns standing behind a cigar counter who squinted at me over his bifocals from between the cash register and a peanut machine; two middle-aged truckers in plaid shirts and blue jeans standing at the back table with their chins drooping; and Bear with two bikers who were both strangers to me.

I'd hoped that Blue Eyes or Mechanic would be there with Bear. No such luck.

My voice cut the silence. "I shoot pool for a living. Anyone here up for some nine-ball?"

"All right," Bear said, appearing delighted to discover opportunity unfolding like free dessert before him.

Granddad sighed and put away his glasses. The truckers put their sticks on the table and picked up their jackets.

"You don't gotta leave," Granddad told them.

They mumbled something about picking up a load. My guess was they put me together with the bikers and smelled trouble. Smart guys. They didn't as much as glance my way as they headed for the door.

That just left the old man as extra baggage. Unless it turned into a bikers come to Jesus meeting like Otis had suggested.

Bear ordered some beers for him and his friends and walked over to where I was racking the balls. His buddies put down their cues, lit up fresh butts, and settled into some chairs to watch the fun.

We heard the truckers start their big rig and pull away.

"Send Granddad to breakfast," I said.

That one caught Bear off guard.

His sluggish brain adjusted and he said, "You heard'er, Granddad."

"I ain't hungry," the old geezer said, because he wasn't even a little bit swift. A look from Bear changed his mind. "Okay. Okay. You buyin'?"

Bear grunted so Granddad cleaned out the register, put on a grungy felt hat, slipped on a ratty old coat the color of dried blood, and shuffled over with his shiny gums showing and his hand out.

"I'll be down at the café. If you get more beers, leave the money on the counter," he said and pocketed the wad of limp greenbacks Bear gave him.

"Take your time," Bear told him.

The old man never looked back. He just shuffled out, pulling the front door closed after him. We looked at each other. It was like we wanted it. Just the four of us. Real cozy.

Bear hadn't changed. He still had yellow teeth and stained fingers from smoking Mexican cigarettes. He looked as if he hadn't bathed since he got out of prison weeks ago; his hair and beard could have hidden earthworms.

Seeing Bear for the first time since Henry's Poolroom created a calm sadness within me. I could still hear the sounds of that night echoing in my head, as I so often did. All from a distance, muted. I felt neither the fear nor the shock that I'd experienced with Scarecrow, none of the anger that I had felt so many times when I looked forward to meeting my attackers face to face.

I was positive that the murders and assault that had consumed my life had been just another evening in Bear's brutal existence of commonplace violence. The sadness I felt was sensing that difference. The pain and grief that Henry and I had gone through were inconsequential to that vicious thug. I was glad for the months of waiting that had given me some perspective.

Revenge, they say, is best served up cold.

How much alike those bikers looked. The way they dressed and acted. Granddad kept the place so warm, they'd all thrown their Lost Demons jackets over chairs.

The short guy looked kind of stylish with a fresh red bandana around his neck. Otherwise, he was in greasy pants and an untucked sweat-stained denim shirt that was indistinguishable from Bear's attire.

The taller thug wore a gray, sleeveless sweatshirt to show off his muscles. That shirt and his twitchy movements defined him. He had a way of lifting and rolling his shoulders, like a gunslinger testing his flexibility. It was what my dad would've called an affectation.

"Wanna lag for break?" Bear asked me.

Billiards as foreplay. It seemed our Bear was a romantic, and we were actually going to shoot some pool.

I said, "Let's discuss business first. Fifty a game okay?"

He shrugged. "Make it a hunerd."

"Fine, a hundred it is."

"Ain't you scared, a little girl like you carrying big bucks, coming into a place like this?"

"Why should I be scared with strong guys like you here to protect me? Winner breaks?"

He shrugged, growing tired of the prelims he had begun.

"Wanna lag?" he asked.

"Nah, go ahead and break," I told him.

So, Bear grunted, laid his beer belly over the end of the table, and punched the cue ball on its way. He dropped one on the crush, did okay with two more, and missed a bumper-to-bumper that he never should have tried.

It was my turn.

I ran the table, racked, broke, and ran it again, double kissing the final nine just to show off. Leaving myself on the far side of the table, I looked across at Bear and smiled.

He had backed up and placed his butt on the edge of the next table when I started slamming balls into pockets. He'd drained a couple of beers, smoked, and watched in glowering silence as I ran through the games. Those biker boys had never seen a woman shoot that well.

Hell. They'd never seen a woman shoot pool, period.

"You owe me two hundred," I said in a pleasant voice, adding insult to injury.

Irritation and loathing were transparent in every aspect of the burly biker: his facial expression, the way his body tightened, the way he gripped the cue he hadn't used since he broke the first rack two games ago.

"I guess you don't want to play anymore, huh?" I added.

That did it. When he stood up, I knew for sure that foreplay was behind us by the way he flipped his cigarette butt across the room to spark against the wall.

"I'll pay the two hunerd in trade," he said.

I gave him a blank stare.

"What does that mean?" I asked.

"I'm gonna take the money outta your ass, that's what it means," he growled.

Bear glanced at his friends. They were pleased to see things on the move. The one with the bandana tossed aside the reefer he was smoking, snorted like a feral hog, and rubbed his hands together in a demented kind of glee. Twitchy, the tall guy, put a grin on his face as he got up from where he was sitting.

I placed my cue on the table parallel with the cushion, never taking my eyes away from Bear, who also began to smile. My guess was they thought raping me was going to be a piece of cake. That's why their amusement was so easy to understand.

"I don't understand," I said and unbuttoned the waist of my short jacket.

Twitchy did his shoulder roll as he rounded the end of the table, coming at me from my left. I turned to face him so my left side was hidden from the others.

He said, "I'll bet you ain't got no underwear on, them pants is so tight."

When he was a step away, I lifted a ball from the side pocket and tossed it straight up to come back down on the table. Twitchy glanced at the ball as he reached to grab me. His mistake. I dipped down and up and used my hidden hand for a little close work.

It was quick.

Twitchy stopped. His blinking eyes came back to me.

"Hey!" he said, not grasping yet what had occurred, but sensing something was wrong. "What?" he added as his attention went to his right hand. His eyes bulged with disbelief. "My—I'm cut!"

Bear and Bandana Man rubbernecked as Twitchy stumbled back and lifted his wrist for them to see.

The blade of my knife was scalpel-sharp and would have sliced the biker's hand right off his arm if the bone hadn't stopped it. I moved away from the blood spewing from the gaping wound above his useless, drooping hand.

"I'm cut," he said again.

Then he realized that high on his inner thigh he had been cut, as well. His pants leg was darkening with blood.

"It's bad," he announced, backing away seriously then, not knowing what to do. "I'm—I'm bleeding."

That took split seconds, and no one had seen the knife. By the time Bear's focus had returned to me, I had a .38 Colt automatic in my hand, and it was pointed at his heart.

"Drop the cue," I told him in the same voice I used to ask for the asparagus.

The sounds in the room came from Twitchy who backed into the wall.

I glanced over to see his baffled stare was fixed on his wounds. His life was pulsing out of his body like rusty sludge from a garden hose. He lost his balance and collapsed to a sitting position, his injured leg folded beneath him, his blood expanding in a black pool around him.

His mouth moved in a grotesque mime ahead of his voice coming back. "You—you gotta stop this bleeding," he whined.

"Shut the fuck up!" Bear snarled, his cruel eyes alert and fixed on me.

The other guy made a bad decision. He reached under the front of his shirt as he started up from his chair, and I shot him.

I must've aimed at the bandana. The bullet hit him in the throat. He went back and down so fast that my guess was the slug cut through his spinal cord. That biker was fertilizing daisies before he hit the floor.

Bear tensed at the sound of the discharge but held his ground. However, his regard for my resolve had been redefined. As proof, he dropped his cue without further prompting. It took a bounce, fell with a clatter, and rolled across the floor.

Twitchy's moans were becoming pitiful as he gripped his wrist, desperately trying to hold back the escaping blood.

I spoke calmly to Bear.

"You have two pistols, one in the back of your belt and one in front. Stick your right hand up over your head. Pull your guns with your left. Push them across the table."

"You fuckin' bitch," he growled.

Then, after confirming glances at the piles of blood and death to each side of him, he did as he was told. When I had his weapons on my side of the table, I said, "You're Roy Birns. I saw you in another place."

His face stiffened with curiosity.

"You had a couple of friends. They were Lost Demons, too. One was a young guy, a mechanic, I think. Fair-haired, broken nose. Know who I mean?"

He scoured his memory for some hint of who I was. He couldn't get it.

"You want to walk out of here, Roy, tell me where I find the mechanic."

That glimmer of hope brought back his surly nature.

"Whatta yuh want with him?" he growled.

"I have a present for him," I said.

Bear pursed his mouth like he might trot out a note-worthy reply, but Twitchy derailed that effort with a gasp and gurgle. They were unpleasant sounds and jerked Bear's attention to him.

When his eyes came back to mine, I saw surrender in them.

"Yeah, yeah, okay. I give yuh that guy and I walk outta here?"

"You tell me where to find him, sure," I lied.

He stalled briefly before he spilled it.

"He hangs out at a honky-tonk called Bobby Ray's."

"Back away from the table," I said and moved my aim to his face.

"What're yuh doing?"

"That was too easy. You're lying to me. Back up."

"No. No. Fuck me if I'm lyin'. I ain't lyin'."

"Back up. I don't want blood on the table."

"It's Bobby Ray's. I'm tellin' yuh. Bobby Ray's over'n South Dallas. He lives there."

"Now, what about the other guy?" I asked him.

"What other guy?"

"The guy with sandy hair and blue eyes. The guy who gives the orders."

He drew in his breath, squinted hard, and said, "You got a present for him, too?"

He wasn't giving up Blue Eyes, and it was beginning to take too long.

"It's time for you to pay me for the games you lost."

He shifted his weight and put a hangdog expression on his face.

"Tell me you're not a deadbeat, Roy. How's a girl to make a living?"

"Yuh got Wayne. That's worth somethin', ain't it?"

"You don't remember me, do you?"

"I'm tryin'. I'm tryin'."

And he was, too. His eyes were working like a Las Vegas slot.

"I—I—who are yuh?" he asked.

His face was flushed and distorted in his attempt to control his rising panic. He must have known by then that he was way into borrowed time.

"Yuh gonna tell me?" he asked, his voice just above a whisper.

"Sure, Roy. I'm the girl you dragged from the Cadillac outside the pool hall over west of Abilene. You and your friends murdered my father, raped me, and set fire to the place. You thought it was funny. Remember?"

His mouth opened, his eyes widened, his shoulders slumped, and he totally shut down. Even his breathing stopped as he stared at me.

"No," he finally exhaled, his eyes telling me what I wanted to see.

"Yeah. I guess I'm what you'd call a loose end."

Bear took that stunned look of recognition directly to hell—along with two slugs in his heart.

15

AS I CROSSED the room, I was careful not to walk in the expanding pools of what James Agee called the precocious grandchild of the sea. No point in leaving boot prints.

Carrying my cue case, I stepped out the back door into a dirt alley and began wading through knee-high weeds toward my car on the street beyond.

After taking a deep breath of the icy night air, I said, "Half the job is done." And across the wintry night, far, far away, like an answer to my declaration, I heard the mournful cry of a train.

It was getting colder. I should've worn my heavier jacket.

A few minutes later, as I drove past the café, I saw Granddad in there. That poor old guy was going to have some day ahead of him.

On the highway back to Sweetwater, my mom and dad were alive. Mom was healthy and in a good mood. We were parked beside the road reading our books—

I caught the car as it crossed the shoulder, got it back on the highway, and let in some cold air to wake me up.

I would have thought that after taking three lives, insomnia would have been a more natural reaction than dozing off at the wheel. Perhaps it was because I didn't feel what I had done was wrong. I had no sorrow for the act. Did this mean my character was strong or weak?

Okay. Enough of that. What did I have? I had a lead on

Mechanic. Wayne, the Mechanic. And after him—Blue Eyes. Somehow, I *would* find him.

I drifted off again. So I opened the window again. That time I left it open, cranked up the heater, put up my collar, and turned on the radio.

"Oh, I'm thinking tonight of my Blue Eyes," was playing.

That coincidence raised the hairs on my neck. Was I supposed to laugh or cry?

I decided to hum along as I watched the dawning light begin introducing long, thin shadows to the desolate prairie careening past.

Jim let Henry know when I started down the county road so they were outside waiting for me when I drove in. Henry didn't look good. He'd found my note and snoozed on and off all night sitting up in the living room. He was anxious to hear where I'd been.

When I told him, he wasn't happy that I'd gone over alone. "Not plan," he said after helping me close the big, sliding garage door.

"The iron was hot. I struck it."

"Who say that?"

"Charles de Gaulle, among others," I told him as I knelt down to work a bur out of Jim's coat.

The morning sky was cloudless and steel gray. The windmill was complaining more than usual, its spinning blades facing north. Maybe my blood was thin from being up all night. I suddenly wanted to get in out of the cold.

"The wind's picked up," I said.

Henry squinted from below the brim of his straw hat as he stared out across his dry fields where the sharp wind rippled the pale grass and moved things that weren't rooted down. I could tell that he was weighing what was important for him to say.

"Next time I strike iron, too. Like Charles."

"Agreed," I said.

"Hit sack now?"

"You got it, partner."

I headed for the *hacienda*.

"Tell more later," Henry called after me.

"Tell more later," I called back.

It was close to noon when I woke up, looked out the window, and saw Otis' primer-coated Mercury.

I bathed and dressed, strapped my .38 on low and to the left, and put on my sheepskin jacket. I glanced out across the colorless winter fields as I walked to the main house, the cold air stiffening my wet hair. I noted that the winter silence seemed more brittle than usual.

I soon understood why Jim hadn't gotten me out of bed when Otis arrived. Henry was at the stove fixing his country breakfast special, and that always captured the big dog's attention.

For reasons known exclusively to Henry, when he cooked his special, he fixed enough food to feed a pack of ranch hands. Pork chops, eggs, potatoes, onions, okra, *poblano* chilies, biscuits, and gravy made up the basic menu, the larger portion of which would not be eaten until it hit Jim's enamel dishpan.

Otis was at the table nursing a cup of burnt muck that Henry had boiled up for him and telling how he had returned to The Riverbank later that morning.

"Something told me to go back by," he said more to me than to Henry. "And surenuff, the end of the road was clogged up with boys from downtown, cars everywhere and a meat wagon."

"What meat wagon?"

"For the dead, Hank. Like a hearse. What d'you call them in Shanghai?"

"Think I know?"

"What kind of Chinaman are you?"

"Meat wagon," Henry repeated, putting it to memory as he tended to his pork chops.

Otis went on. "I didn't see that Mexican jalopy of yours

parked anywhere. However, that didn't mean your young corpse wasn't in there attracting maggots."

"You make Otis scared," Henry wanted me to know.

"Uh huh," I let out under my breath as I tried to imagine Otis ever being scared of anything. Of course Henry meant concerned. And that was sort of touching.

"I knew the detective in charge. Told him I was working a case nearby, heard the ruckus, and in I went. I still have friends. There were a few guys I knew there. I even saw your good buddy Hansard. He moseyed in before I left."

That was a name I hadn't heard for a while.

"Otis see bodies," Henry told me as I hung my jacket on a hook by the door and went to the cabinet for a glass.

"I sure did," Otis confirmed, eyeballing my gun and holster. "What're you packing there? Colt .38?"

"That's it," I told him and poured myself some orange juice.

"Not all that accurate at a distance. Effective up close, though."

I didn't tell him I could plug his eyeball out at twenty-five feet. After a pause, he started up again.

"You should've heard the mangy cuss who oversees that crap hole, Hank. He was flapping his gums fifty miles an hour. The truth was he was down at the café when it happened. I had to laugh. He was the closest thing they had to a witness, and they was telling him to shut up."

"Flapping gums," Henry said.

I could picture the toothless old man getting in everyone's way.

"He had it all figured out, the Einstein. He was convinced the dolly—that's you—was there to get the bikers off guard before the shooters came in. That old fart couldn't describe hisself if he was looking in a mirror. So I'd say you dodged another one, Missy."

When I didn't say anything and Henry didn't move, it grew quiet enough to hear Jim's stomach grumbling. Otis was giving me a hard stare.

"How'd that go down exactly?" he asked.

I looked him in the eye to make sure it was clear that I'd out-waited him.

I said, "I asked Bear where I could find Mechanic. He told me, I left, and the shooters came in."

Henry smiled. Otis groaned.

"You gonna make a habit of being ornery?"

I shrugged. It was nice to win one.

"Mechanic's name is Wayne," I told him.

"Baby Girl get name." Henry confirmed proudly as he set a heaping plate of food in front of Otis.

I thought of the starving children in China that my mother used to tell me about.

"You know a bar in South Dallas called Bobby Ray's?" I asked Otis.

"I do," he clucked. "And I can tell you it ain't a fit place for proper society."

He doused his fried eggs and potatoes with hot sauce.

"That's where we find this Mechanic?" he asked.

"According to Roy, he lives there."

"That's a nasty thing to consider," Otis said and paused with a knife in one hand and a fork in the other. "You're not eating?"

"I'll have something later," I told him.

Henry sat down with his plate full, too. Jesus. Watching those two as they stuffed dishtowels in their collars and started putting it away was enough to give *me* indigestion.

The situation gave me a chill. It wasn't Otis and Henry eating like farmhands that made that moment surreal, it was how they'd accepted what I had done merely hours before.

I thought of Sarge and tried to put things in perspective the way he would have. He'd say it was as if we were at war, and I had gone out on patrol to seek and destroy.

Henry, who had seen to my training, expected my success.

Otis, who had witnessed the results, was in awe.

My military analogy began to fall into place. We were

at war, and the first battles had been fought in skirmishes, reprisals for the initial attack. Larger engagements lay ahead. What wasn't so apparent was with whom and where those next battles might be fought.

However, one thing was clear, I was past wrestling with moral issues.

Otis began talking in between bites.

"Hank, you been wondering if you two being witnesses was a bother to them bikers. You can quit wondering. Just the fact that lover boy shows up lying to Missy here is enough to say they're gunning for you."

That gave my stomach a twist.

"Gunning for us," Henry repeated.

"That's right. You being witnesses is all the reason they need to come after you," Otis said and took a bite.

He began chewing while waving a beefy hand holding a fork to keep the floor. Finally, he swallowed and said, "Who's behind all this cover-up don't matter."

"It does matter," I said.

"Sure it does," Otis corrected himself.

"I damn sure want to know who's behind the cover-up," I said.

"I said that wrong," Otis assured me. "What I should of said is the cover-up part is trickier'n the witness part. That means maybe we'll find out what that's about, or maybe we won't."

I knew Otis was telling it to me straight. It just didn't sit right.

"Like I say," Otis went on, "*in a way*, the cover-up don't matter right this minute. What matters most now is keeping your asses from getting shot up."

"Take fight to gang," Henry insisted. "Not wait like sheep."

"I think you're right, and you've got one big advantage," Otis said.

"What that?" Henry asked.

"They don't know who killed that guy Scarecrow, Hank. And they don't know who got Bear, either. And—*and*—they was killed a year or so apart, so they don't know they was done by the same people. This is the advantage I'm talking about. They don't have a clue they're being hunted. They especially don't know they're being hunted by you."

Henry and I looked at each other. Hunters. The word had power.

"My advice is get on with it," Otis said. "Before they know who's doing what. I'd say they've put you and Hank together now since this San Angelo thing."

This San Angelo thing.

That embarrassment made me grimace.

"And I figure that's why they ain't done something before," Otis went on. "I mean, think about it. A Chinaman can't be no problem to them. Who's gonna believe him? Who's gonna care? And a scared girl hiding somewhere? Again, who cares? The two of you together? Maybe that's different."

"Maybe different," Henry agreed.

"Living to-hell-and-gone out here is just asking for midnight visitors. I'm surprised you ain't already had some. Of course, you got that big dog to warn you."

Otis' timing was off, since Jim was fat as a tick with breakfast leftovers and wouldn't be awake much the rest of the day. We all agreed in principle that he was a good watchdog.

"You know, Otis," I said. "The truth is, you don't know what Mechanic looks like, and I do. We'll save time if I help you spot him."

"That makes sense," he said.

I concealed my amazement, but Henry's jaw dropped.

"Don't look so shocked, Hank. I can work with the little maverick. We just gotta fix her hair."

As short as my hair was, I had no idea what he thought he was going to do with it.

"What about hair?" Henry wanted to know.

"That straw-colored mop of hers sticks out'n a crowd,"

Otis said. "A mousy brown wig. Some eye glasses. A big sloppy purse. You know, carrying a big purse'll lump up your figure, Missy. You know. Maybe blue jeans that don't fit so tight. Disappear instead of stand out. That's what we want."

That little outburst gave Otis away. He'd been thinking about me working with him. I could see it in his eyes. And best of all, he knew I knew. So we had that out of the way.

We moved to the living room after the men finished gorging themselves. Henry and I took the comfortable chairs. Big Otis dominated the sofa, and Jim was doing a dead dog imitation on the floor at our feet.

I felt friendlier toward Otis than I'd ever felt.

"We'll have to watch ourselves," I said. "This guy Wayne, the Mechanic, is crazy. He's a born killer."

"What happened that night at Hank's poolroom?" Otis asked me. "I wanna know what we're dealing with here."

I was speechless. I felt a flame rushing through me. The events of that night still plagued my thoughts. What I'd seen and experienced—the sounds, the smells. I deplored reliving that night, but deplore it or not—I did relive it. All the time.

"I've never talked about that night."

"Maybe now it's time," Otis said.

They didn't rush me, and after a while I knew I could tell them.

"It's been two years, and thinking about it still makes my skin crawl."

I spoke quietly. I told them about Bear dragging me inside and about seeing Henry on the floor. Will on the counter. The biker dying at their feet and being ignored.

I saw it again myself as I told about my father kicking Scarecrow and breaking his cue across Mechanic's face. I heard his argument with Blue Eyes and how Bear held a gun to his head. I saw Mechanic ram a splintered cue through my dad's heart when Blue Eyes gave him the order.

I told what happened to me. What Blue Eyes, Bear, and Wayne, the Mechanic did to me.

"I was screaming when they threw me down on a pool table and they hit me in the mouth until I shut up. They chopped my clothes off. They used their big hunting knives. They cut me as they did it. They were laughing like it was a contest. Blue Eyes was the top dog. He did everything first. They all made me do things. They did whatever they wanted, one after another. They made me do things."

I had to stop for a moment. My throat felt dry. Otis and Henry waited.

"They never stopped hitting me. They beat me as they raped me. My eyes were almost shut and my ears were ringing. They took turns beating me, laughing at me. Telling me how stupid I was. They knocked me out, I guess. I woke up on the floor. They were kicking me and urinating on me. I tried to crawl away. You know, hide under a table, but they dragged me out and kicked me again and again. I kept passing out. I woke up and Henry had me in his arms and there was fire everywhere."

I finished talking, and neither man spoke nor moved for the longest time.

Otis let out his breath and said, "I want them all dead."

That summed up our thoughts that afternoon.

Before Otis left, I agreed to meet him that evening to start our stakeouts at Bobby Ray's.

He warned me, "We could be up all night. You better get some more shuteye. You know how to dress. And bring them big Navy glasses of Hank's. I think we'll need them."

Jim, who normally chased cars the quarter of a mile out to the county road, gave Otis' departure a cursory glance, belched, and moseyed over to his spot by the cellar door.

Henry loaded some tools in his truck and drove off to meet his installation crew at a job site over south of Abilene.

I ended up with that cold, drab day all to myself.

After some time at the kitchen table cleaning and oiling

my .38, I returned to the *hacienda*, built a new fire, and put on Bill Evans and some Modern Jazz Quartet.

Jim couldn't resist the fireplace and came in to join me. I had a feeling that things were about to get rough, and I wanted to spend the day in front of a cozy fire enveloped by mellow jazz and Somerset Maugham as a way of preparing myself. It was my calm before the storm.

16

"YOU LOOK LIKE a cat burglar," Otis said when I entered his office that evening.

That was true. My boots, Levi's, turtleneck sweater, and denim jacket were all black.

"I have a black stocking cap to hide my hair, too," I said to him.

"Good girl. And you brought Hank's big spy glasses."

"With instructions to bring them back unbroken," I said.

"Not a problem," Otis said. "I got some Dr Peppers. They're in the icebox if you want one."

That was a shocker.

I put the binoculars on a chair and stood by them. Otis was at his huge old desk. As usual, his .45 was in a shoulder holster rig hanging on the back corner of his chair. He was having a cup of coffee and smoking a cigarette.

"I drove over to Bobby Ray's before I came here," he told me, using his conversational tone of voice like last night in the car.

"Uh huh," I said.

"I thought I recalled a parking lot up the street. It's still there. So I stuck my jalopy in a space in back that has a clear shot of Bobby Ray's and grabbed a taxi back here."

Otis, I was learning, thought things out.

"That's why the spy glasses. We have a perfect spot for as long as we need it, and there's no chance our boy Wayne or anybody else'll see us. I like getting what I need without a fuss. Of course if it comes to a fuss—"

A buzzer sounded.

Otis nodded at me, snubbed out his cigarette, and said, "That's Madame Li downstairs. She's letting me know I got company. Why don't you wait in the other room? Let's see who this is."

"Did she buzz me?" I asked.

"Everybody gets buzzed," he said.

He pulled his .45 out of its holster and placed that hand in his lap. I picked up the black leather case that held the Navy binoculars and took it with me through the open door into the dark adjoining room.

At first glance, it was as dreary in there as I thought it would be. Although the big wolf hide thrown across the large iron-framed bed was attractive in a manly sort of way. I placed the binocular case on the bed, ran my hand through the thick wolf fur, and glanced around.

The walls were bare except for an out-of-date girly calendar from an auto dealership and a few grainy 8x10 boxing photos from 1934 that I found were of Clyde Chastain and Maxi Rosenbloom, a couple of light heavyweights.

Besides the sturdy bedstead, there were some old, straight back chairs, a worn out table or two, and a hefty antique oak armoire that no doubt had a story attached to it.

Across the room was the open door that I usually saw reflected in the freestanding, full-length mirror near the bed. I'd assumed that was the door into the bathroom. It wasn't. The bathroom was beyond.

The unlit space that I always saw reflected was a dark-room where Otis developed his pictures. The strategically placed mirror was no accident. From his workspace, I could see into his office. I realized also that since I was wearing all black, if I were to pull on my stocking cap—which I did—I could step back into that darkness and watch Otis and his visitors without being seen.

Otis continued to surprise me.

By changing my angle, I discovered slump-shouldered Detective Hansard standing in the middle of the office, speaking to Otis. He was alone. He was wearing the same shameful fedora I remembered and a long, brownish-gray topcoat.

I hadn't seen that contemptible human being since the hospital. I had, however, thought of him many times. I was too far away to hear what he was saying and too curious to stay where I was. I eased back over to the door.

"So you're saying you ain't backing off?" Hansard was mouthing in his tough voice as I peeked into the office through the crack on the hinge side of the open door.

"Yeah. I'm saying that," Otis snarled back. "You and whoever's pulling your strings ain't telling me what to do."

"That's your problem, Millett. You've always been bull stubborn."

"And your problem is you're a whore. You always have been."

"I come here to give you a friendly warning, and you insult me," Hansard said, and brought a long-nosed revolver from under his topcoat.

"You pulling a rod on me?" Otis growled.

I caught my breath, drew my .38, and cranked one into the chamber as I spun on my heel to get around the protruding door.

I heard the loud report of Otis' big automatic as I rounded the door and saw that he was in motion with his smoking .45 in his hand. He had sprung to his feet, slamming his rolling desk chair into the wall behind him. I brought my pistol up as I cleared the door and squared my shoulders to the doorframe.

The unholy blast of the .45 must have masked Hansard's gunshot, because I didn't realize that Otis had been hit until I saw the blurred motion of his body falling. The impact of the slug had knocked him back and down, this time sending the rolling chair parallel to the wall to crash into a bookcase, scattering books and file folders full of papers.

As I stepped full into the doorway, Hansard was bounding toward the desk, his long-barreled pistol extended before him.

I let one go and hit his shooting arm below the elbow. His high-pitched screech of surprise and pain seemed loud. The blast of Otis' .45 going off again in those close quarters was louder.

I'd saved the detective's life because he stiffened when my bullet slammed into his forearm. So, instead of the big hunk of hot lead from Otis' .45 taking his face off, it burnt a groove into his forehead and sent his fedora sailing.

My next round hit him high in his right shoulder. It was a through-shot. I saw the blood mist spray out behind him. With all the clothes he had on, I wasn't sure how solid that hit was.

He cried out again and began backpedaling at once, gasping and grunting with fright. He knocked over a chair, stumbled, and caught his balance as he ducked and ran like a man ten years younger. His topcoat flapped out behind him as he ran, his damaged right arm flailing in a bloody sleeve.

I fired at him again as he flew through the door. I missed. I heard him clatter down the front stairs.

"All right," I said to Otis as I came around the desk and saw him on the floor.

He was leaning up on one elbow, his head and shoulder against the wall, his .45 still clutched in his big fist. The front of his shirt and pants were soaked in blood.

"Do I call a doctor, an ambulance, or what?"

Otis spoke to me in the same voice he always used.

"I think I caught some luck here, Missy. Why don't you get some towels? Make one of them good'n wet."

When I re-entered the office with the towels in my arms, I discovered a timid young Chinese man wearing a long white apron standing at the door, looking into the office.

I didn't think he could see Otis behind the desk. He saw the overturned furniture, the scattered papers the fan was blowing about; he, Madame Li, and everyone else downstairs had heard the shooting and Otis hitting the floor.

I stopped near the desk and spoke to the waiter in a calm voice. "Everything's okay," I said.

I remembered I was dressed like a burglar.

When he remained silent, I added, "I'll give you a call if I need any help."

He nodded his head.

"Thanks for coming up," I told him and smiled.

With a long glance back, he walked away.

My heart was thundering as I rushed around the desk and got busy getting Otis' bloody shirt out of the way. He had taken the hit low in his belly, and his big silver buckle was immediately a problem.

"Cut the leather," Otis grunted. "You ain't getting the buckle open."

I got a knife out, cut the belt, and worked the big buckle out of the way. It was then that I discovered the luck he was talking about.

"The slug went through your buckle."

"That's what I thought," he said.

I used the wet towel to clean up around the wound. He was in pain. A few sharp intakes of breath gave him away.

"Christ," I said. "I don't believe this, Otis. I think the slug's right here. I think I see it."

When he stood up the bullet that was aimed at his heart hit his stomach. His heavy buckle and two layers of thick leather belt had stopped the lead from penetrating his stomach too deeply.

I cleaned the area around the wound and got Otis to press a folded towel against it to help control the bleeding.

"What now?" I asked.

"In that drawer over there," he indicated. "There're some needle-nosed pliers."

"Hold on now."

"Just get them, Missy. And in the bathroom, there's some rubbing alcohol. Should be a couple of bottles."

"You expect me—"

"I'm bleeding here. There's a box. Alum and stuff."

I went after the things Otis asked for, came back, and used a lot of alcohol as I cleaned around the wound again. The alcohol must have stung like crazy, but he didn't complain.

When I was finished cleaning, I picked up the pliers and looked him in the eye.

He said, "Don't pantywaist around. Just get in there and get it."

I was scared out of my wits, but I concentrated like crazy, performed surgery with a pair of pliers that had been God knows where, and I did it without pantywaisting around.

When I pushed the pliers into the open wound, Otis sucked in his breath with a hiss and mouthed, "Goddamn it," under his breath. But he held still.

There were some dreadful moments of fishing around until I snagged the little chunk of metal. I brought it out and dropped it in the palm of Otis' hand.

"Thirty-two," he said, squinting at it.

I poured more alcohol into the wound, which wrenched, "Goddamn it! You could've warned me," out of him.

"It was just nestled there, right under the skin," I said.

"Plumb wore itself out," he managed through clinched teeth.

The small cardboard box that I'd found in the bathroom had suitable bandages, tape, and some alum powder that stopped the bleeding. I bandaged him as well as I knew how.

He seemed to be breathing easier, but I knew he was still in pain.

"Wrap it tight," he said.

When I was finished, I said, "You're going to a doctor."

"Sure, I am. D'you think I want gangrene? I ain't going right this minute, though. Go wash up and get me a fresh shirt out of the closet. Would you, Missy? We got things to do."

I cleaned up, found a faded blue work shirt and a dark

gray cardigan sweater in Otis' armoire, and helped him get them on. By not tucking the shirt in, it covered the top of his bloodstained pants. After we got his suspenders over his shoulders, I helped him strap on his shoulder holster.

He looked a little odd without his white shirt, vest, and tie. So what. Looks weren't the issue. He stood by his desk and washed down a handful of aspirin tablets with a slug of cold coffee. He cupped a match in his hand and lit a cigarette.

After a couple of deep drags, he squared his shoulders and asked, "Did he get a look at you?"

"Nah. He was too busy running."

"Did I hit'm? I got off two."

"You must've missed with the first one. Your second grazed his head," I said.

"You fired three shots."

"Yeah, and nailed him twice. In his shooting arm and the same shoulder."

"Oh, you nailed him. He left a trail," Otis said, indicating the blood splatters on the floor that started in the middle of the office and continued into the hall. "You did good. I owe you."

"Let's call it even. You've done a lot for Henry and me."

I could tell that Otis liked that answer.

He said, "You don't cry and carry on like most girls."

That was a backhanded compliment. Although, I don't think he meant it as one.

Otis took a deep breath and glanced around at the disorder that was his office. I picked up and set straight the chair the detective knocked over during his retreat, and Otis stepped over and redirected the fan that the bookcase had bumped.

I gathered up the papers the fan had blown about, and also picked up the shell casings and put them in an empty coffee cup on the desk.

"Ain't that cute?" Otis said discovering Hansard's weapon covered by the paper mess on his desktop.

"What is it?"

"A nickel-plated .32. You ain't touched this?"

"Nope."

"A silencer means for sure he was here to rub me out."

That's why I didn't hear the shot.

I leaned over and looked because I'd never seen a silencer before. I wasn't impressed. It wasn't more than a short piece of pipe added to the barrel.

"Get me a paper sack," he said, nodding at his coffee area. "On the bottom shelf there."

Otis picked up the little revolver by sticking a pencil through the trigger guard. I brought the sack over and he put it in.

"You know Ava Gardner's birthday?" he asked me.

"Do I? Nooo, can't say that I do."

"You will from now on."

Carrying the sack with the pistol in it, Otis led me into the other room and showed me that the table beside his bed that was draped with an ecru crocheted shawl was in reality a beautiful old safe finished in black enamel with Murray Allenby lettered in gold script on the door.

"It's a Boston series, triple hard plate," Otis told me proudly as he stood back and waved his hand for me to open the safe.

My school locker was my total experience with combination locks. I knelt down and spun the knob on Otis' Murray Allenby as if I were in the hall at Central High.

"Twelve, twenty-four, twenty-two," he said, and I opened his safe.

I wasn't surprised to find a sexy, autographed photo of Ava Gardner taped to the inside of the door. He handed me the sack containing Hansard's shiny little pistol, and I put it on a shelf inside.

"Your Colt's a Super, ain't it?"

"Yeah."

"I got one of them, too. Look in the hardware down there and find a fresh barrel. He may be a bad cop, but he's a cop. You don't want the pistol that shot him."

I found a new barrel and sat on the edge of the bed, broke my weapon open, and changed the part.

"Stick the old one in there. We'll get rid of it later."

I did as Otis told me, shut the safe door, spun the knob, and stood up.

"How come I get the combination to your safe?"

"Hell, Missy, the way we're going, we ain't gonna be alive this time next week, anyway. What difference does it make?"

"Fair enough," I said.

I helped him get on a heavy coat.

We locked the place up and departed cautiously down the hall. Otis carried his camera and lenses in a small canvas bag in one hand and his .45 in the other. I kept my pistol in my hand, too, and hung Henry's Navy binoculars over my shoulder.

He went down the front way because he wanted to lean in and thank the woman behind the register at the Mandarin Palace. I took the back stairs down and hid my pistol as I cut through the kitchen to the back door. I smiled at the curious cooks and nodded at the waiter that I now knew personally.

Otis was up against the building having a smoke when I drove around to pick him up. He flipped his butt aside and strolled over. He got in carefully and I pulled away.

"What did Madame Li tell you?"

"She said Hansard had his collar pulled up to hide his face. He came up to bump me off. Pure and simple."

"What did she see when he left?"

"She saw him get into his car. She gave me that. A two-tone DeSoto."

That rang a bell that I couldn't put together right then. It was quiet as we drove along, except Otis' breathing was labored.

"I'm worried about you," I said.

"I'll be fine after we get a couple of things sorted out."

"Where to? South Dallas?"

"Not yet, Missy. I'll give you directions."

We didn't drive all that far before we were on a dark, residential street lined with large old elms and two-story homes. Otis had me slow down at one of the houses where the lights were off, and there was no activity in the area.

"Okay," he said, "this was the closest. There's another place."

We drove to an area of pawnshops, beer joints, flophouses, and secondhand stores.

After a couple of turns he had me stop at the curb near an alley so he could gaze back at a dozen or so cars parked helter-skelter behind an old brick building.

"I think that's it," he said. "The DeSoto."

I stared back into the dark area.

"The blue and white?"

"Yeah. That's what Madame Li said Hansard was driving. Pull in. Park near him."

I parked where Otis said.

The light in the deserted area came from an illuminated window or two at the rear of the old structure and a dim bulb above a doorway. Farther down the murky alley, some guys were hanging around the back door of a beer joint.

We watched them through our front window as they had a smoke and talked. No one was paying any attention to us parked there in my dark car.

"How'd you know he'd be here?"

He tipped his head toward the door in the brick building behind us.

"There's a doctor in there. Just like the first place we tried."

I looked back over my shoulder at the unremarkable door with the lit bulb above it. The entrance was set flat into the weathered brick wall in front of a plain cement stoop at the top of three or four steps. There were no windows to either side of the door and there was what looked to be a small metal plaque to one side. The doctor's shingle, maybe.

"Some doctor's office," I said under my breath.

"You ain't choosy if you get shot and don't wanna report it," Otis said.

"You're right," I said, realizing my experiences with doctors was not in the least relevant.

"There're a few places he could've gone. This one and the other was the closest. We got lucky on our second try."

"More like an educated guess," I said.

We didn't speak for a while. Otis cracked his window and fired up a smoke. With his glass down that inch or so, we could hear the music from the beer joint. And, like it happens when you don't think about it, I remembered what had rung the bell before. I looked over at Hansard's car.

"Otis."

"Yeah?"

"I think we saw that car when we were at The Riverbank. It pulled into the café down the street. I'd swear that's the same car."

He stared at the DeSoto, took a deep breath, and said, "Nobody ever got out of that car, did they? Ain't that funny? The reason I remember that car now is because nobody ever got out and went into the café. What was I thinking about that I missed that?"

"You were already there," I said. "He must've followed me."

"That slimy bastard followed you in, and when he saw me, he followed me out. That's how come he showed up later. He followed me to a motel I was checking out near Mineral Wells and back to that piss hole where you was busy offing Bear. I just thought he was one of the men working homicide that night. When was it Hank saw you and the Mackenzie fella together? Last week, was it?"

"Yeah. Well, three days ago. Thursday," I said.

"That's when Mackenzie got Hank's license number. Hansard ain't been on us long, but he *has* put us together. He's put us together, Goddamn it."

"I know he came up to your office to shoot you. What did he say?"

"He said I was messing with the wrong folks, and I should back off."

"Those were Lost Demons at The Riverbank. Was he warning you off the gang?"

"We're gonna find out, ain't we?"

No more than fifteen minutes later, the doctor's door opened creating a wedge of light. Detective Hansard stepped out and was framed in that light as he paused on the small stoop to speak to someone inside.

His head was bandaged, and his left hand was hidden because his overcoat was hung over his shoulders like an Italian film actor.

When the door closed behind him and he started down the steps, Otis shifted in his seat, preparing to get out and confront him. That was when we heard the roar of motorcycles starting up.

From the far side of the dark area, two bikers rolled out from behind some cars. Their bright headlights swung across the building as they roared up to where Hansard was standing at the foot of the steps, a deer on the highway.

They shot the wide-eyed detective in the face and chest, at least a half a dozen times. The discharges were like firecracker snaps almost lost in the roar of the motorcycles. The barrage sent Hansard tripping back over the steps before he collapsed.

"Can you make them out?" Otis barked at me during the attack.

"The one with long hair. That's Mechanic. On the red bike," I shouted.

Otis opened the door and stepped out with his .45 drawn.

Using both hands, he leveled his weapon and fired several times at the bikers who were hunched down and leaning over as they rounded the corner into the dark, narrow alley. They were heading for the street at reckless speeds, the raucous growls of their machines echoing hard off the walls of the buildings.

The roaring engines almost masked the hard pops from Otis' big automatic. He missed them.

I fired up the Caddie while Otis was shooting. As soon as he was able to get his damaged body back in the car, I burned rubber backing around and fishtailed up the alley.

The bikers had disappeared by the time we got to the street. It was anybody's guess which way they went. We made a couple of turns with our windows down, straining to hear the machines.

The luck we'd been riding had run out. We'd lost them.

"We got caught with our pants down," Otis said. "Okay. So this Mechanic guy was one of them. Who was the other one?"

"Never saw him before. How'd Mechanic know Hansard was there?" I asked.

"Hansard told him, most likely. The fool called somebody to report what happened at my place and signed his own death warrant. Whoever he talked to figured I'd find him and make him talk."

"When you say 'whoever they talked to', you mean the Lost Demons, right? So, that *is* who's being protected from that night at Henry's."

"Sure looks that way, don't it?" he agreed.

"And another thing," I said.

"Yeah?"

"We just saw a police detective murdered. We saw it happen, and we know one of the guys who did it."

"Call the police, you're thinking. You see there's a hitch in that gitty-up, Missy. If he's in police custody, somehow he'll end up dead, or somewhere up the line a judge signs a paper and he's out of the hoosegow, pissed off, and looking for us."

"Is this 1854 or 1954? A gun seems like the preferred justice," I said.

Otis was silent for a breath or two before saying, "You

know, Missy, I'm getting a little tuckered out." He put his head back, closed his eyes, and murmured, "A sawbones might be just the ticket 'bout now."

"Not back there, though. Right? That place'll be crawling with cops."

"No, no. I don't want no drunk. We'll go to Doc McGraw's over near Lake Arlington. You know where that's at?"

"Kind of," I said and Otis began to snore.

I had to wake him several times to clarify directions and ended up not certain where we were even after we got there.

17

DOC McGRAW'S PLACE was set back in the middle of several hundred acres of blackjack oaks.

After I left the paved county road, I followed a narrow dirt trail that looked as if it had been cut through jungle instead of woods. It was pitch dark in there with the foliage interlacing above our heads. It was like leaving a tunnel when we burst out into an open area awash in moonlight.

"Otis," I said, loud enough to wake him.

He lifted his head to see that we were crossing a meadow.

"Are we where we're supposed to be?" I asked.

"Yeah. Yeah," he said. "This is it."

In my headlights I saw that the trail bridged a wide creek and ended at several whitewashed frame houses, a barn, and what looked like horse corrals and other animal sheds and enclosures.

When I drew closer to the buildings, several mongrel hounds charged out from somewhere to greet the car, chasing around us, baying, barking, and jumping up to offer their sorrowful gazes.

As we pulled up, bright lights came on above the spacious porch of the main house, and a big man pushed open the screen door. He had on overalls, a wool plaid shirt, and sported untied work boots on his big feet.

"That's Doc," Otis told me.

Doc called out something in Spanish, and the dogs calmed down and moved away.

The man of medicine looked more like a farmer with his leathery, sun-browned skin. He was easily as big as Otis with broad shoulders and muscular arms. I guessed that he and Otis were about the same age, too. Pushing fifty.

As he left the porch and came down the steps toward us, I saw his tough face. He'd seen some hard knocks. Like Otis, he displayed a nose that had been broken at least once. He held up a big hand to shield his eyes from my high beams.

I turned off my lights and cut the engine.

Otis sighed and opened his door.

"Wait for me," I said.

"I can handle it," he said to reassure me and then worried me by groaning under his breath as he pulled himself up and out of the car.

"Oh, it's you," Doc said when he saw Otis. "Didn't recognize the car. What's wrong this time?"

"It can't be very serious if I'm here to see you," Otis replied.

He was unsteady as he closed the door and held onto the car to regain his balance. Doc reached him at that moment and took his arm.

Like giant warriors leaving the field of battle, the two big men clung together and made their way to the house, neither of them speaking.

When the screen door opened ahead of them, I was taken off guard. I shouldn't have been. Why wouldn't there be someone else there? Or ten people, for that matter. It was just that nothing had been said about anyone besides Doc McGraw.

I closed my door and started for the house with the curious dogs trailing along.

A tall woman held the screen door open for the men as they made their way inside. She was big-boned, as well as tall, and wore a maroon ankle-length robe. I could see the bottoms of white pajamas over fluffy pink slippers.

I couldn't tell her age. She had a pale blue beauty mask

smeared on her wide face, and her hair was up in pin-curlers. She smiled at me, and I thought of a traveling min-strel show I'd seen once. She motioned with a wave of her hand for me to come on.

I walked a little faster, crossed the porch, and entered what I guessed had once been a farmhouse. It was close and warm inside.

"I'm Kristin," I said.

The big woman nodded, took my hand and gave it a little pull so I would follow her. She talks less than I do, I thought, and fell in behind her.

We left the small front room that served as an office and waiting area and entered a long hall. It was where they displayed framed degrees, licenses, and other documents. Doc McGraw, I learned, was an M.D. *and* a large animal veterinarian.

Otis was on his back on a large stainless steel table in the center of a very clean, glossy white, windowless room bright with light and rife with the unmistakable scent of disinfectant. He was taking fluids through an I.V. from a bag that was hanging from a ceiling hook.

Against one wall were large stainless steel sinks and counters with stacks of trays, containers of liquids, and surgical instruments and paraphernalia. Near Doc was a small table on wheels that held surgical instruments in trays and the syringe and needle that he'd already used.

Doc was cutting away Otis's clothes with a pair of scissors. Without looking at me, he said, "So you met Loretta?"

"Yes, I did," I said.

Loretta went to a cabinet and took out bedding. She put a pillow under Otis' head and, while she moved around and got him covered with blankets and an operating sheet, the doctor paid attention to me.

"He told me you saved his life."

"He tells big ones," I said.

"And she's ornery," Otis mumbled, and Loretta's smile caught my eye.

"You be quiet and take a nap," Doc told him.

Doc gave me the once over. His evenly-set, dark, intelligent eyes were the only handsome feature in that fearsome face. He had what I guessed would be called a piercing gaze.

I didn't look away.

"How old are you?"

"I'll be twenty pretty quick."

Loretta was keeping an eye on me from across the table.

"You pulled the bullet out?" Doc asked.

"With some pliers, yeah. It was right there. His belt buckle pretty much stopped it."

"Then what did you do?"

As I told the doctor what I had done, he sterilized instruments, and Loretta worked beneath the edges of the blankets to get Otis' shoes off and cut away and remove the rest of his clothing.

"Did he take any medications?" Doc asked as he turned away from me and ducked his head down for Loretta to hang a fresh white butcher's apron on him.

"Some aspirin," I told him.

"How much?"

"A handful."

"He never makes it easy," Doc said.

When Loretta moved around Doc to tie the strings in back, he faced me, and I asked if Otis was going to be okay.

"Nothing to worry about," Doc told me. "You did fine."

Loretta, still looking ridiculous in her mask and curlers, confirmed the doctor's assessment with a sincere smile and a nod as she tied her own apron.

Otis began snoring.

"What's your name?" Doc asked.

"Kristin," I said. "Kristin Van Dijk."

"You don't mind waiting in the other room, do you, Kristin?"

"I may leave for a while, " I said.

Doc said, "Good idea. Why don't you go get this guy a

change of clothes, and we'll see you tomorrow."

I picked up Otis' key ring before saying my thank yous and goodbyes.

The dogs were gentlemen; they saw me to my car. I drove out through the forest primeval to the county road and stopped there to make a decision before turning onto the highway.

I figured it was early for Mechanic to call it a night. Especially since he had a successful killing to celebrate.

Bobby Ray's address was in the phone book.

I found it while an old guy in greasy coveralls and his young helper filled the tank, checked under the hood, and scraped the bug juice off the glass. The old guy was the owner of the gas station, and he apologized for the cost of ethyl. It was up to 26 cents a gallon, and he said he didn't know where it was going to stop.

"I've seen it up to 29 cents in some places," he said. "Folks're mad."

"I'm not mad at you," I told him, and asked how to get to the address I'd found.

While he was inside his office writing down the directions, the young guy admired my fender skirts and dual exhaust system.

"Glasspacks," he said to himself. "Swell paint job. California," he said to me, a toothpick clenched in his teeth. "Can't get nothing like gat around these here parts."

The big parking lot near Bobby Ray's that Otis had told me about had a thin-as-a-rail, middle-aged Negro man ensconced in a chartreuse canvas lawn chair at the entrance.

"Mm, mm, mm," he said. "That's some paint job."

"Thanks," I said.

"How long y'all plan to stay, miss?"

The rates were displayed on a board above his head. I

paid him for one day. As he took my money, he offered a word of advice.

"Y'all lock up, now. I'm leaving pretty soon. Ain't nobody here till I get back'n the morning."

I located Otis' '50 Mercury tucked way back against the fence. I found a space for my car and stuck it in. I grabbed the binoculars and walked over to see if the vantage point was as good as Otis said it was.

The view was perfect. Bobby Ray's well-lit entrance was just down the way—less than a half block from the back of the lot. There were over a dozen motorcycles parked in front of the joint, and while I was standing there, several more arrived.

I unlocked Otis' car, put the binoculars inside, and looked around to make sure no one was watching me before climbing up on the Mercury's fender.

Using my stocking cap to protect my fingers, I unscrewed a light bulb to put the back section of the lot in darkness. I wouldn't have walked on my lacquered finish, but I didn't think Otis' primer job would suffer from my footprints.

After I jumped down and looked around again, I discovered that the big two-hundred-watt-bulb that I'd just removed had been the light for that section of the dark street *and* the back of the parking lot.

That's when I realized that the entrance to Bobby Ray's was located in a paved alley. It wasn't on a street at all. That's why there were no streetlights. Fine. The darkness would work to my advantage.

Using Henry's big binoculars from the back seat of the Mercury, I could look out through the windshield and get a close up of every slimy biker who entered or exited the beer joint. Little by little, as Otis would say. Step by step.

The snarl of revving motorcycles woke me up.

I was confused for a moment. But I got the sleep out of my eyes when I realized that the gathering thunder rumbling down the alley was coming from the guys who had closed Bobby Ray's.

"Damn it!" I grumbled, found the glasses on the floor, and got them up and working.

As the bikers left the joint, they were throwing beer bottles, laughing, and roughhousing. They were getting on their machines and preparing to ride. A bike got knocked over and a fight started. A hard little mama slapped one of the combatants several times and broke it up.

"Be there. Be there," I murmured as I moved from one biker's tough face to another. I noticed as I worked my way through the guys that no one was leaving. They were all just holding it there, gunning their engines, making noise.

"There you are," I whispered.

I'd found Wayne on his idling fire engine red Indian. His face looked as vicious and empty of common decency as I remembered it. I was pleased to see his nose was crooked and notched from where Dad had hit him.

"There you are, you bastard. Who's this?"

Long dark hair, blue jeans, a short white leather jacket, and a heavy scarf. She put her hand on Mechanic's shoulder, swung her leg over, and snuggled into the seat to ride behind him.

When she looked up the alley, I saw her face. She was older than I was—not by much—and could've been cute as a cheerleader. But she looked drunk and had a tough edge to her. Thin nose, square jaw, and full lips.

Mechanic had on the same dark brown pilot's jacket with a fur collar that he was wearing when he shot Hansard earlier in the evening. The way they were dressed made me think they weren't going far.

The bikers began turning and adjusting their machines.

They were going to leave as a group and ride past where I was. I had no time to get to the Caddie. I scrambled over the seat, stuck the key in the ignition, and got Otis' jalopy going. I'd never driven a Mercury before. It didn't seem that different from my car once I got the seat adjusted.

I heard them as I was driving out of the lot. A pack of a

dozen or so rounded the corner out of the alley and streamed by at the end of the street.

I floored it up to the corner and made a right turn. I found myself about a city block behind the noisy parade. The idea was to stay behind them without arousing suspicion. It was late and there weren't many cars, so I stayed well back, relying on the street lamps at the corners and mid-blocks to help me keep the white jacket in sight.

The group began breaking up one and two at a time until there were two motorcycles remaining. Mechanic and his girlfriend were on one of those bikes.

They were pretty far ahead of me, and there was still some traffic, though it was residential by then. When they made a right turn off the big street that we'd been on for the last mile or so, I slowed down as I approached that corner and saw the machines and riders swinging into the drive of a large, two-story frame house.

I drove past that turn, hung a right at the next corner, took my time circling the block, and found a tree-shaded spot to park a few properties up and across from their house. I took out my .38, held it in my lap, and lowered the front windows so I could hear better.

I had to pull my collar up and my stocking cap down against the cold. Peering out across the hood, I grasped the advantage of the primer coat finish on the car. Its dull, smoky-gray finish absorbed light. That's why Otis called it his invisible car. It didn't reflect light like my car.

No wonder everyone complimented my paint job. They noticed it.

I hung around for a half-hour or so, but it was getting colder and I was getting a little tired. I didn't want to fall asleep again like I did at Bobby Ray's. Besides, nothing was happening.

So, I 'cranked up the jalopy,' as Otis would say, and pulled away.

As I drove by, I heard a Johnny Cash tune coming from somewhere back in their brightly lit house. I didn't put on my lights, roll up my windows, or holster my weapon until I was past their place and turning the corner. My plan was to drive out of there the same way I'd gotten in. I couldn't get lost if I just reversed the route.

As I drove along, I began to think that the night had gotten darker. And in a way, it had. What few businesses had been open before were now closed, and there were fewer cars on the streets, too. I shrugged off the weird feeling it gave me to be alone and just told myself to get home. I glanced at the fuel gauge.

The best laid plans.

I didn't have enough gas to get me home and I hadn't seen any open filling stations in that area.

"Wake up," I said.

I wasn't in the Cadillac. *My* car had a full tank. And I should trade cars anyway. I'd just leave the Mercury where I found it. That was no problem since I was on my way to the parking lot because of the reverse route that I was taking.

"Wait until Otis hears how I tried to get away with his car," I said.

I'd just gotten behind the wheel and took off and found out where Mechanic lived. Or, at least where he was staying. I knew that Otis would've had some method, some moves he would've made to keep from being seen. But I'd done okay.

I felt good about doing what I did, following them, getting away with it. I also felt a sense of relief because Mechanic and the guys he rode with were stone cold killers. I didn't think they would be as easy to take as Bear and Scarecrow.

Albert would shoot them right off the bat and ask later if they were the right ones.

Something caught my eye.

Something happened in the rearview mirror. I picked up my speed, just a little, not enough for anyone to notice.

There it was again.

There was something moving behind me.

While keeping an alert eye on the rearview, I became conscious of being on that first main street that I had taken when I started following the bikers. The street that in a few long blocks would return me to the lot where my car was parked.

I saw them.

Two motorcycles without lights.

"Shit!"

I hadn't gotten away with anything.

They were still pretty far back, but they were picking it up. I punched it and the powerful Mercury jumped like a rabbit. Okay. I had power, but they'd still be faster. And where was I going to get gas? I had to figure things out in a hurry. I was in a deserted commercial area. There were no people around.

"Nobody, nobody, nobody," I mumbled, keeping an eye on the bikes behind me.

I thought about what they would do.

The street was wide enough for them to come up on each side of me and murder me just like they murdered Hansard. They didn't know who I was. How could they know that? I was just someone who had followed them. That's all they knew and that was enough for these guys. They were murderers.

I'll slam on my brakes. I'll do it very suddenly, and as they overtake me without meaning to, I'll shoot them. I rolled down my windows to get ready.

"That won't work. Don't be crazy. Think. Think," I said.

They were gaining on me. They were coming up for the kill. I saw the parking lot corner just ahead and that's when I got an idea. A good idea.

"This'll work," I said. "This'll work."

And it all seemed so clear to me as I entered the intersection with the parking lot over on the far left corner. I lifted my foot from the accelerator because I was going to turn into the paved alley behind the parking lot, the alley that led to Bobby Ray's.

Two could play at this no lights business.

They were just entering the intersection behind me as I hit my brakes hard. It was going to be close. My tires screeched and the car began to drift as I counter-locked the wheels.

I could hear my dad when we were practicing on ice, "Cut hard the opposite way."

And that pointed my nose into the left turn that I needed. I got off the brakes, down-shifted, punched the gas, and left enough rubber on the street for a whole new tire as the reliable Mercury lurched, got its grip, and shot me smoking into the dark alley.

Showing that machine no mercy, I stomped the brakes. The tires screamed as the brakes took hold, and the car began sliding to a stop in the darkness that I had created when I unscrewed the parking lot bulb.

Before the car could stop, I clutched, ground the poor baby into reverse, popped the clutch, and stomped the gas pedal as hard as I'd hit the brakes.

While the transmission was deciding whether to give me what I asked for or explode, I doused the lights. The transmission made up its mind and, with its shrieking tires smoking, the big car lurched backward down that narrow, pitch-dark alley.

I twisted around and, from over my shoulder, began directing three thousand pounds of *invisible* primer-coated Detroit steel toward the alley entrance. The transmission whined up the scale as the car picked up speed in reverse.

The bikers rounded the familiar corner, leaning hard into the turn without their lights on—lights that would have told them the odds had changed.

I kept the accelerator to the floor and must have been doing over thirty miles an hour when I collided with the two bikes. The collisions weren't as impressive as I had expected. It must have been the difference in weight. Yet something definitely happened.

One of the motorcycles and its rider flipped across the roof of the car and clipped the left front fender before careening off into the darkness as the Mercury moved under. At the same time, on the right side, there were flashing shadows as screeching debris ripped shards of sparks from the brick façade of the building that bordered the alley.

I was sideswiping the building, and steel fragments were careening back and over the Mercury breaking the side windows. It all happened very fast.

I jammed the brakes again and felt a wheel bounce over something before the car shuddered to a stop. I threw the overheated transmission into neutral, set the emergency brake, and with my heart thundering went out the door with my .38 in my hand.

The damaged motorcycles and both bodies were up the alley some distance with pieces of torn metal and other debris strewn about, as one would expect. There was a strong odor of gasoline.

The first rider I came to I recognized as the accomplice in the Hansard killing. He was alive and was pulling himself up as I got to him.

I shot him twice in the chest and kept walking.

The other biker was on his back farther up the alley near the crushed and smoking remains of his fire engine red Indian. He was still alive, too, and missing an arm. I glanced around as I crossed the dark alley. I didn't see it anywhere.

He was emitting a feeble groan and struggling to sit up, using his one elbow for leverage. He couldn't do it and fell back into the blood and spilled fuel that was gathering in an iridescent sheen around him.

I wanted that murderer to see me, so I stepped closer. As our eyes met, I thought he was going to speak because his mouth quivered open. Instead he shimmied in the oily muck and began regurgitating blood.

My guess was things hadn't turned out the way those boys had expected.

"Give my best to Scarecrow and Bear," I said and pumped two into Mechanic's chest.

I holstered my weapon and walked away while the hot cartridges were still bouncing around. I took a few deep breaths to help settle my nerves as I looked at the damage to the Mercury. I recognized it as evidence that would lead to Otis and made a decision.

I maneuvered the car out of the alley and drove around to the parking lot. The attendant was long gone, of course. I found an open slot against a wall, as far away from the alley as possible, and backed into it to help hide the damage.

I left the car unlocked and lowered the unbroken windows. We'd wait a few days. If it didn't get stolen or the police didn't put it together with that mess in the alley, we'd drive it home. If it was discovered and connected to the incident, so what? We'd call it stolen. Otis had an airtight alibi.

As I walked to my car, carrying the binoculars by the shoulder strap, I sensed the tension within me begging to let go. The familiar fluttering at my temples. I swung the binoculars over my head a couple of times like a cowboy with a lasso. My feelings were so mixed up I couldn't identify them.

Step by step. I was in the Caddie. I was out of the parking lot. I was out of the neighborhood. I was on my way home. And in my head I could not shut out the lines I was hearing: *"And if you wrong us shall we not revenge?"*

I was too tired to drive out to Henry's. So I made it into Fort Worth and parked in front of the Mandarin Palace. I found the key to the outside door on Otis' ring, climbed the dark stairs, and opened the office door.

Something was wrong.

What was it?

The fan wasn't running.

18

I MOVED AWAY from the door as I pulled my automatic. I squatted down to make myself less of a target. My heart was racing. If someone was there, his eyes were accustomed to the dark. So, I was already dead and just didn't know it yet.

My eyes had adjusted coming up the dark stairs, and as I searched the room, I realized it didn't matter. It wasn't as dark as it should be. The Venetian blinds that Otis always kept closed had been raised. Streetlight was coming through the window.

I scanned the room. Nothing. No movement.

I listened as hard as my flawed hearing allowed. Nothing.

I strained harder for sounds from the other room. Still nothing.

There was a scent that was foreign to Otis' office. I realized that I'd noted the smell before I opened the door. What was it? It was sharp, almost a medicinal odor. I thought of the alcohol that I'd used on Otis' wound. That wasn't it.

Okay. I was alone in the office. So I turned on the lights and looked around.

I began to understand things.

The floor had been scrubbed clean. The bloodstains were gone from the office and out in the hall. The office had been straightened up. The bookcase was back in place with the books and papers arranged neatly on the shelves. The coffee area was no longer a disgusting mess, and the noisy fan had been turned off. The pervasive odor was that of cleaning solutions.

I closed and locked the door and turned out the overhead light before going to the window and lowering the blinds.

After that, I went into Otis' apartment and snapped on a bedside lamp. That room, too, had been cleaned and dusted. The blood-soaked towels that I had left in the bathtub were missing, and the bathroom had been cleaned top to bottom.

Otis' landlady, Madame Li, had overseen the transformation. I was certain of that. The cleaning job had a woman's touch: the toilet and mirrors were spotless.

I'd been sleepy when I climbed the stairs. Thinking I'd been ambushed had snapped me out of it. I had a look around and found myself in the darkroom. On the counter were several stacks of photographs and a box of envelopes. Otis appeared to be behind in his filing.

The photos were of men and women leaving or entering motels, hotels, houses, and apartment buildings—though, several were of a tall blonde holding a man's hand as they left the train station. Initials, dates, and times were noted in wax pencil on the backs of the shots.

Those candids were Otis' stock in trade. They were offered as indications of infidelity and were used in divorce cases.

I was drawn to the faces in the photographs. It seemed curious to me that pictures that were destined to shatter bank accounts and lives, for the most part, simply showed lovers at unguarded moments of happiness, sharing gentle touches, adoring glances.

"It's never simple," I said, catching myself in the glaring light of the strange contrasts that I knew were a part of life. I considered myself a good person, but I had arrived at a place where I could justify killing.

"Like a soldier," I consoled myself in a whisper.

My heart turned over when I saw the first picture of Mac, but I wasn't surprised. I knew that was how Otis operated. He followed, he staked out, he photographed.

Mac had the even features of a movie star, eyes that were made to melt a woman's heart. Looking at those pictures of him in downtown Dallas stepping out of his truck, striding across a street, entering a building stirred my senses in ways that I wished were not true.

"It's never simple," I said again and sighed.

Another series of photos of Mac showed him with a man in a dark suit and fedora. A man I shouldn't have recognized dressed like that. But I did.

The man was Blue Eyes.

I felt that discovery throughout my body. The familiar pulse at my temples began again. The two men knew each other. That was clear. My knees were vibrating. I left the darkroom, went over to the bed, and sat down.

Those pictures were a confirmation of my worst suspicions about Mac. I didn't know whether to cry or scream. Since I never cried, I let out a scream. It was good that it was so late; Madame Li didn't need any more excitement. I grew angry again as I recalled how Mac had conned me.

There was no going to sleep after I discovered the pictures of Mac and Blue Eyes. I gathered up the clothing for Otis, turned on his cleaned and oiled fan, locked up tight, and drove out to Henry's. I knew it would be mid-afternoon before I got back to Doc McGraw's.

So what. Otis would probably sleep the day away in any case.

Jim was waiting for me out by the gate beneath a brilliant sky crowded with orange and red clouds. The sun would show its face soon. That sky said it would.

I opened the door and let the dog in to ride with me to the house. He always behaved well in the car once he finished his hello and settled down. I knew that Henry let Jim hitchhike, too. Neither of us ever discussed it. We knew we were spoiling him. He was such a good boy.

Henry wasn't outside. I knocked and then used my key to open the kitchen door. Jim pushed past me and into the warm house. He knew his way into Henry's bedroom.

"That you?" Henry called out from the other room.

"No, it's someone else," I called back.

"You okay?"

He came in wearing slippers and pajamas and putting on his robe.

"Yeah, I just need to talk."

He went to the door, opened it, and looked outside.

"Some sky, huh?"

"Gorgeous," I said.

He closed the door and went over to the sink to get his teapot.

"You hungry?"

I was. I couldn't say when I'd last eaten.

"Sure. How about you?"

"I could eat," he said.

Because I knew Henry's habits in the kitchen, I could help him without getting in his way. It wasn't long before we were at our table enjoying breakfast, soft morning light whispering through the windows.

Henry fixed a ground beef hash with chopped onions, potatoes, sweet peppers, and a selection of seasonings I could never seem to get straight. It was delicious. He served his hash with a side of pan-fried Brussels sprouts.

He knew my mother couldn't make me eat that vegetable and took pride in watching me have seconds. It would have been perfect, except he insisted that I drink a glass of milk.

"Keep skin pretty," he said.

As we ate, I told Henry about what happened to Otis and Detective Hansard. I told him that we were pretty certain now that it was the Lost Demons who were being protected.

I said, "It's too bad Otis couldn't have gotten to Hansard

before they killed him. We might've gotten the names that we want."

"Otis get shot. He okay?"

"He'll be fine," I said.

"Otis good man," he said. "We lucky to find."

I told Henry all about Doc McGraw.

"I think we have a family doctor now, Henry."

"Jim, Baby Girl, and Henry all same doctor?"

"Works for me," I said.

"Works for me," he said and laughed.

"Something else happened last night that I need to tell you about," I said.

"I finish sprouts and listen," he said.

He was quiet as I explained going over to Bobby Ray's, then scrunched his face up a time or two when I told him about the chase and what happened to Mechanic and his buddy.

When I finished he said, "Know how drive on ice save life."

"I guess it did," I said.

I told him about the rest of the evening, including how I'd found the pictures of Mac and Blue Eyes. I showed him the picture that I'd kept.

"Know building in picture?" Henry asked.

"No," I said.

"Newspaper building."

"The Star-News Journal?"

"You bet," Henry mumbled, studying the photo. "Too bad. I want Mac be good man," he added.

"Me, too, Henry. Now we know better, don't we?"

"Blue Eyes only Lost Demon left," Henry said with a certain amount of satisfaction. "Baby Girl be careful. Blue Eyes bad egg. Not always have ice to drive on."

I slept until after noon. When Henry knew I was awake, he knocked at my door and said he would meet me at our pistol range. That was a good idea. We had fallen out of our routine.

For pistol practice, I wore a t-shirt under my jacket, waiting to put on a turtleneck until I was ready to leave. It was a cold day, but the early afternoon sun was warm.

After practice, I changed shoes and ran out to the old well and back. Jim and I both needed the exercise.

It looked busy at Doc McGraw's when I arrived. I saw several men standing around a horse in one of the corrals. There were a couple of pickup trucks and a station wagon parked near the main house.

As I got out of my car, Doc came from around the corner looking even more like a farmer than he had the night before. A floppy-eared mutt and two nanny goats trailed along behind him.

"You need any help?" he asked.

"If you'll carry this."

I handed him a three-piece suit on a hanger and gathered up the clothes that were folded and stacked in the back seat. I also grabbed a small paper sack and fell in behind Doc as he started away, following a wide gravel path that led out toward some whitewashed cabins.

"How is he?" I asked.

"The bullet stopped subcutaneously in the preperitoneal fat—"

"Is that a fact," I said.

Doc frowned at me and said, "It stopped before breaking through the abdominal wall. That was fortunate, since you could have had a very different situation on your hands."

I noticed Loretta coming from the back of the main house. She was wearing work boots and overalls over a pink blouse. Our sheepskin jackets could have made us twins if mine hadn't been black and hers natural.

Her face without the beauty mask was a broad, happy face. I think she smiled a lot since it seemed easy for her. Her eyes were large and brown, but her best feature was her thick and wavy auburn hair that cascaded over her shoulders.

As she drew near, she brought her hands up and began making signs. Loretta was mute. Of course. There had been clues last night.

We paused and Doc said, "Loretta wants me to tell you why she can't speak because she knows you must be curious."

Before I could respond, she tipped her head back and showed me some scars on her neck below her chin.

"It was an accident that almost cost her her life," Doc said. "We were extracting an infected tooth from a young mountain lion, and he surprised us by coming out of anesthesia early. During the scramble to hold him, he tore out her larynx."

Loretta signed and Doc said, "She wants to know about your scars. She wants to know what happened to you."

"I was mauled by some animals, too," I told her.

She wrinkled her brow and tipped her head, sympathetically.

"I'll tell you about it sometime," I added.

She nodded at me, her face full of understanding, and took the suit from Doc. He and his loyal entourage moved away to join the men in the corral.

"Maybe I'll see you again before you go," he said over his shoulder. "If not, thank you for what you did for my friend."

He paused.

"Oh, yes. If there's ever a next time."

"Yes?"

"Don't let him have aspirin. It thins the blood."

"I'll keep that in mind," I said, and off he went with his goats and dog hot on his trail.

I followed Loretta as we approached a house the size of a motel cabin. It was the nearest of the three little buildings that were nestled back away from the main house in a park-like gathering of oak trees and shrubs, a calendar picture in the mottled late afternoon sunlight.

Without breaking stride, Loretta stepped onto the small porch, opened the door, and entered. As I entered behind her, I saw that the cabin was a hospital room.

Otis, who wore a white terrycloth robe and bedroom slippers, was perched on the edge of a hospital bed smoking. Our entrance startled him. Loretta took the cigarette out of his mouth, stepped into the bathroom, and tossed it in the toilet.

Otis made a grouchy face at me. "You took your time," he said.

Loretta hung his suit on a hook on the closet door near his shoulder holster and .45. I put his folded shirt and other fresh articles of clothing on the foot of the bed.

"I bought you a tie," I said, indicating the paper sack.

"Why'd you do that?"

"Have you looked at your ties lately?" I asked him.

Pleased with my response, Loretta, who probably weighed in at something like one-ninety, slugged Otis on his shoulder. He winced and she gave me a big smile, just to let me know whose side she was on.

When she picked up and shook out a pair of olive drab boxer shorts from the things I brought, I said, "I'll wait outside."

Later, Otis looked like his old self in his suit, tie, fedora, and scowl. He told me his tightly-bound mid-section wouldn't have to be touched until he went back in a few days to have the stitches removed.

On the drive back to the office, I tried to bring him up to date on what he had missed. We stalled out when I told him about following the bikers and what happened to his Mercury. He was instantly annoyed and had me explain twice how I backed into the motorcycles. He wanted to know why I even thought a crazy idea like that would work.

"Hell, I didn't know if it would work, I was desperate," I told him.

"Why didn't you just get out and shoot them?"

"You tried shooting them. I don't recall that being so easy to do."

That wasn't fair. He'd had a bloody wound in his gut and was in a lot of pain when he was shooting at those guys.

"We ain't finished with this, Missy," he huffed and launched into me. "You did so many things wrong, you gotta have an angel on your shoulder. Just tell me right now you ain't gonna follow nobody else till I learn you some art to apply to that skill."

"Fine," I snapped, annoyed about getting a lecture.

"Good," he said.

"There's only one of that gang left now," I threw out at him, figuring that would be the last word on the subject.

"You mean only one more from that night at Henry's. We ain't got no idea how many a them dirt bags is in that gang."

"That's what I meant. You got me pissed off."

"I'm glad it turned out good for you, Missy. Don't get me wrong. It just worries me how you keep going forward as if you had good sense. Here's the thing; there ain't no number of them shitheads worth your life. You hear me? I'm sorry I got myself shot, okay? Next time you wait."

"Fine," I said again, still upset. I realized he was concerned for me. I bit my tongue and added, "You're right. I should've waited."

There was a long pause that I didn't want to mess with. Finally, he grinned and said, "Tell me again how you backed into them."

Otis was okay. He just had a quick temper, which I got to see again when I showed him the photo of Mac with Blue Eyes.

"Here's the one that's left," I told him. "Look who he's with."

He flipped the print over, looked at his grease pencil

notations on the back and, using a tone of voice I didn't care for, said, "You was in my darkroom."

"Not me," I shot back. "You must be thinking of that other person who took you to the doctor and went back to get you a change of clothes."

That stopped him.

He narrowed his eyes at me, mumbled something about me being a pisser, and asked, "You know who owns the Star-News Journal, don'cha?"

"Old man Belmont?" I guessed, going for the obvious.

"You're right about that, and the dandy that Belmont's son is talking to is the guy you call Blue Eyes?"

"Yeah, who is he?"

"I don't know, but they came out of the newspaper building, and I know a reporter there. All reporters have one thing in common, Missy. They're nosy. They're snoopy. They're like you. They think everything's their business."

"Stop grousing. I didn't know anybody in your pictures except Mac and Blue Eyes."

"My photos are private, like doctor-patient stuff. That's all I'm saying."

"Okay, you've said it. Just keep in mind, you asked me to work with you. You're the one who gave me Ava's birthday."

Otis heaved a sigh and looked out his side window.

"I reckon I'm just feeling tired and useless maybe. Not on my game," he said.

"That's why you're being so grouchy?"

"After telling you and Henry we oughta go after these guys, I'm somewhere else while you're going after these guys."

"I get it. Don't go all sniffles on me. Let's just find out who Blue Eyes is. That's what we need to be doing."

We locked eyes.

"I want him, Otis. He's the one. He was behind it all."

"I want them, too, Missy. I want them, too."

When we got to his office building, Otis took me into the Mandarin Palace to meet Madame Li.

A woman in her fifties, she ruled her establishment from a high black lacquered stool between an ancient cash register and the front glass window. Though I'd often read the description, Madame Li was the first woman I'd ever met with porcelain skin. If she had pores, a microscope would be needed to see them.

Part of her allure was a glowing complexion, part was impeccable hair and makeup, and part was her fashion sense. The silk Chanel suit she wore fit her small, slim frame perfectly. Madame Li exuded an overall impression of delicate Asian beauty with French highlights.

After we were introduced, she said to Otis, "How handsome you look in your new tie. It's quite tasteful." Flawless, unaccented English. She added, "Your choice, Miss Van Dijk?"

We were instant conspirators.

Otis had dined at Madame Li's for years. It was certain that she knew his wardrobe. Of course he had already forgotten what tie he was wearing and pushed his chin into his chest to see it. That gave Madame Li and me another reason to exchange a smile. Men.

I stood aside while she and Otis discussed a problem her dentist cousin was having with a client who refused to pay a bill and had said something threatening. Otis seemed to know about the situation and said he was looking into it, which was an obvious relief to her.

I complimented the pale yellow dahlias that were in a cloisonné vase on the black lacquered table near the door, and asked her where she'd found them that time of year.

Other pleasantries followed; food to go was forced on us by an adoring kitchen staff, and eventually we were through the restaurant, up the back stairs, and into Otis' office where he stashed the food in the refrigerator and started some coffee sludge boiling.

He opened a fresh pack of Luckies, lit up, and sat down at his clean desk to call his newspaper contact.

Little by little the place was starting to smell like it used to.

We met David Rushford, Otis' friend and newspaper contact, at Crocker's, a well-established old saloon down the street from the newspaper building.

It was a good meeting place, since the dark bar was caught in its late-afternoon doldrums. We had the leaded glass, polished wood, and padded leather pretty much to ourselves.

Otis told me that Dave had toiled as a reporter at the Dallas Star-News Journal for close to three decades.

I saw as he walked up that he was a dapper little guy who spent money on his clothes, wore trendy black Xylonite glasses frames, and dyed what hair he had left. He was trying pretty hard, but all his effort wasn't keeping him from looking sixty-five.

As he took a seat to join Otis and me at a table against the back wall, his drink arrived without him saying a word.

"Thank you, Linda," he said to the waitress whose bosom attracted and briefly held his attention.

Otis ordered coffee. I asked for a Dr Pepper.

"Ol' Dave was a lady-killer in the thirties, those years after the Depression. Quite a dancer, too," Otis had told me on the drive over.

"On through the war years, he had the passion that makes a good reporter. Always getting in places where he wasn't supposed to be. Telling tales on business crooks and cheaters. He's wore down some since then. You know, he ain't young now, and then there was that marriage. He should've got hazardous pay for living all them years with that woman."

"He outlived her?" I asked.

"She fell off something up high, if I've got my facts straight. Another household accident. Anyway, he mostly does research these days and gives advice in a column. Aunt Somebody."

"Aunt Ruth. He writes that?"

I'd been impressed that our contact was Aunt Ruth and was thinking about that when Otis introduced me by my full name for the second time that day.

"My pleasure," Aunt Ruth said in a deep, gravelly voice that I assumed had been fashioned from years of scotch and cigarettes. He proffered a soft, manicured hand as he peered at me through glasses so thick they enlarged his troubled eyes.

Two things stood out about him: he was accustomed to speaking privately in public places, so he didn't let his voice carry past the table, and he held my hand too long. I turned my head to compensate for the former and remained passive in reference to the latter. He finally let go of my hand and got out his Pall Malls.

He growled, "So, Otis, who's this individual you think I may know something about?"

Otis put a photograph of Mac and Blue Eyes on the table. The newspaperman tipped his head back to accommodate his bifocals and gave the picture a quick once over.

"What's your interest in those naughty boys?" he asked.

"I know the one dressed like a rancher," Otis replied, putting the photo back in his pocket. "It's the one in the suit I'm asking about."

Dave offered Otis a cigarette, and as the men lit up, he said, "They're brothers, my friend."

Otis was as blindsided as I was.

"You don't say," he said under his breath.

"That's right. The one in the suit is Martin Belmont. The younger brother you say you know."

"I know him, all right," Otis said. "Alexander Mackenzie Belmont."

My head was spinning. They didn't look alike. Did they? Mac sure didn't have blue eyes.

"I call him Alex, like his father does," Dave said. "Well, I've known him all his life. I repeat. What's your interest in these boys?"

I had to wonder how one of the wealthiest ranchers in Texas could have a worthless murdering biker for a son.

"I have reason to believe the older brother, Martin, committed a crime over in Abilene a couple a years ago. A serious crime."

"And you're working for someone who's interested in solving that crime?" Dave asked, and motioned to the waitress to bring another.

"You're on it, Dave. And, knowing who sired them boys— well, you might could see how I'd wanna know all them cows was mine before I start brandin' them."

"I'd say that was wise, yes. All right, I've told you who he is, what else do you want?"

"This Martin works at the paper?"

"In a manner of speaking."

"He ain't been there all that long. Am I right?"

"Not that long at all, Otis," Dave said, and put his oddly enlarged, bold eyes on me. "And how do you fit into this, Miss Van Dijk?"

"I'm with him, Dave," I said. "And let's make it Kristin, okay?"

"Kristin," he said and looked at Otis.

"She's with me. Is there a problem?"

"We go way back, Otis. I not only don't have a problem, I must say that your timing is rather splendid. I just happen to feel like answering questions about the elder Belmont brother."

"Damn," Otis said and took out his little notebook and a yellow number two pencil stub.

"Scotch and water," Linda mumbled as she placed Dave's drink in front of him. "More coffee?" she asked Otis. "Another

Dr Pepper," she asked me, her eyes perusing us while Dave's eyes perused her.

When Otis and I shook our heads, the waitress retreated.

After slugging down most of his second drink like it was *all* water, Dave said, "I have followed Martin's rebellion for a number of years—"

Otis cut in with, "You call the things he does rebellion?"

"We can do it your way, Otis, but it'll take more time than I can give you today."

"Whatever you say, Dave," Otis said.

Dave turned his strange eyes to me and toyed with the ice in his glass.

"Do I know you?" he asked. "Have we met before?"

It was like a bad line from some young guy in a pool hall.

"Maybe we were classmates," I replied. "Did you attend Our Lady of Mercy High School?"

Otis rolled his eyes toward the ceiling, but Dave wasn't annoyed by my reply. He just found Linda and motioned for another drink.

"I have followed Martin's rebellious activities for a number of years," he continued, his weird eyes going to Otis. "Here and across the state. In point of fact, I have detailed notes on a goodly portion of his nefarious career. I'm happy to say that I possess information that may be useful to you."

"Good," Otis said.

"Of use, yes. I would have to say, dangerous, too, Otis. Dangerous, too." Dave's odd eyes shifted to me with a look that put a chill up my back.

19

AS DAVE TALKED, it became clear that he had incriminating evidence against Martin Belmont that he had done nothing with. Another interesting thing was he appeared to have put much of this information to memory. That was impressive, as well as curious.

As he talked and talked, Otis and I began to realize that Dave was telling us more about that murderer than we would ever need to know. We had discovered Dave's obsession.

The question for me, regardless of his longstanding friendship with Otis, was why was Dave so ready to spill everything that he knew about his boss's son? Especially after keeping it to himself for so long. What had broken the camel's back?

I didn't have to wait long before I found out.

Dave made it clear that he was upset about Martin's newly created-position at the paper, a position that had been designed to allow the owner's son to float until he found where he was comfortable. A cynical, world-weary journalist like Dave had worked hard to gain his position.

That Blue Eyes had so easily gained a better position offended him and the other journalists.

"You won't hear any complaints above a whisper," Dave said. "Because he is obviously unstable. When he doesn't get what he wants, there's always hell to pay."

"The old man's eldest is a lunatic, and everyone at the paper's staying out of his way. Is that it?" Otis asked.

"Yes, but don't think of him in simple terms. Martin is clever and ruthless. Underestimate him at your peril. My presumption is that whatever it is that you believe or even *know* that he has done, you'll find it impossible to prove. That is his *modus operandi,* and I have seen it only grow more sophisticated over the years. This is why I've done nothing with the information that I've gathered. Knowing and proving are two different things. Two different things. And, too, one would always have his father to contend with."

"Clever, ruthless, troubled, and connected," Otis said, reading from his notes.

"Yes," Dave confirmed. "Poor Martin's young life was full of turmoil. He had a mother who would have made Tennessee Williams blush. A raving drunk, died in a fire. And there were all those stepmothers, none of whom seemed to like him."

"The boys had different mothers?" Otis asked.

"Oh, yes. Different mothers. However, all Logan Belmont's wives were alike in one respect. The more neurotic they were, the more he was attracted to them. He sired two sons, but he never fathered them. Oh, the younger one—the one you know—got a few scraps of attention, because of his love for horses. Nothing for the older one, ever, that I was aware of. When Martin wasn't being ignored, he was being mistreated."

"You're saying the father mistreated the boy?"

"I'm saying the father did nothing about the way the mother and subsequent wives treated his oldest boy," Dave said. "Of course, Martin was no angel, either. He asked for most of the trouble that came to him."

I knew that journalism attracted brainpower; still I was amazed at Dave's meticulous memory. He talked and drank nonstop for close to three hours. Poor Otis got finger cramps. I asked Linda for a pencil and paper and I took notes, too, until my hand went numb.

The old reporter who wrote Aunt Ruth didn't refer to any notes. He just drank and spoke of the troubled life and evil deeds of Blue Eyes.

The reporter never showed even the slightest tendency toward a sense of humor, never made the mistake of speaking in front of the barmaid, and never failed to admire her figure. Hands down, he was a peculiar duck; a very smart duck that had an ax to grind—and he ground it.

The last thing from him was to ask Otis if he could make Martin Belmont disappear. That was the first hint I had that Dave was three sheets to the wind.

Otis said, "Now, Dave, I'm gonna forget you said that, because that sounds a lot like solicitation to murder, and I'm certain you'd never mean a thing like that."

That caused Dave to stare at us in confusion, his eyes more bizarre than ever. He pushed his chair back by standing up, touched the edge of the table with the tips of his fingers to get his balance, spun about, and started for the door.

He weaved through the maze of tables and chairs without a single mishap, crossing the dark room with the agile competency of a professional drunk. He slipped out the door and he was gone. That was the last time I would see Dave Rushford alive.

"Let's go over this, Missy," Otis said when we were in the car on the way back to the office. "Blue Eyes rode back into town this last spring from a trip he took to the Gulf."

"Dave said they were mostly in Louisiana," I said.

"That figures. Scarecrow showed up about then with Peggy, that blonde Frenchy."

"Hell, no wonder you couldn't find them," I said. "They were out of the state for a year and a half."

"That sure gave Hansard the time he needed to cover things up."

"He even got the insurance company to pay off," I said.

"That hush up was slicker'n pig snot," Otis said.

"Who told Hansard to cover things up?"

Otis stared out the car window.

"I'm thinking that beau of yours, most likely. Him and his brother looked tighter'n thieves in those pictures."

"I think you're right," I said, whether I liked it or not. "That means the insurance payout was part of the cover up."

"Like I said. Slick."

"That check was for thirty thousand dollars."

"Chicken feed to an insurance company. I'm figuring it like this; Hansard's been on the Belmont payroll for years, see, so when he hears Martin's gang was at a pool hall that got torched and some people died—"

"He calls Mac," I said.

"Fast as he can dial a phone, Missy. He tells Mackenzie his brother's in some deep shit, and your boy arrives with a briefcase full a moola *muy pronto*. He had that cover up under way before the ashes were cold at Henry's place."

"He bought off the police *and* the fire department?"

"Why not? There's the money on the one hand and the Belmont name on the other. Don't you see? Cash *and* the chance to call in a favor sometime. That's a hard one to pass up over a no-account pool hall, a couple of drifters, and a foreign guy nobody's gonna miss."

"The cover up wouldn't be complete until they found me," I said.

"Yep. A witness is a horse of a different color. Mackenzie found out Hank didn't know shit from Shinola about what happened that night. He wasn't so sure about you."

"So he's been looking for me to find out."

"And being the natural maverick you are, you just plum disappeared."

"Until I rode my Harley into San Angelo. But that doesn't explain how Mac knew I was Baby Shark."

"I don't know how he knew that, Missy. But we know now why Martin's been trying to find you. You're a danger to him. He wants you outta the way."

Otis had more to say, but he waited until I'd pulled up in front of the Mandarin Palace and turned off the motor.

Otis said, "So the gang comes back to town, and Scare-crow buys the farm right away, thanks to Hank."

"And Bear went back to Huntsville," I threw in.

"You don't wonder anymore how Bear got outta stir do you?"

"Mac, or maybe even Daddy, called in a favor from some judge somewhere," I said.

"And in the meantime, our naughty Martin's giving up the wild life and starting to be the wealthy rancher's son again."

"From gypsy criminal to Dallas upper crust," I said.

"That ain't much of a change," Otis grumbled.

"I'll tell you something that makes sense now," I said.

"What's that?"

"When Blue Eyes was talking to my dad that night, he said it wasn't about the money he'd lost. He said he'd always had more money than he needed."

"I guess so, if your daddy's old man Belmont."

Otis opened his door and started getting out. He still wasn't moving well because of his stomach wound and by the time I'd gotten around the car to help him, he had his summary ready.

"So it turns out our Mister Blue Eyes was doing nothing more'n just having a little fling on the wild side. Kill a little here, rape a little there until he gets bored with it. I'm sorry if what Dave was saying's true and Blue Eyes got shoved around as a little guy, but he ain't a boy no more. He's a spoiled, nasty rich, grown man going around hurting folks. And I'm thinking that Mac ain't no better."

"You're probably right," I said.

I still got a catch when I saw his picture.

As we approached the building, Madame Li smiled at us through the restaurant window. Her greeting reminded Otis of the food he'd put in the refrigerator.

"You hungry?"

"I could eat," I said as I followed his slow progress up the stairs.

His heating up supper for us took care of the few remaining odors that were needed to restore identifiable character to his office. Now I understood why the fan ran constantly. I washed my hands while Otis burned pans and spilled things.

We ate our delicious meal with our chairs pulled up to Otis' clean desk. We'd put our collected notes in a pile over to the side, neither of us anxious to try and make sense of them yet.

"Where do you think we slipped up?" I asked. "Out of nowhere Mac appears in San Angelo knowing who I am, and, not long after that, Hansard's on my tail and coming around to kill you."

"Blue Eyes gets back, kisses up to his daddy, and starts to work at the paper. Attacks on us ain't no coincidence."

"How'd he know?" I asked again.

"And you know what else?" Otis asked, ignoring my question. "I say it won't take our boy long to get bored with all that workaday sissy shit. That's not the blood sport he's been used to playing. You know he's already looking around for some excitement."

"Yeah, I agree with all that, and I think Blue Eyes sent Mac to me. But that's not the answer to my question. What tipped him in the first place? How'd he find out who I am?"

"I ain't got that one figured out yet, Goddamn it. Quit asking. But Dave's given us a bucket full of stuff to sort through. Only not tonight. You get on home now."

"But first."

"Go ahead," he said.

"Knowing who Blue Eyes is makes him untouchable, doesn't it? It wouldn't matter if I could prove he killed my dad and Henry's son and twenty other people. Old Man Belmont's not going to let him serve a day behind bars."

"I'll never hear it put better," Otis said.

"So, knowing that he'll kill us if we don't kill him makes this a neat little dilemma, don't you think? How the hell are we supposed to handle this? I mean and you keep your license and me keep my freedom."

Otis sighed big.

"It's damned if you do and damned if you don't, that's for sure," he said.

What I was thinking was how to get Blue Eyes alone and get this thing over with. I wasn't about to debate with anyone about what happened that night two years ago at Henry's. Blue Eyes and I knew what happened.

"I want us to get some stakeouts going on the elder Belmont brother. Now that we know who he is, we need to start watching where he goes and what he does. Can you get back around noon tomorrow?"

Otis wanted to lie down and rest. He never complained, but I knew that's what it was.

"Sure," I said.

I got up and started cleaning up our luncheon mess. It took no more than a couple of minutes to get everything thrown away and put away. Otis didn't move. I could tell he liked having a woman wait on him—probably for all the right reasons.

"Missy."

"Yes, Otis?"

"I want you watching your young self around the clock. You hear me?"

"I hear you. Thanks for supper, Otis."

"Wait a minute," he said, and got up with a little groan and pulled that cannon of his from its holster. "On second thought, I'm walking you to your car."

"Down those stairs and back up again?"

"And I ain't putting up with no backtalk about it."

"Fine," I said.

"And I want you to have a rod in your fist every time you come here. Let's just make that a rule for you and me both till we get this all behind us. Agreed?"

"Agreed," I said and pulled my .38, cocked and locked it and started for the door.

Otis followed in my wake, a very large, wounded angel.

The next morning, Otis phoned me at Henry's.

"Get on in here. Dave came by and told me some stuff you should hear."

I arrived at the office shortly before noon. It smelled like burnt coffee and the Lucky that was smoking in the full ashtray. Otis was behind his desk, wearing the same clothes he was wearing last night. His fan was humming and rattling.

I had on my winter uniform: boots, blue jeans, turtle-neck, and shoulder-holstered .38. I threw my jacket aside and started paying attention. I could tell by the look on his face that Otis wanted the floor. He'd taken notes while Dave was there and had them spread out before him.

He was talking before my jeans hit the chair seat.

"Dave did recognize you the other day; he just couldn't place where. What he recollected was Martin Belmont saw a picture of you."

"Of me?"

"Yes, Ma'am. Last spring. He told me—"

"What picture?" I cut in.

Otis pushed around some papers and came up with a torn piece of newspaper that he shoved across his desk.

There I was all right, lined up with a bunch of pukes holding cues. It had been taken at Whirley's One Stop during the West Texas Nine Ball Tournament. I'd flown over with Harlan. That was the week Jim had the fight with the coyotes.

"You remember it?" Otis asked, watching my face.

"Yeah," I said. "I won. I couldn't get out of the picture."

"Dave said Martin's brother came up to the paper. After Mackenzie left, Martin asked Dave to research Baby Shark. Where was she from? What name was she using? Dave said he was never able to learn much about you or pinpoint your schedule."

"Because I didn't have a schedule."

"So Martin sent Mackenzie looking for you. Your pal Mac told Dave that every pool hall led to another pool hall in another town. It was making him crazy. He said it was like a wild goose chase."

"I flew to those places, Otis."

"Lover Boy was driving, so he was racking up some real miles."

"And he was telling people that he was a reporter with the Star-News Journal."

"Yeah, and Dave said he was promising money to find you."

Mac was the *reporter* Harlan mentioned over the phone last September.

"I think he talked to Harlan."

"He did," Otis said.

"Guaranteed he got nothing out of him," I said.

"They found out he had an airplane. Harlan told Mackenzie he'd given you a lift a time or two."

"All right. So Mac goes wherever he thinks I might be. So, when I'm dumb enough to show up in San Angelo—"

"Don't do that, Missy. These guys had eyes everywhere. It was just a matter of time."

"Okay, so he hears I'm riding a bike and, because it's cold, figures out the rescue business, and moves in. My hero."

"You're talking to yourself. I don't know about all that."

"That's okay. I know enough for both of us."

"Listen, Missy, Blue Eyes didn't know your whereabouts until Hank showed up in San Angelo and snatched you out of Mackenzie's truck. You've been safe out at Hank's place all this time because they didn't know you was there. And they're seven *cucarachas* shy because they didn't know about you. Seven. Jesus. You're a one woman extermination squad."

Otis shook his head, stood up, took his holster rig off the chair, and started trying to get in it. I didn't say anything; I just went around and helped him with that, and his suit coat, too.

"Doc McGraw wants me out for a check up. I'll be a couple of hours. Hang around. We'll go for some late lunch when I get back. We got some more talking to do."

"I'll meet you back here," I said and put on my jacket.

I got my .38 in my hand and held it out of sight as we left his office. I felt like his bodyguard getting him down the stairs, into his car, and on his way.

20

IVY HAD AN opening and saw me without an appointment. I knew Otis wanted me to have a wig or two, and she had some. I tried a few that weren't flattering and then couldn't bring myself to buy them. Ivy told me I was "bugnuts" for even trying them on.

I ended up with two: a raven pageboy that Ivy said made me look "alluring" and a curly brunette that she swore made me look "exactly like Gloria DeHaven."

"I'm not that pretty, and you know it," I told her.

"You don't know how pretty you are," was her reply. "And I don't know why you let your nails get like that. You're not leaving here till you get a manicure. You may be a ranch hand, but you don't have to look like one. And why don't we just shampoo that hair and shape it some, too, as long as you're here?"

She had just cut my hair three days ago. She also insisted on doing my eyes.

"Just a little bit, and I have a perfect lipstick, too."

Ivy took all the fight out of me. When I left her shop I felt and looked like a girl for a change. And for sure I smelled like one.

"Evening in Paris," she'd said when she dabbed perfume on me from a blue, cut glass bottle. "It's all the rage again."

It'll make Jim sneeze, was what I thought as I walked away from her little torture chamber. I needed time to myself. Ivy hardly shut up while I was there, and I wanted a few minutes to think things over before meeting Otis back at the office.

Taking a walk seemed like a good idea. I needed to see into the future. What was Blue Eyes going to do next?

I didn't need Dave's confirmation that Martin Belmont was sick and ruthless. I knew that. And Dave saying that Martin had always made an effort to clean up after himself—and that he had simply gotten better at it—virtually assured that he would try to kill Henry and me. Especially me. So, trying to figure out his next move was something worth concentrating on.

I paused in front of a department store window. I didn't look at the display. I was trying to understand something, something significant about Blue Eyes that was rattling around in my head.

He didn't just clean up after himself, he moved fast to get it done. The fire that night at Henry's. The attempt on Otis' life. The assassination of Detective Hansard. He didn't put those things off. He didn't hesitate. He moved at once to protect himself, to cover up his crime. That was an important detail within the *modus operandi* that Dave talked about. Blue Eyes acted at once.

Okay, so what made that seem important to me?

"Kristin."

The voice jolted me from my musing. I looked at the store window.

The voice was unmistakable, and his reflection in the glass confirmed it. My heart turned over, but that didn't keep me from getting my defenses up. I'd removed my shoulder holster before going to Ivy's. That left a .32 in my sock and knives to protect myself if it came to that.

Anyway, it was broad daylight, and we were on a city street.

"Out selling insurance today?" I asked Mac's reflection.

I couldn't bring myself to turn around yet. I wanted to keep a distance between us.

"I deserve that," he said.

"You deserve more than that, you liar."

"C'mon, Kristin. I just want to talk."

"About what? Do you want to pretend you don't know me again?"

"I acted like a jerk."

"Worse than that," I said.

"Look, there's a café just down here. Please. Let's sit down for a few minutes. Give me a chance to explain."

I turned, looked up at him, and felt my cheeks grow warmer. He was closer to me than I'd expected, and that caused my heart to flutter. If I was reading his face correctly, my sarcasm was affecting him. Of course, I'd seen him do some pretty good acting.

I was confused about what to do next. I meant *exactly* what to do.

I knew better than to trust him, regardless of how it felt to be close to him. I had to keep that stuff to myself and watch my step since he could be as deadly as his brother.

"Sure, we can do that," I said, "but you utter one false note and I walk. And believe me, mister, I'll know if you're lying."

"Right," he said and stepped away in the direction of the café he'd referred to.

The instant he looked away, I scanned the street to see if he was alone. I knew he was going to pretend that our meeting was accidental. Surely he'd been following me. I didn't see anything unusual, but I didn't quit checking as we walked toward the café.

I knew that I could hurt him if I had to, though I didn't want to. I'd put to memory some lines that I planned to use if I ever saw him again, but they weren't surfacing. So what. I didn't mind impromptu.

Did Mac realize that I knew Blue Eyes was his brother? I'd know soon enough what he knew and didn't know. My heart was making a remarkable recovery. Things were starting to feel like business, as Sarge would say.

We walked together, but not too close. He held the door for me. The place was more than a café. It had tablecloths and nice settings. The luncheon crowd, made up of business-men, was thinning out.

An older, uniformed waitress, her gray hair pulled into an attractive French twist, indicated that we could sit wher-ever we liked. I chose a table back from the front windows. I wanted a clear view of the front door and the street outside. I didn't want to be seen from outside—or shot by someone from out there, either.

No more surprises. I shouldn't have been daydreaming on the street. Otis would have a fit when he heard that Mac had snuck up on me.

"You look different," he said, "your hair's shorter."

"I'll worry about my hair."

"If ya'll're having lunch, our special's done," the waitress said, holding out menus.

"I'd like a Dr Pepper," I told her. "Plenty of ice, please."

"We just got Coke, honey."

"That'll do. Thank you."

"Coffee," Mac said.

The waitress went away, leaving us staring at each other. Mac looked tired. I hoped that his conscience was causing him to lose sleep.

"You're not an insurance man. Why'd you tell Henry Chin that you were?"

"I kind of was. My dad got a call from Western Empire, the company that wrote the fire policy on Henry's Pool-room."

"You mean, Logan Belmont? He's your father, right?"

His eyebrows lifted, then he nodded.

"Yeah. He's one of the owners of the insurance company. Look, my dad asked me to go over, take a look at the build-ing, and see how bad the fire damage was. I used to do that kind of work summers when I was in college. The thing was, the policy was fairly new and large. The disbursement represented a substantial loss to the company. They just wanted to know if the fire was on the up and up."

"What did you tell them?" I asked.

"The building had burnt to the ground before the fire engines could get there," he said. "I spoke to the Fire Department investigator and got a copy of his report. He told me he thought a short in the heating system caused the fire. They sent Mr. Chin's check to my dad, he gave it to me, and I delivered it. That's all there was to it."

"All there was to it? Three men died at Henry's that night. What about that? And what about the motorcycle gang that was there?"

"Mr. Chin told me about the bikers. He told me they'd made trouble and he wasn't able to identify any of them."

"Did he tell you why? Did he tell you they shot him and beat him unconscious?"

"Yeah, Kristin, he did tell me that. And I told him I'd look into it, and I did. Can you back off a little and give me a chance to explain things?"

"Sure, if you tell me about how you looked into the beatings and murders."

"Okay. I spoke to the Abilene police, and they said they were investigating. They weren't so sure there'd been any murders."

"By Abilene police, do you mean Detective Hansard?"

He paused before telling me that he'd spoken to Hansard. He said that he was the detective who had headed up the investigation. I told him that I'd seen in the papers that he'd been shot to death.

"I was sorry to see that, too," Mac said. "He was a nice guy."

"You must've known him better than I did. Did you ever ask him about the Lost Demons, the biker gang that was there that night?"

"I can't say that he ever named the motorcycle club, but he investigated the deaths."

"And you weren't interested in the biker gang?"

"Look, I'm not a policeman, I can't—"

"You could say you were. You told Henry and my Aunt Dora that you were an insurance man. You told pool hall people all over West Texas that you were a reporter. Why can't you be a policeman?"

That stopped him. And his pause was well timed, too. The waitress returned with our drinks. I offered her a pleasant, relaxed smile, and she responded with one of her own.

Mac witnessed those smiles and gave me a long, hard stare before ruining with cream and sugar what looked to be a perfectly good cup of coffee.

"You seem to know a lot of things," he said in a tone of voice less conciliatory than before.

"Do I?"

"You've changed."

He was sliding toward a sullen belligerence. I'd carried it too far. If I expected to get anything real from him, I needed to stop being a threat and get vulnerable.

I relaxed my face and dipped my head so that I was peering up at him. "You broke my heart, Mac. When I found out you were lying to me, I didn't know what to think."

I kept my eyes on his, and showed no anger. He watched me for a moment before answering. "I made a mistake. I wasn't trying to hurt you."

"Why'd you lie to me? Why couldn't you be honest?"

That was enough to loosen him up, which made me think he must've been in a confessing mood. He told me that he was trying to get to know me, that he didn't like pretending, and that he'd just handled things the wrong way.

He admitted to having a picture of me that he'd gotten from Aunt Dora, and took it out of his billfold to show me. It had been taken for the school yearbook. I'd never liked it, but mom sent wallet-sized copies to everyone.

"It was because of this picture that I decided I wanted to meet you."

Uh huh. I pushed the photo back across the table, and asked how his brother fit in to all that he was telling me.

He tightened up again, and mumbled, "What do you mean?"

I told him that I knew his brother was a member of the

Lost Demons. He flinched; he was going to protest, but thought better of it.

"Not any more. He's finished with that life."

"He was there that night," I said.

Mac gave his head a shake. "He told me he wasn't there when all the violence happened. He wasn't a part of all that."

Scarecrow said the same thing. It was the other guys. He hadn't done anything.

"I was there, Mac. I know who did what."

"Then you know my brother didn't kill anybody."

He was right. Technically, Blue Eyes hadn't killed anybody. He'd just ordered it done. He'd been cleaning up as he went along.

Mac leaned forward and put a lot of sincerity into his voice. He said that the guys who his brother had been with at Henry's that night were all dead. He said they'd been feuding with a rival club and had gotten themselves killed.

They lived violent lives, he told me. That's why his brother didn't want anything more to do with them.

He did sincere convincingly. Was that because there was a lot on the line? I asked him what his brother had told him about the other things that happened that night.

"What other things?" he wanted to know.

"The things that happened to me, for instance."

"Detective Hansard said that you were pushed around. Is that what you mean?"

"Pushed around?" I looked him in the eye. "Let's clear that up. I was left for dead."

Mac's face fell. His response seemed genuine, so I asked him what his brother had said.

"He didn't—," Mac began but stopped, realizing, maybe, that he'd be talking out of school.

I could see his mind working as he grew silent and cocked his head a bit.

I lifted my index finger and watched his eyes follow it as I gave him a tour of the much faded, but still visible, scars around my face and below my jaw. I didn't need a mirror. I knew their locations.

Mac was the man that I'd dressed up for a week ago, the man I'd wanted to please with my looks. Now I was showing him my flaws.

He was right. I'd changed.

I pulled back my hair and showed him my cauliflower ear. The angry red had diminished many months ago, but the puffy ugliness that defined my deformed ear remained. I gave him plenty of time to visually digest one of the results of the vicious beating I'd received.

When his eyes returned to mine, I brought my hair back to disguise how I truthfully looked. I believed then he understood that those weren't my only scars.

When he spoke, his voice was soft and earnest. "I want to make this up to you. My brother, too. He wants to apologize. He does, Kristin. That's why I searched for you. He asked me to find you so he could set things straight."

That put a chill up my back since I knew what Blue Eyes meant by *set things straight*, even if Mac didn't. I was beginning to believe that the younger brother did not know the depth of the evil the older brother represented.

He added, "He wants to do the right thing about what those bikers did that night."

Those bikers.

It seemed obvious that the subject of my assault had never been broached with Mac. Hansard had told him I'd been *pushed around*, and Martin mentioned me as a *survivor* who needed an apology. Mac wasn't made of the same stuff as his half-brother. Detective Hansard knew that, and so did Blue Eyes.

And now, I knew it.

I said, "My father was murdered by those bikers, Mac. Are you so naïve to think an apology from your brother will mean anything?"

Mac drew in his breath and exhaled, grimacing. "Look," he said. "I wanted to get to know you, and I wanted you to get to know me before I tried to arrange a meeting with Martin. That's why I lied in San Angelo. I just wanted some breathing room before I got into the serious stuff."

Mac wanted me to talk, but I just nodded and he went on.

"Martin told me he wanted to apologize for what happened at that poolroom. I trusted him. I can see now that I haven't been told everything."

"You're right about that, Mac."

"Give me a chance to make this right, Kristin. I don't know yet how I can do that, but I want to try. I want us to have another chance."

I remained silent. When he saw I wasn't going to speak, he pushed his chair back and stood up.

"I told you just a few minutes, so I'm going to leave. Think about what I've said about us having another chance."

I wished that my heart would settle down, but I was still in control of myself, still mistrustful.

He went on, "I know that as soon as Martin hears what I have to say, he'll want to get things worked out. He doesn't like to let stuff stew."

As he turned away, I got it. I understood why Martin moving fast was important.

"Mac," I said.

He stopped and turned back to face me. "Yes?"

"You could be right. It's been a couple of years. Maybe it *would* be a good thing to talk with your brother, if he'd be willing to meet with me. Do you think we might be able to work this thing out?"

"I do, Kristin. Believe me. He's a different guy. He's sorry about his past and wants to do the right thing now."

"Will you make the arrangements? We'll have to meet someplace neutral, someplace where we both feel at ease. No people. No interruptions."

"I can do that."

"All right," I said. "I'll get your number from Wilma and call you later." I smiled. "*You'll* be there, won't you?"

Mac's smile was brilliant. He was pleased to hear my change of heart. He nodded his agreement as he turned away again, and left the restaurant a hopeful guy.

I sat where I was, staring through the front windows, watching him stride down the street as I thought over what I'd realized about Martin's habit of not letting stuff stew.

What had come to me was that Martin cleaning up after himself was always in direct response to his need for survival. In his case, a lifelong necessity.

The way Dave told it, Martin's mother used any excuse to beat him. Cleaning up a mess quickly, before she found out, was a way to avoid catching hell. Never being caught off guard, making sure someone else got the blame, easily grew into moving fast to hide his bad deeds from the law.

That implied to me that he could be conned into moving faster than he should, if he felt threatened enough, moving so fast that he'd make a mistake. And I thought I knew a way to make him feel very threatened.

"Excuse me," I said to the waitress.

"What is it, honey?"

"I don't want to run into him again. Is there a back way out of here?"

"Sure, Sugar. Follow me," she said, and led me off toward the back.

"You're a lifesaver," I told her and gave her some money.

"Stuck you with the check, did he? You gotta watch out for those handsome cowboys without means."

"I hear you. I'm still suspicious of him. But he's so darned cute."

"Well see, that's the thing, isn't it," she said, pushing open the door to the kitchen.

21

OTIS AND I drove over to Sylvia's Steaks, a down-to-earth, twenty-four-hour-a-day workingman's meat and potatoes place near the stockyards. Otis was comfortable there. The portions were large and the service straightforward.

Henry treated vegetables with more respect than Sylvia, who boiled or fried them, but she couldn't be faulted on her trademark giant mesquite-grilled porterhouse steaks smothered in sweet onions and mushrooms. Since Otis liked to spread out and we were ahead of the dinner rush, we ate at one of her big tables that seat six grown men.

"I can't leave you alone for a slim minute without you getting in trouble," Otis said when I told him about meeting up with Mac and all that we discussed. "Do you think he just happened along?"

"Of course not," I said. "He either followed me or staked me out. Why do you think I went out the back door of the restaurant?"

"You look different. You wearing makeup?"

"Not really. I got my hair washed and cut a little."

"So running into Lover Boy turned out okay."

"How do you mean?"

"You confirmed he knew Hansard, which just proves what we was jawing about earlier. It was Hansard who Mackenzie called to get the lowdown on Hank's license plate, don'cha see? And after Hansard told Mackenzie where you lived, he told Martin."

"And Martin told Hansard to tail me."

"That's how his DeSoto shows up down the street from The Riverbank. You got that piece of the puzzle, too, Missy. Later Hansard tells Martin that he saw me and you at that rat hole where you bumped off Bear and them other two. You following this?"

I nodded, but I had my face in my plate.

"You ever taste a better steak?"

"Never."

"Them home fries is killer, too. Ain't they?"

"Killer," I agreed. Although, I had some uneasiness about becoming as big as Otis.

"Hansard, who had the brains God gave a goose, believed the story the old fart at The Riverbank was telling about you coming in first and the killers coming in next. So, that's what he tells Martin."

"You think he told Hansard that I set it up and you killed the bikers?"

"That's gotta be it, don't it? That's why Martin fingered me."

"Sounds right," I said.

Otis enjoyed some steak and potatoes before he continued.

"But when rubbing me out turns to cow patty, Martin calls this Mechanic and has Hansard knocked off before I can get to him. But your Mister Blue Eyes, he's cooking along on all burners and cuts off his nose to spite his face. Because now who's he got, since you backed over that Mechanic guy and his buddy like they was dogs sleeping in the driveway?"

"Moving too fast is his weakness, Otis. I see that happen when I'm shooting pool. Guys get in a hurry and mess up."

"Uh huh," he said, his mouth full of steak.

"Blue Eyes and his boys went into Henry's that night two years ago to beat up everybody and murder and do as they please and felt like they couldn't be stopped. When they left, Blue Eyes thought Henry was dead and I was beaten too senseless to survive the fire. He was right about me, but wrong about Henry."

"He knows better'n that now."

"He's trying to cover his tracks," I said, "and he's moving too fast again. Killing Hansard wasn't the right thing to do. Protecting him would've made more sense."

"Protecting ain't his habit, killing is."

"So you see. He makes mistakes when he moves too fast."

"And you got some slick idea how to get him moving too fast, do you, Missy?"

"I do. I'm calling Mac as soon as I get home and setting up a meeting with him and his brother for tomorrow. The sooner the better."

"You plan to discuss this with me before you jump head-first into it?"

"Here's how I figure it. Neither Blue Eyes nor Mac has a clue that I know how to handle myself. I mean, how would they know that?"

"So?"

"So, in any kind of meeting with Martin Belmont, he's going to figure me for the girl he remembers. A little older, sure, but still a girl he can abuse. He won't know I'm dangerous until it's too late."

"So, the mistake you think he'll make is just flat coming up against you. Simple as that."

"That's it. And, with his brother as a witness to say I acted in self-defense—"

"His brother, Hank, and me. You ain't going there without me and Hank."

"We'll work out the details. I've been a little shy of crowds since Helen's Bay Side," I said.

"Okay, I can understand that, but I still don't like it."

"No?"

"No. What you're saying ain't no more'n staking out a goat filled with dynamite. Looks good over a couple of beers. Only problem is once you're into it, it don't never turn out the way you think. You know why? Because you don't know what *he's* got up *his* sleeve."

"I've done this in pool rooms. I'm aware it wasn't life or death. Nevertheless, I know how to make guys get antsy and do things they might not if they were thinking straight."

Otis put down his knife and fork, pushed back from his plate, and gave me a stern look.

"We ain't done talking about your goat and dynamite trick," he said.

That night, or rather very early the next morning, Henry came out and woke me.

"Otis on phone."

I pulled on some Levi's and boots over the long underwear and long sleeve cotton shirt that I was sleeping in, and slipped on my black lamb's wool jacket. Sunup was still a couple of hours away and it was cold.

Jim and I didn't waste any time getting to the main house.

"I'm guessing you ain't seen the morning papers," Otis said the instant I answered the phone.

"What's going on?" I asked.

"It's on the front page. Dave Rushford was murdered."

That put electricity up my spine.

"How?"

"It happened earlier tonight, about when we was having our supper. A neighbor heard some palaver and called the police. I talked to a detective who told me they're gonna be looking hard into this one. Dave was tortured."

"That bastard," I said.

"This might've been our fault. We're talking about watching Blue Eyes, but he's already been on us a day or two. That step ahead ain't good news. I think you and Hank–"

The line went dead.

I clicked the receiver a couple of times.

"What matter?" Henry asked, standing there in his long johns, boots, and jacket.

"The phone lines have been cut. Get your guns, Henry."

"Get guns," Henry said, moving away at once.

I crossed the living room in a bound, turned out the kitchen lights, and headed for the back door. Jim knew something was up and was right on my heels as I threw open the back door and ran headlong for the *hacienda*.

I wanted to get the lights out. If they thought we were in bed asleep, we might get the jump on them. They must have cut the lines down the road, away from the house, or Jim would've known about it and told us. Maybe we had some time.

I dashed into my little house, doused the lights, and went for my guns. I pushed two .38 automatics into one of my big jacket pockets, grabbed a handful of loaded magazines, jammed them into another pocket, pulled on my black wool stocking cap, and tore back outside.

Jim was staring toward the county road, growling.

I put on the steam then, running full out along the edge of the drive that leads to our gate. I was racing to get to the big switch that operated a defensive device that Henry and I had constructed not far from the house. There was a pit that we'd dug beside the drive, next to the switch. I wanted to be in that pit.

The hole was waist deep, had cement walls, a gravel floor, and was roomy enough for the dog and me.

The switch was a spring-loaded, thick steel bar the length of a baseball bat that was held in place by a notched plate of steel. All I had to do was put some muscle behind moving the switch rod out of the notch and it would spring over with furious force, releasing two counter weights on each side of the drive.

The action of those falling weights would snap up a braided steel cable from a buried trough; a cable that would lock in place as it stretched across the drive like a heavy clothesline. That medieval apparatus had lain buried since last summer when Henry and I fortified the homestead.

Still, there was no reason to believe that it wouldn't work just fine.

We got to the location, I dragged off the wooden cover, and we jumped into the hole. Jim put his head and front paws over the edge of the pit and stared through the lower branches of the scraggly shrub that concealed our position.

Jim's eyes were steady; his ears were at firm points. I looked, too. It was dark, and I was trying to see across a quarter of a mile of flat prairie to where our drive met the county road at a right angle.

It was a dark night. There were only stars in the sky. If there had been a moon earlier, it was already gone. I couldn't see a thing. However, Jim knew something was happening out on the county road, and his low growl told me so.

Henry ran up and took a position on the other side of the narrow drive.

He whispered, "What you see?"

"Nothing yet," I whispered back.

We saw the lights of a slowly moving car. It stopped near our gate and the lights went off. It appeared that we had done the right thing to get the house lights out. There was a good chance whoever was out there didn't know we were awake.

However, I gave some consideration to being wrong about that. If they did know we were awake, this could be a trick to pull our attention away from the real direction of attack.

"Henry," I whispered.

"Baby Girl," he whispered back.

"Watch behind us. Watch that no one comes up behind us," I whispered.

"Also watch behind," Henry said and I heard him change his position under the shrub where he was lying prone.

A motorcycle came grumbling down the county road from the highway. It pulled up on the far side of the car and turned its light out and left its engine running. Even with my hearing, I could hear the distant low rumble of the bike.

It was so reminiscent of that night at Henry's Poolroom.

That bit of light on the other side of the car had given me a silhouette—maybe. Or shadows through the car windows made me think I saw something. What had I seen? I was staring too hard, and it was all too far away for me to be certain of anything.

I felt that vibration at my temples that always accompanied tension. The dog and I were staring toward our gate. I couldn't speak for Jim, but I couldn't see anything.

When the bike cut its engine, I became aware of the cold winter silence. There was no breeze, and the fog I made as I breathed hung for an instant around my face before it was gone. I was glad that I'd grabbed my wool stocking cap.

Jim stirred, aware of something new.

I searched the darkness and saw nothing. His growl was deep and muted. He was onto something. I touched him with my knee to stop his growling and strained to hear what had his hackles up. And finally, I *sensed* what he had known for some time. There was motion on our long drive.

Something was moving toward us. I felt a little tingle at the base of my neck as I took my hands from the switch bar and stuck them in my pockets to warm my fingers. There wasn't going to be a motorcycle roaring toward us to be stopped by a braided steel wire.

I brought out my guns, cocked them, thumbed off the safeties, and held them at ready. All I had to do was rise up from my kneeling position, straighten my arms, and begin firing.

"Stay boy," I mouthed.

I heard the familiar sound of gravel crunching underfoot and began to see a lone figure walking down the center of the drive, his breath visible in rhythmic bursts. A few steps more, and he would be no farther away than our targets.

Jim growled. The man stopped and held his breath.

I touched the dog with my knee and we, too, stopped breathing.

To see us, the man would have to know that we were in

a hole in the ground at the foot of a large shrub. Watching his head move, it was clear that he didn't know what he was looking for; he just knew that he'd heard something from our side of the drive.

After a long pause and not hearing anything else, he started forward again, resuming his quiet, measured pace. I could see that he was holding something across his chest with both hands, a sawed-off shotgun maybe.

It was time. In a single move, I rose, straightened my arms, pointed at his chest, and began squeezing off shots two at a time. I heard Henry cut loose, too. I'd anticipated the blasts of our weapons, but I wasn't prepared for the rattling thunder of a Thompson submachine gun.

Frightened out of my wits, I ducked, pulling Jim down with me.

As the fatally-wounded man collapsed with the automatic weapon clutched in his frozen fist, he released a burst of fire that haphazardly slammed lead into the ground around us. His aim swept upward, and he attacked the night sky with stuttering bursts of fire as he fell back.

I heard the last of those slugs whistle back to Earth before I dared stick my head up.

"You okay, Henry?"

"You okay?" Henry called back.

"Stay here, Henry. Keep watching behind us," I said.

"Watch everywhere," Henry said.

I muscled myself up and out of the pit and started running toward the car lost in darkness, the car I knew was parked on the road near our gate.

There was no reason to believe whoever was in that car could see any better than I could on that dark night. I was all in black, and I felt in my gut that surprise would be on my side. Jim was used to running with me and took up his position a few feet out to my left.

We didn't push it, just steady, the same way we always ran together, except this time I had a .38 in each hand. I strained my eyes to see in the dark, and began to make out our leafless jacaranda trees—gray spidery shapes against the blue-black sky.

I saw a white flash, heard a little pop, and realized that it was time to start shooting. There was another flash, another pop, as I brought up both pistols and started firing. And I kept firing as I ran, left, right, left, right. I was too far away and I knew that.

So was the shooter in the car too far from me. I began to see the blurred outline of the car. Best of all, no more flashes came from it once I started shooting.

The automobile came to life with its headlights whipping around. It was on a rutted dirt road, and the driver was not finding it easy to reverse directions.

I kept running as I released my empty magazines, got full ones in, and began firing again. I was getting close enough to see that it was a big car, dark-colored.

It got turned around and aimed for the highway and was throwing up a rooster tail of dirt by the time I was able to get its make. A Packard. A new Packard convertible. Jim kept barking, and I kept firing at the departing car until I'd emptied two more magazines.

"You coward," I shouted after the car that I felt certain was being driven by Blue Eyes. "You coward!"

At daybreak, we pulled the tractor out and together got the would-be assassin and his motorcycle on a cart. Henry buried man and machine out past the oil well, a good half-mile off his property.

"Plant out yonder," Henry told me when he got back.

I'd cleaned the biker's bloody pockets before that to see who he was. His name didn't ring any bells. He was an older guy with a Fort Worth address. A picture he carried disturbed me. He was younger in the photo and had a couple of children hanging on him. He had a big wad of cash strapped with a rubber band.

"Pay in advance," Henry said. "No refund."

We showed the submachine gun to Otis, who arrived in time for breakfast.

"Thirty round magazine," he said. "A Thompson's one nasty problem up close."

"We know about that," I said.

"Bullets come down all around, hit garage roof, ping, ping," Henry said.

"The Chinese used Thompsons in Korea, Hank. Did you know that?"

"Think I know what Chinese do in war?" Henry snapped.

"What in tarnation's wrong with you?"

"Always think I know Chinese things," Henry growled.

He stood back from the stove and stared at Otis.

"Henry's lived in Texas for thirty years. He's not Chinese. He's American," I said.

"Okay, I'm sorry. Don't pitch a fit on me, Hank. I was just making small talk, that's all."

Otis set the heavy weapon aside and looked at me.

"Hell, I didn't know he was so goldarned sensitive."

"Now you know," I said.

Otis sighed, let a minute pass, and picked it up.

"This gang's a bunch of termites, ain't they? You keep thinking they're all gone, and quicker'n gossip another one shows up."

"*La cucarachas,*" Henry said, which caused Otis and me to look over at him.

"The guy last night was older, you say?" Otis asked.

I put his license and other stuff out on the table.

"It's like Blue Eyes pulled him out of retirement," I said.

"Look at that. Maybe the ranks are thinning out for Mister Blue Eyes. Lord knows you've been doing your part to help them."

"Baby Girl tough tomato," Henry threw in.

I said, "That assassin last night was here to kick down our doors and murder us in our sleep. If you hadn't called about poor Dave Rushford, it might not have mattered how tough we were."

"And you're sure the jalopy was a Packard ragtop?" Otis asked me.

"Yeah. A new one. Dark color. Can't be too many of them with bullet holes. I threw a couple of dozen shots at it."

"I'll look into it. Did you put the call into Mackenzie last night?"

"Yeah. He said he'd get it set up."

"I knew you was gonna do that, even if I did talk against it. And now I'm less in favor of your loco idea."

"You think they know now that I can shoot?"

"I ain't reflected about that. But *I am* thinking how desperate he is. Look what lengths he's going to. Coming all the way out here to kill you two. Bringing along some granddad."

Otis and Henry exchanged a concerned look.

"All right, gentlemen," I said. "What are we going to do? Sit around and wait for him to try and kill us again? You said it yourself, Otis. It's damned if we do and damned if we don't. I say nothing will happen if we don't get close. This arm's length stuff works best for him, not us."

"Not good stand around," Henry agreed.

"Hell, with all the money he has to throw around, we don't know who to trust," I said.

"Longer wait, more dangerous get," Henry said.

"How about Albert Sun Man? Has he sobered up?" Otis asked.

"Albert in Las Cruces," Henry said.

"Wouldn't him and some of his ducktails just drive up beside Martin and do him in his car? Just like another day's work."

"That's the problem, Otis. Albert and his boys would get a stink on in some cantina and just go do it. And maybe they'd do it right and get away with it, or maybe they wouldn't."

"Maybe talk too much get caught," Henry summed up.

"That's what I'd be afraid of," I said. "And with Belmont money behind an investigation—"

"Mmmm. Good point. The boys downtown would be running some tough interrogations if Old Man Belmont was hollerin' at them."

"Police hit *pachucos* with rubber hose," Henry said.

"Of course they do, Hank," Otis said.

I said, "Albert's dad has been Henry's installation foreman for over fifteen years. I don't want to put that family in jeopardy again. One mistake was enough. You said yourself we were plain lucky last year. Albert is reckless enough without our help."

"Okay, Albert ain't an option," Otis said.

"Let's just keep it at home. I can do it. Mac said he'd put this meeting together for today or tonight. He's supposed to let me know."

"Now your phone's out. As I was driving in, I saw where they pulled down your line. I'll report that for you, if you want me to, Hank. Is there an office in Sweetwater?"

"Abilene," Henry replied in a friendly voice, maybe trying to make up for his show of temper earlier.

I got up from the table to leave.

Otis said, "You ain't having breakfast with us?"

"After that supper with you last night, I may not eat again for a week."

"Where go now?" Henry asked.

Two mother hens.

"To doctor my feet, Henry. I was running barefoot in my boots last night. I have some blisters to take care of."

"I was wondering why you was in your socks and slippers. It's like injury and insult. How does that go?"

"Adding insult to injury," I said.

"Yeah," Otis said.

"Who say that?" Henry wanted to know.

"Otis," I said.

"Bob Hope, maybe. Not Otis," Henry said, slapping his knee and laughing.

Otis grimaced and said to me, "So, you're gonna call him again?"

"Yeah, I'll use a pay phone in Sweetwater after I fix my blisters."

"You ain't going over there alone," Otis grumbled, and helped himself to another pork chop.

"No go alone," Henry echoed, sounding much too much like Otis.

Henry had some work to finish at his lathe. So Otis drove and I made my phone call in Abilene while he reported the downed line.

When I reached Mac, he told me that he hadn't spoken to his brother yet. He said he'd tried, but he hadn't caught Martin at home or the office. As soon as he reached him, he'd arrange something and let me know.

"And you think he's on the up and up?" Otis asked.

"Anything's possible," I said. "I told him to leave a message with Wilma in San Angelo."

"He ain't messing with you?"

We were on our way back to Henry's, and I was looking out the side window. I was struck with how the winter landscape we were passing seemed so flat, so one dimensional under the gray, cloudless sky. Everything seemed to be the same distance away, fence posts, barns, windmills, the occasional tree, the horizon. It seemed unreal.

"Missy?"

"Yeah, I heard you. He could be messing with me. I don't know for sure. My gut wants me to believe he's sincere, but the thing is—. Hell, I don't know if I can trust my gut with this guy."

Otis remained silent as I listened to the hum of the heater and watched the landscape slide by like a sketch on paper.

He surprised me with, "That's the way it was with me and Dixie."

I turned and watched him as he continued talking.

"Problem was, I was birds-a-flying in love with her, you know. I couldn't no more rely on my own thinking than I could trust her. I was more messed up'n nine bulldogs in them days, wondering who she'd sleep with next. It's like being burnt with hot grease. You think it's awful when it happens, then it starts getting bad."

"Been there," I said.

"I used to lay awake nights. Big guy like me. Makes a fool out of you when you care too much."

We were quiet for a few miles.

Then, as we turned onto the county road toward Henry's, he added, "It's hard not to think about him all the time, ain't it?"

"Yeah, but the worst part for me is, if I kill his brother—even in self-defense—how's that ever going away?"

"Mmmm," Otis hummed, thinking about it. "He knows what they did to you, don't he?"

"I'm not so sure he does. Or at least I don't think he knew the last time I talked to him."

"Ain't that something? They just never told that kid the truth."

Otis didn't speak again until we'd passed the spindly jacaranda trees and were turning into the drive.

"You ain't had what I'd call a run of luck these past two years, Missy."

"So what. I'm alive. I have you and Henry and a few other friends. I'm doing okay."

We were almost to the house when I saw Jim beside the road.

"Stop!" I shouted and was stumbling out the door while the car was still moving.

The big dog was on his side, but his position was unnatural. Something was wrong.

"No, no, no, no," I was saying as I rushed up and knelt beside him.

There was blood on his head and ear. One of his front

legs looked broken and had been bleeding. He was breathing, but it wasn't easy for him. His eyes weren't blank, but they were heading that direction. I couldn't tell if he recognized me or not.

"Jim, don't you do this. Don't you die on me."

"Is he alive?" Otis said as he puffed over to where we were.

"We've got to get him to the doctor fast."

Otis and I thought the same thing at the same time. "Henry," we said together.

"Let me help you get him in the back seat," Otis said.

Henry's shop door was open and his lathe was running, making that loud whine it made. No Henry. I turned off the machine and we looked everywhere, fast, with our pistols at ready.

His truck was there. He was gone.

Otis said, "No signs of a struggle. My guess is he was taken at gunpoint. With his machines going, they was on him before he knew it. Come on. Let's get your shepherd to Sweetwater. I know a clinic. We can get to a phone over there, too."

I rode in the back with Jim's head on my lap, talking softly to him and loving his face.

I was sick with worry that he wasn't going to make it and equally worried that something awful was happening to Henry. I hardly had room for the anger I felt for Blue Eyes.

"I think Henry's alive," I said from the back seat.

"Why're you thinking that?"

"He'll try and use him as bait."

"That's one way to look at it, but he's a sick bastard, and Hank could be a handful. You know how Hank can get his back up."

"I don't want him to hurt Henry," I said, thinking about Dave Rushford.

"Me neither, Missy. I'm gonna call in some favors from police friends in Abilene and Dallas. This kidnapping business might be the straw that breaks his back."

22

WHEN WE GOT to the Laurel Lane Medical Clinic, some helpers came out with a stretcher board and carried Jim inside. His breathing was still weak, and his eyes didn't look good.

A small, middle-aged man introduced himself as Doctor Epperson, and told me after a quick examination that Jim had been shot three times. One bullet had grazed his skull and torn off a piece of his ear, another had broken his front leg, and a third shot had entered his body and lodged somewhere inside.

The doctor said, "I would normally recommend that you take him to a veterinarian in Abilene—but he's lost so much blood. I've handled gunshot wounds before, though never with a dog as a patient. Look, I'll do the best I can. That's all I can promise."

He excused himself and went in to start surgery.

I felt helpless, desperate. I didn't want Jim to die, and I felt guilty that I hadn't been there to protect him when he needed me.

Otis found me in the waiting room. He'd located Doc McGraw on a horse ranch over near Weatherford. "Doc says he'll be an hour or so getting here."

"That's good," I said.

But I knew in my heart that an hour from now wasn't going to make the difference. Whether Jim lived or died was being decided right then.

"Did you call the police in Abilene?" I asked.

"Yeah, I'm meeting my detective friend there. Are you staying?"

"No, I'm going with you. I can't do anything here. We have to find Henry."

In Abilene, we drove to a Mexican restaurant where the owner, a stout man with a sparkling smile, greeted Otis with a handshake and me with a polite, "*Senorita.*"

He took us to a back room, away from his other customers, where a hard-faced, plainclothes detective in shirtsleeves, tie, and suspenders was seated by himself at a big, round table eating refried beans, rice, and chunks of meat in a green sauce. The detective's jacket was hanging on the chair next to him. His cowboy hat was on the table.

When we sat down across from him, he moved his hat to the chair seat below his jacket.

The owner took our drink order and left. Otis pulled an ashtray over, took his time lighting a cigarette, and tipped his head at me.

"This is Kristin Van Dijk. She looks innocent enough, just don't shoot pool with her."

"Doug Gustman," the detective mumbled with his mouth full.

I nodded.

"How's the pork?" Otis asked him.

"Check with me later today," he replied.

He was an intelligent man. I could see it in his dark eyes. I could also see that he was tough as nails. I guessed that went with the territory.

"You got a permit for that?" Detective Gustman asked me, his glance indicating the pistol in a shoulder holster under my jacket.

"Her life's in danger. But that's not why we're here," Otis told him.

"That means you don't have a permit," the detective said, looking at me. "You can talk for yourself, can't you?"

I nodded again, and his jaw twitched when he clenched his teeth.

"You're in a good mood," Otis commented, and held his tongue until the waitress that brought our coffee and Dr Pepper was out of earshot.

"You have a crime you wanna report," Gustman said, "but you don't wanna do it at the station."

"That's the size of it," Otis said.

"I'm listening," he said.

Otis explained that a new, dark-colored Packard convertible had been out at Henry Chin's last night, and that the person driving that car had shot at Henry and that Henry had shot back. He said that Henry's phone line had been pulled down last night, too. And today, Henry's dog had been shot and maybe killed.

Otis reported Henry as a missing person, foul play suspected. The name Belmont was never mentioned.

The Detective said he knew who Henry Chin was. "He's the cabinetmaker that made the new front desk at the station house."

"That's the guy," Otis said.

"Same guy had a pool hall fire a year or so back."

"Same guy," Otis said.

"Same guy," Detective Gustman repeated. He looked interested as he took out a pad and pencil, wrote down some details, and asked a few questions.

When he and Otis were finished, the detective agreed to start an immediate search for Henry and the Packard, and said he would be in touch with any results.

Nothing was said about me. Otis knew better than to say I was living out at Henry's. Admired as Henry might be for his woodworking skills, to most folks he was still just a Chinaman. I was still an American girl, and narrow-minded bigotry hadn't all of a sudden flown the coop in those parts.

When we were ready to leave, Detective Gustman said to me, "Get that weapon permitted, or leave it home. Understand?"

I nodded.

On our way back to Henry's, we drove by the clinic in Sweetwater to check on Jim.

A nurse told us that Doctor Epperson was still working on him. She didn't say that it was looking bad, but I could see she knew it was serious. Doc McGraw had arrived and was assisting, so that was good news.

I called Mac's number while we were there. I didn't get an answer. So I called Wilma. She was in a talkative mood. She said Mac hadn't left a message yet and that she knew we were having problems. She could hear it in my voice.

I told her it was over between us.

"I'm sorry to hear that," she said. "And I sincerely mean it."

"I know you do, Wilma. Thank you," I said.

Wilma told me Mac was going to be one of my "what-might-a-beens."

"There ain't a woman alive who don't have a trunk full of them," she said, snapping her gum. "Just means you're growing up, hon. And why should being a woman be any easier for you than it is for the rest of us?"

When we got to Henry's, I gathered some weapons and clothing and personal stuff and we closed and locked things up. I left a note in case Otis and I had gotten it all wrong and Henry just showed up out of nowhere with some weird UFO story or something.

I drove my car and followed Otis back to his office.

It was well after dark when the phone rang in the other room and woke me.

I had curled up with the wolf skin and fallen asleep, worn out. The early arrival of the veteran hit man had been demanding physically, the emergency rush to the hospital with Jim had been emotionally draining, and the anxiety of Henry's abduction had filled the balance of the day.

I was groggy as I opened my eyes and lay listening for Otis' voice to carry from the other room. I could hear him, but I couldn't make anything out. He was just grunting now and then. Whoever he was on the line with was doing all the talking.

I sat up. I could hear the fan rattling in the background. I smelled burnt coffee.

I stretched and yawned, shook my head, got up, slipped on a wool plaid shirt over my t-shirt, and joined Otis in his office just as he hung up the phone. He was standing behind his desk, his coat and vest off, his tie loose, his sleeves rolled up. A Lucky was smoking in the ashtray near his coffee cup.

"That was our boy Martin."

"I had an idea it was," I said.

Otis was strapping on a second holster. He was going to wear two .45s, one on his right hip and the one he carried to the left of his heart.

"What did he say about Henry?" I asked.

"He says Hank'll be all right as long as we don't do something stupid and so on and so on."

"Did he say where he was?"

"He gave me a location where he wants us to be in an hour."

"He plans to kill us," I said.

"No shit. The real question is how he plans to do it. Figuring that out'll give us a half a chance."

He opened a drawer, removed several loaded magazines, and placed them on the desk.

"How would you do it?" I asked.

He took a swig of coffee.

"First off, the phone call is just to make sure we're up here. I'd be lying about the meeting being in an hour. I'd be downstairs right now to shoot us as we go for our cars. I'd do it with a shotgun. That's how I'd do it. If you want somebody dead, there ain't no rules."

"I'm glad I asked. What about the police helping us?" I was referring to Detective Gustman in Abilene and another police friend of his in Dallas.

"I decided against it," he said.

He stuck a cigarette in his mouth, snapped a match with

his thumbnail, lit up, and mashed out the butt that was smoking in the ashtray.

"They wouldn't mean to, it's just they'd get Hank killed if they found out it was a Belmont they was supposed to arrest. We gotta get Hank out on our own."

I picked up my jacket, put it on, and asked, "Where's this place he wants us to go?"

"I wrote down directions," he said.

He picked up a scrap of paper, and I motioned that I wanted it.

"What're you doing?" he asked.

"Calling Mac. If he's there, he's not a part of this. If he's gone, we'll know where he is."

Otis dropped the paper by the phone and moved back.

I was relieved when Mac answered.

First, I asked him if he'd made arrangements with his brother. When he told me he was never able to reach him, I told him that I was on my way to meet Martin. He asked for the directions, I gave them to him, and we hung up.

Otis had heard everything. He put out his cigarette, picked up the directions, and stuffed them in his pocket.

"We have to go now," he said.

I said, "Martin's got the advantage. It's dark, he knows the setup, and we're the last to arrive."

"You're right," he said and handed me his jacket so I could help him get into it. Then he winked at me. Otis *winked* at me.

What did the Apaches used to say? *Today's a good day to die.*

Less than an hour later, on the outskirts of Fort Worth, I left the highway and followed Otis in one of his big four-doors into an area of abandoned factory buildings that had last been active some ten years ago for World War II airplane production.

Otis told me that thousands of B-24 bombers had been built out there. Now the area was overgrown with weeds and had that eerie, neglected feeling of someplace that time's forgotten. A little moonlight might have helped. No such luck.

I followed him back into an area where deserted buildings surrounded by acres of land appeared in our headlights. They grew to monumental sizes as we approached them. Each mighty structure was grand enough to accommodate the dimensions of an airplane that went in one end as parts and came out the other as an assembled, ready for combat Air Force bomber.

I was ten years old at the end of WWII and was aware of a lot of things, but wartime manufacturing wasn't something that I knew anything about.

I tried to imagine what it had been like in this park with thousands of workers coming and going, the lights, the bustle, the roar of countless airplanes moving, their propellers turning. I could only conjure up the ghosts that Hollywood had fed me through film—Greer Garson, William Bendix.

When we were downstairs from the office, preparing to leave, Otis had told me, "Ain't nothing out there now; just big empty buildings. You stay behind me, and when we get where we think he's at, we'll take a look and talk it over."

The time to do that had arrived.

Otis stopped beside a huge structure and turned out his lights. I switched off my lights and stopped, too. I got out, walked over, and joined him where he stood looking around the edge of the building.

He was looking at another big structure. It had its giant doors open, and just inside the massive space, there was a car parked with its lights on. It looked tiny a quarter of a mile away from us. The taillights faced us, its headlights shined inward.

Said the spider to the fly.

Otis said, "Okay. I reckon the asshole's got Hank in there tied to a chair or something. He's got a flair for the dramatic, ain't he? Too many Cagney movies."

"I hope Henry's not too cold."

"It's pretty damned cold tonight, ain't it?"

We were silent for a few minutes, just watching the distant building, maybe expecting it to do something.

"You know Blue Eyes is not alone," I said. "He hasn't shown any stomach for working by himself."

"He always comes up with another one, don't he? You think Mackenzie's here yet?"

I looked around the dark park. There was nothing to see.

"He drives that big pickup," I said, rubbing my hands together to warm them.

"Let's don't worry about it. Here's what we're gonna do," Otis said. "We don't know what's gonna happen when we get in there. We oughta have something in mind."

"Like what?"

"Like I'll take care of getting the car lights out. If Hank ain't already dead—"

"Don't say that."

Otis shrugged and made the face cynics make when confronted with naiveté.

"Okay. If they ain't got lights, maybe we got a better chance of saving him. That's all. And maybe they don't know we got two cars, and they'll think we're coming in together."

"What's your idea?" I asked.

In a few quick sentences, he told me a plan. But it was flawed. I should talk. I sure didn't know what to do.

"Look," he said, after explaining his plan. "He grabs Hank and uses him to drag us out to this no man's land. He's asking for a shootout, ain't he? And he thinks he's got the edge. What else is he doing?"

"I think that's it. His gang's been killed around him. He's feeling threatened, and he's in a hurry. This is the bad decision we've been talking about."

Otis squinted at me.

"You don't know the first thing about picking locks, do you?"

"Not the first thing."

"It don't matter. Break a window if you got to."

We stared at each other, our hands in our pockets, both of us doing battle with the cold by shifting our weight from foot to foot, neither of us saying anything. His plan appeared to be as good as it was going to get.

"You're driving without lights, so take your time. I'll wait a while before I go over," he said.

"I'll know when you get there?" I asked.

"You'll know."

He lit a cigarette.

"And, Missy," he said in a somber tone of voice, exhaling a plume of smoke into the wintry night air.

"Yeah?"

"I know I ain't never told you how much I admire your grit. I mean what happened to you that night at Henry's. Another girl might have given up, blocked it out of her memory...or just rolled over and died. Not you. You hitched up your britches and took care of business. I just want you to know, in case this all goes south, it's been a real pleasure knowing you."

"Oh, for chrissake. Let's get on with this cockamamie plan of yours."

As I walked away, I heard Otis laugh.

"Too many Cagney movies," I said.

I was thinking, though, if something *did* happen, I hoped that Jim survived and ended up out at Doc McGraw's with the goats and horses.

23

I DROVE WITHOUT lights to the factory building, parked along the side, and made my way to one of the doors. It was standing open a foot or so. No lock picking necessary.

I grasped the knob and lifted as I leaned my shoulder into the door. It creaked as it opened inwards, but so quietly, it was like a little secret between the door and me.

I hustled through the opening and into the building, kicking up a swirl of coarse dust. I stopped and squatted down to the cement floor to give my eyes a chance to adjust.

I felt hair prickling at my neck and was aware of cold sweat beneath my clothes as I held myself motionless in that foreign space that smelled of dirt, iron, and rot. The car lights were a long way from where I was. There was only a dim wash of light everywhere, a muted glow reflecting from the high walls and ceiling of that huge space.

My eyes adjusted, and I moved into an area of shelves.

There were rows and rows of tall, raw wood shelves. I moved through them. Each section of shelving was maybe thirty or forty feet long, and those sections, end on end, went back into the inky depths of the building—hundreds upon hundreds of empty shelves with wide paths between them.

A gigantic library without books, an idea that Kafka might've crafted.

My boots were crunching. If *I* could hear the scratch of sand and dirt on concrete, it was certain others could. I sat down where I was in the shadows, removed my boots, and left them on one of the lower shelves for safekeeping.

I was quieter in my heavy wool socks as I stole along beside the shelves and moved toward the lighted end of the building. As I advanced toward the light, I also moved inward through the rows of shelving, until I was closer to the assembly floor that ran the length of the building.

It was becoming easier to see.

The sound of an approaching truck cut the silence. I froze in the shadows and watched as Mac's pickup entered through the big open doorway and stopped near the Packard.

I wasn't sure what it meant having him there. Hopefully it would make the situation less dangerous for Henry. Knowing all the attention was focused on Mac's arrival, I moved faster. I heard Mac's door slam as I arrived at a place where I could see everything. Mac had left his lights on, too.

It was getting downright cheery in there.

I moved until I saw Henry. When I saw that he was tied somehow to a heavy chain that hung down from above, I got the notion to do something crazy. His arms were stretched up over his head, his body was hanging limp. I couldn't tell if he was alive. He was an easy target if someone in the shadows wanted him dead.

Mac walked toward Henry and spoke to him while he was still some distance away. I heard concern in his voice. "Is that you, Mister Chin?"

"My name Henry Chin. You insurance man, Mackenzie."

"My God, Mister Chin, are you all right? How'd you get tied up like that?"

Otis came roaring through the door and skidded to a stop near Mac's truck. He left his lights on and his engine running as he stepped out and took a stance like policemen do, with his arms over the top of the open door, his pistol at the ready.

Mac was out in the open, maybe halfway to Henry. He

raised his hands to show that he wasn't armed and called out.

"Hey. Hey. Hold on. What're you doing?"

"I'm a licensed officer of the court. I'm here to get Henry Chin. He was kidnapped by your brother."

"Kidnapped?" Mac said with disbelief.

"Martin Belmont here," Henry shouted. "He has gun."

"Don't worry, Mister Chin. Nothing's going to happen to you," Mac said, and gazed into the darkness of the building and shouted. "Martin! Where are you? What the hell are you doing? If you're here, come out so we can talk."

There was a clank of iron from the dark side of the factory building, followed by silence. I saw Otis turn his attention to the general direction of the sound.

I, too, began searching the darkness in that direction.

Mac said to Otis, "Maybe if you put your gun down."

"That ain't likely," Otis said. "I don't trust him. Look what he's done to Hank."

Mac started toward Henry again.

"Okay, Mister Chin. I'm gonna get you down from there right now."

My opinion of Mac was going up fast. He had such calm authority in his voice that I began to believe that things might play out like a British mystery story—the police chatting amiably with the murderer about how he did it.

A rifle shot put an end to that fantasy.

From where I was, I saw both the muzzle flash and the bullet impact against the concrete floor between Mac and Henry. Otis, too, had seen the flash and was looking the same place I was. A rifle meant that Blue Eyes had accuracy.

That was not good.

Blue Eyes yelled out from the darkness, "Leave him be, Mac. I want him where he's at."

I couldn't have located Blue Eyes with just his voice alone; having seen the muzzle flash made a difference. I acted at once.

The assembly floor was crisscrossed with work trenches covered by steel grillwork. I could get to the other side of the factory without exposing myself.

I heard Mac say, "Watch out where you're shooting there, Martin. You're gonna hurt someone. I'm positive you don't wanna to do that."

Otis chimed in with what he might have to do if there was any more shooting. Blue Eyes spoke up again. Then Mac began pleading with his brother. I didn't believe that all that talk was going to change Martin Belmont's mind. It was just buying time.

As I ducked down the stairs that led to the trenches, I remembered the city tunnel near my grade school that we children streamed through to get across a busy street. It was an adventure because it required you to hold your breath and run.

At least the work trench in the abandoned airplane plant wasn't rife with foul odors, only the chance of violent death.

I knew I was an easy target while running in my stocking feet through that trench, so I held a pistol in my hand as I ran. If someone started something, he'd better be ready to finish it.

As I eased up the stairs on the dark side of the building, I began hearing the voices again. From where I was I couldn't see Mac, Otis, or Henry.

Mac was shouting, "You're gonna have to kill me, Martin, because I'm not going to allow you to keep Mister Chin hanging up here like an animal."

Mac was playing with fire. I knew his brother better than he did. I was moving to a better position when Blue Eyes spoke up.

"Don't push me, Mac. Get away from him."

My heart jumped. Blue Eyes was close to where I was.

There was enough reflected light for me to see a spacious platform about fifty feet from me, that looked to be constructed of steel mesh and plate. It was raised above the floor ten feet or so with an unobstructed view of the assembly area. I strained to see where he might be on that platform.

"Get away from him," Blue Eyes warned Mac again.

I concentrated on where I believed he might be. I still couldn't see him.

Otis called out, using police language. "Martin Belmont, this is a warning. If you discharge your firearm again, I will fire on you. Put your weapon down. Put your hands up and come out where I can see you. Do it now."

Otis didn't know where I was. He was warning me that he was getting ready to shoot.

Mac yelled, "You tell me you've changed, Martin. So, prove it. Do as the officer says and come out here."

"Goddamn it, Mac!" Blue Eyes shouted.

I saw the muzzle flashes when Blue Eyes began firing, and ducked back as Otis let go. It was like the Lone Ranger radio show with bullets ricocheting off the steel plate. I stayed down even after the shooting stopped. I had a feeling it wasn't over.

"Hank!" Otis shouted. "Get back."

"He shoot brother," Henry called back.

It was like a dagger in my heart. Mac had been shot. How badly was he hurt?

"Get back, Hank," Otis barked. "Get down."

The shooting started again, lead flying in both directions. When it stopped, I rose up and tried to see what was happening down on the floor where Mac had been hit.

I don't know if I saw a motion from the corner of my eye or if I sensed someone. But by ducking as I snapped around to look over my shoulder, I caused the steel bar to miss my head. It hit an I-beam with a deafening clank and landed a glancing blow off my shoulder and down my arm that sent my pistol flying.

I twisted away with my weight on one foot and kicked at my assailant with the other.

I was lucky; I connected. I heard the steel bar hit the floor and bounce away as I caught my balance and lunged forward to follow up the first kick. I was surprised to find out that my assailant was a woman.

While she was trying to recover from being knocked on her butt, I kicked at her again. I aimed at her knee. I wanted her immobilized, but she was moving, and I didn't connect.

She scrambled away, got to her feet, and stepped into enough light for me to see her thin nose, square jaw, and full lips. It was the tough girl who had worn the white leather jacket—Mechanic's girlfriend. She was in black leather pants, boots, and a wool shirt.

We were almost twins, except I was tougher.

I was expecting a knife or a gun to come out. She either didn't carry a weapon, or she was under the impression she could take me without one. She came at me, hands out like she thought I was going to wrestle with her. Her experience had been honky-tonk catfights. My experience had been Sarge.

I grabbed one of her hands with both of mine and broke her wrist as I moved her past me. She cried out, staggered, and tried to catch her balance. I snatched a handful of her long hair, swung her around, and slammed her face into a steel I-beam before dropping her to the floor, unconscious.

Something smashed against my head, just over my ear. There was a burst of light and a split-second when I thought I knew something.

24

*"YOU'RE FLYING HER," Harlan says. "You've got the stick,"
he says. But I know I can't be flying the plane. I'm in the canvas
sling back seat behind him. "You're stalling out," he tells me. "Feel
how soft and floppy she's getting? Can you hear me?" he shouts.
"You're stalling out. Can you hear me?" And his voice gets farther
and farther away. "Can you hear me?" Farther and farther away
until I can't hear him at all.*

Something was bumping against my face—carpet against
my cheek. It was dark. I was cold and in a cramped space—
scratchy, wool carpet. I had a crashing headache. There was
the scent of rubber.

I was in the trunk of a car—a moving car.

Besides my headache, I felt bruised and scraped all over.
I'd been thrown around while I was unconscious.

I wasn't wearing my jacket. My shoulder holster was
empty. My boots were gone. My ankle holster was empty.
I had my jeans on, and my shirt was torn in front—buttons
were missing. My bra had been pulled up above my breasts.
The straps were cutting into me.

As I struggled to get back into the thing, I discovered
an abrasion on my neck and chest. I was sticky with blood.
Someone had pulled hard at my clothes—maybe to drag me
around. My heart picked up steam as I began getting a better
picture of my situation.

Christ almighty, my head hurt. I felt where I had been
hit, just above and behind my ear. I was sticky with blood
there, too.

I was in the trunk of a car being driven down a dirt road. How long had I been knocked out? Where was I being taken? I felt around me. My boots and jacket were not in the trunk.

Think. Think.

I didn't know about my jacket. I'd taken my boots off. Okay. No guns, no knives. I had my hands for weapons. I was shivering; it was so cold. I felt around the trunk latch to see if there was a way to open the lid from the inside. If there was, I didn't know how to do it.

The car stopped.

The engine was idling. What was next? Was it better for me to still be asleep, or should I be ready to act when the trunk opens? What made me think the trunk was going to open? What if it didn't open?

There would be tire tools. I began feeling around again. The car rocked, and a door slammed. I waited for another door slam. It didn't come. Maybe the driver was alone.

A key was put in the trunk lock.

I moved back as far as I could and got ready to use my feet. The lock released, and the lid sprung upward. The light was from the night sky, which was almost as dark as the closed trunk. A cold breeze shivered in, and I could hear water slapping against a shoreline.

Water? Where am I?

I kept my eyes half-closed so I could see, and not give away that I was awake. I held my body as still as I could. I was so cold I couldn't keep from shaking. There was movement, and I saw a figure at the back of the car. It was dark, but I could tell that it was a man. He stood there doing nothing—watching maybe to see if I was awake.

I didn't dare move for fear he would shoot me.

He reached in, grabbed the bottoms of my Levi's, and pulled me toward him. I was on my back, and he only got my legs out and my butt up off the floor of the trunk. He would have to reach inside, and lift my torso up to get me over the edge and out of the trunk. When he did that, I would attack him.

Then I learned that wasn't what he was trying to do. He began undoing my belt buckle.

"I was your first fuck, you little bitch, and now I'm gonna be your last," he growled.

It was Blue Eyes.

Who else but a *sick* man would think of raping an unconscious woman outdoors on a cold winter night?

It wasn't going to happen there or anywhere else. When he ducked his head under the trunk lid to deal with my tight-fitting blue jeans, I rammed my hands into his face and felt two stiff fingers go deep into his eye socket.

He jerked away and cracked his head against the open trunk lid. I saw his hand go to his face as he backed away from the car, cursing. I'd hurt him. Good.

I had to move fast. I scrambled around to change my awkward position. I was halfway out of the trunk when he was back on me with fists swinging. He punched me several times before I caught one of his hands, forced it to my mouth, and bit away a substantial chunk of flesh.

"Goddamn it," he growled, and landed one hard on the side of my head.

I saw flashing lights. That was where I'd taken the earlier blow that knocked me out. I tried to kick him. I was dizzy from the punch he landed, and I couldn't get it done.

He caught my leg and pushed me back into the trunk. "Get in there, you little bitch," he growled and slammed the lid shut. "You fucking bitch," he shouted at me through the closed lid. "You're going swimming now, you fucking bitch."

I was still lightheaded, but I began moving as fast as I could because I'd learned a couple of things during my attempt to escape. I had seen the tail fins and knew that I was in the trunk of my own car. Blue Eyes must have dragged and carried me out the back way, the same way I got into the factory. That's how he got my car. And being in my own car was a revelation of huge importance.

The other thing I learned was we were next to water. A

river. A lake. And he was going to drive my car into that water with me locked in the trunk. I had to move fast.

Damn it. Move. Move.

I reached back and felt along the ceiling of the trunk. If I'd known I was in my own car, I could've already killed that bastard.

The car's moving.

I could feel that he was turning the Caddie around. If he was going to drive me into the water, I didn't have much time.

When Henry and I were fortifying the homestead last summer, we hid weapons and ammunition in several different places, including sawed-off Remingtons in his truck and my Cadillac.

I found the flap of carpet and released the 12-gauge pump from the clamps that had kept it in place. I gripped it and racked a shell into the breach. It was loaded with double ought buck that blasted fist-sized holes in our targets.

The car stopped.

I hunkered as far back as I could in the pitch black, cramped space, felt again where the trunk latch was, and put the end of the barrel against the latch area. The noise was going to be horrific in that closed space, and who knew where shot and torn metal might go?

I pushed my face into my shoulder and got ready.

A door slammed. The car lurched forward. There was pressure against the back of my head. The car was going front-end-first down a sharp incline.

I'm going into the water!

My heart was thundering. I reached up and found the latch area again as I felt the heavy car tipping nose first. The car was picking up speed.

The car was submerging in deep water. I was sinking fast.

I tucked my face into my shoulder, pulled the trigger, and pain raced up my arm.

The recoil damn near broke my wrist, and the sound was

as close to unbearable as I ever wanted to get. Sharp pain sliced through my ringing ears. Very cold water spewed on me through the hole that the blast tore through the trunk lid.

I pushed. The lid was holding. The hole I'd made was above the lock.

"Goddamn it!" I shouted through the frigid water that was spraying on me.

The car was sinking faster. I racked another shell into the breach, aimed straight up over me, below where the water was rushing in, braced the powerful gun as best I could, and fired again. The noise and recoil were awful.

I held onto the weapon as a flood of icy water rushed into the trunk. I filled my lungs with escaping air and shouldered the heavy lid out of the way.

I wiggled out of the trunk, found the car bumper with my feet, and pushed off. I kicked hard. The cold water soaked through my clothes. It was like being packed in ice. It was pitch black. I could feel air bubbles going the same direction I was going and kept kicking. I kept kicking. It was taking forever, and I was growing fearful. My lungs were aching.

I broke the water's surface and gulped the cold air.

Hold on to the shotgun. Hold on to the shotgun.

Lord help me, I was freezing. I looked in every direction. It was dark in all but one. I saw light. I paddled toward the light. I was only a few yards from the shore, but it felt like a mile. My water-soaked wool shirt weighed a ton. I was shaking hard. I was so cold and growing weak. I felt like giving up. I wouldn't, though.

I would not give up.

I dragged myself over sharp-edged rocks and crawled up a hard-packed dirt slope toward an idling pickup truck with its headlights on. Adrenaline and anger were keeping me going.

I began mouthing a command through chattering teeth, "Don't you drive away. Don't you drive away. Don't you drive away."

I wasn't about to let go of the shotgun, so I had one hand to help myself up. Getting my balance was difficult. I fell a time or two before getting to my feet, shaking and panting for breath. I staggered off toward the pickup, my legs stiff and feeling unattached to my body. The involuntary chattering of my teeth was making my whole head shiver.

I saw him.

Blue Eyes was in the pickup truck.

I could make him out through the clouded glass. He had the cab light on. He was looking in the rearview mirror at the eye that I had gouged.

I walked up to the idling truck and stopped outside the driver's window. I was close enough not to miss. The double ought buck would go through the window glass and his skull like paper and cantaloupe. I pumped a shell into the chamber, prepared myself for the terrible recoil, and pulled the trigger.

Nothing happened. Something was wrong.

The water had damaged the paper casing. The primer was wet. I pumped in another shell, took aim, and pulled the trigger. Again nothing happened. The shotgun was useless.

I wanted to scream. Instead I focused on the back window of his truck. Every pickup in Texas had a gun in the gun rack, and this old pickup was no exception. Most of them were loaded, too.

Blue Eyes wasn't aware of me. He no doubt felt safe in his warm, lighted cab, concentrating on the damage that I'd done to his face. I was a dim memory to him, another little bother solved with murder.

We'd see about that. I jammed my sawed-off shotgun under my arm. Maybe it wasn't useless after all. Using both hands, I stepped up onto the running board, swung my leg up, and pulled my dripping, shaking body into the truck bed.

When the truck rocked on its springs, Blue Eyes almost leapt out of his skin.

He grabbed up a pistol and jerked his head around in every direction, using his one good eye, his face grotesque, his right eye a bloody black mess. He wiped at the fogged side window. He was trying to look from a lighted space out into the dark.

Holding my sawed-off weapon by the barrel, I swung it like a club. I swung it with all my might into the back window of the truck cab. The shock of the noise and the spraying glass took Blue Eyes by surprise. He jerked forward, hunching his shoulders.

I dropped my window-breaker to the truck bed and snatched the shotgun from the window rack with both hands. Blue Eyes saw what I was doing. He grabbed at the gun to keep me from getting it.

We struggled, grunting and huffing with the effort. He was reaching back over his shoulder. I had leverage. I won. I pulled the gun through the window and out of the cab.

He was panicked. He twisted about and began firing his pistol. Wild shots burst through the cab roof. Each near miss threw up a fine residue of hot metal to sting my face.

I pumped the shotgun, hoping I was chambering a shell, stepped back, and brought it to my shoulder. When Blue Eyes saw that long barrel coming up to point at his face, he cried out. He clawed for the door handle and slammed his shoulder against the cab door. He was tumbling out by the time I'd braced myself and fired.

The deafening blast of buckshot tore through the steering wheel, ripped a jagged trench in the steel dashboard, and took a softball size chunk out of the hinged edge of the open door.

I swung the hot barrel over the top of the cab and brought it to bear on Blue Eyes. He was scrambling in the dirt beside the truck, frantically trying to get to his feet. In his panic, he continued squeezing off wild shots into the night. He was turning his head like an owl, his one eye wide with fear.

He finally saw me—and recognized me. I was standing above him in the bed of his truck, a shotgun in my hands.

Martin Belmont screamed his outrage at the impossibility of me being there. Surely his scream of frustration was because I had become more than he could comprehend. And I heard another high-pitched shriek, an unknown cry of anguish. It lasted until I choked and realized the sound was coming from me. I was screaming, too, with hatred and rage.

And just as Blue Eyes squeezed off a final, wildly unaimed shot into the winter night, I delivered a load of buckshot that hit him just above the groin. It drove through his body. It dissolved bone and tissue in an area the size of a saucer plate.

It was as if a horse had kicked him, and he was airborne. His body wrapped around the shock, his feet just touching the ground. He pitched backward light as a feather and landed hard, his legs twisted and forever useless to him. His injured face, illuminated by the dim light from the truck cab, was a broken jumble of sharp shadows.

I looked for his pistol. He'd lost it as he fell. It wasn't close to him.

The arteries for the legs divide where I shot Blue Eyes. There was no coming back from that injury, and death would not be instantaneous. The pain I could see he was suffering made me glad. Shivering with cold, I stepped from the truck bed, to the running board, to the ground, and moved over to glare down at his damaged face.

"Who's laughing now?" I asked him.

I felt no sympathy for him or any of the others I'd killed because of him.

I hated Martin Belmont for more than his cruel and heartless actions. I despised him for what he had made of me, for driving me to a level of barbarism that allowed me to kill without remorse. I had relinquished an irreplaceable piece of my humanity when I chose revenge, and he was to blame.

His last breath would mean that a horrible chapter of my life would be over.

And I wanted to witness that last icy breath.

He was in the dirt at my feet. Frail, stuttering gasps formed brief veils of gossamer mist above his mouth. His one eye stared blankly into the cold dark sky.

My mind went to all the damage that man had done. I thought about Henry and Otis and Mac, too. I wondered if they had survived the gunfight, and I thought about Jim and felt such an ache in my heart. And almost before I knew I had done it, I jacked another shell into the Winchester and jabbed the end of the long barrel into Martin's open mouth.

"Deliver this to Satan," I said.

I heard the motor of an approaching car. I turned to find myself captured in headlights and brought the shotgun to my shoulder.

"Don't shoot! Don't shoot!" Henry cried out.

I looked back at Blue Eyes in time to see the dissipating mist of his final breath. I was still staring at his corpse when Henry got to me, a .45 in his fist.

"Baby Girl," Henry whispered.

How was this possible? "How did you find me, Henry?"

"Girl at factory tell Otis she bring truck here. He pinch her broken nose."

"And Mac?"

"Al Mackenzie dead."

"No," I said—maybe to myself—knowing the pain had only begun.

"Holy Jesus," Otis said as he joined us.

He stared at the destroyed body at my feet.

"He lived and died by the gun," I told Otis.

"Holy Jesus," he said again.

He took the shotgun from my hands and threw it aside.

"Get the car door, Hank," he said as he took off his big coat, and wrapped it around me.

He steered me toward his car. I moved, but not well, and Otis and Henry together finally got me in their arms. All of us groaned with the effort, Otis from his stomach wound and Henry and me from our scrapes and bruises.

They carried me to Otis' idling car, got the back door open, and shoved me inside, pushing me across the seat like a fragile bundle of laundry.

"Get outta them wet clothes," Otis said.

"Get outta clothes," Henry said from the front where he was cranking up the heater.

They closed the doors, and it was silent.

They'd left me behind fogged windows in the warm interior of the car.

I was so tired.

I concentrated on my chattering teeth, tried to stop my body from shaking. I felt so alone. I thought of my dad, and I looked up like I might see him holding his book, peering over his glasses at me from the front seat.

"Listen to this," he would say.

I missed my dad so much it hurt.

And for him—and for all I would never have and all I could never be—

and for all I had become—

finally—

finally, I cried.

Capital Crime Press

offers you an excerpt from

Robert Fate's newest crime

adventure

Baby Shark's
Beaumont Blues

September 1956

CHUCK PARKED THE Cadillac under a stand of huge, white-barked sycamores near a new Chevy pickup, one of those big three-quarter ton trucks. He got out and told me to come with him. I smelled cattle on the heavy night air as I followed him to the middle of the spacious yard. He stopped there and glanced back. We were waiting for Cecil, who was still struggling out of the car.

"This guy we're here to pick up don't like strangers," Chuck said to me, keeping his voice down. "He's a little peculiar, see, and he may get rowdy. So, stay out of the way. Don't get involved. Don't look 'im in the face. Don't talk to 'im even if he talks to you. Just open and close doors, you know, help out like that until we can get 'im in the car. Then, you'll do the driving. Me and Cecil'll handle the rest of it. You understand?"

I nodded, and Chuck spun his keys for a moment. Ching-ching. "You ain't gonna have trouble driving a new Caddy, are you?"

"Can't imagine why I would."

Chuck nodded his approval. "What kind of work do you usually do?"

"Rodeo," I lied, probably because of the cattle smell.

"Rodeo?"

"Yeah," I confirmed, punching my ticket to hell, so to speak.

Chuck squinted. "How old're you?"

"If it's any of your business, twenty-one."

"I doubt that," he said, which taught me a lesson about telling the truth. He spun his keys, and squinted at me some more. "What's your event?"

"Calf roping."

Chuck made a face indicating his disbelief, and shook his head. "First pool, now rodeo." He looked over at Cecil who had caught up with us. "Did you hear that?"

"What?"

"Our driver girl here ropes calves in the rodeo."

"She does, huh?" Cecil chuckled.

In fact, they both had a good chuckle as they continued on to the house. I thought it was kind of funny, too, but I kept that to myself.

Chuck was across the big porch and to the front door before his partner could pull himself up the two steps.

"I can't remember a September this fucking humid," Cecil reminded us, as if we might have forgotten.

"We're due for a rainy spell, I reckon," Chuck told him.

As I waited in the yard for the football player to take the high ground, I had a chance to look around.

There was a sky full of stars, though with the moon so bright they weren't too showy. About the only sounds that far out in the country came from the insects. Although, I did hear some coyotes yipping off in the distance when we first got out of the car.

I followed the lumbering lineman across the porch. Chuck already had the front door open.

"You wait here, Rodeo," Chuck said, and relinquished the squeaky screen door to Cecil before stepping into the quiet house. "Bobby Jack. It's Chuck, Bobby Jack. Chuck and Cecil," he called out as he started up the dark hall, his boot steps resounding on the hardwood floor.

Cecil was short of breath from conquering the porch stairs, so he gathered himself before giving me a hard look and issuing orders. "I'm giving you a piece of advice. Don't say another fucking word till we're back in the city."

He clumped away after Chuck up the dark echoing hall.

I closed the screen door and stepped into the entryway where I was determined to be quiet. I glanced around. The only light came from the dim, bug-covered porch light and the soft glow of the lamp in the front window.

So far, things were going as planned. Using these guys to locate Bobby Jack had been the first challenge.

Now, if the rest would go as smoothly.

I waited where I'd been told for a few minutes, listening to the silence, before moving into the parlor.

The table lamp provided passable light for the small space. There was a door to an adjacent room. It was closed. The wallpaper and furniture was Montgomery Ward, circa 1930. Someone's grandma had done the crocheted doilies displayed on the backs and arms of the prim sofa and traditional wingback chairs.

There was a group of framed photographs arranged on top of the old upright piano, and I was just starting to look at them when I heard voices. Arguing voices. I heard glass break, and the voices growing louder.

I moved back to the hall, and made sure I could get to my .32.

Heavy footsteps. I listened.

They were coming up the hall.

No, they left the hall. A door slammed somewhere.

I heard something scrape across the floor—maybe furniture being pushed around.

The door on the other side of the parlor slammed open. I hadn't expected that. My narrow view of the room through the hall door didn't allow me to see much.

I moved farther back out of the light, which constricted

my view into the little parlor even more. So I was surprised when Cecil limped backward into view. He was terrified of something that I couldn't see from my angle.

The big man scuttled back until he knocked over the table and lamp.

And then a shotgun blast rang out, hitting Cecil in the chest, and startling me out of my wits.

I was pulling up my pant leg and grabbing my pistol as Cecil tumbled back, crashed heavily through the front window, and fell out onto the porch with a sickening thump. He was surely dead before the thin cotton curtains that he pulled with him through the demolished sash had time to float down and settle around him.

It grew quiet. The smell of burnt gunpowder was thick in the air.

It was even darker where I was with the only remaining light coming in from the porch. Sweat dripped from my face. I held as still as I could, but adrenaline had my knees trembling. I couldn't hear a sound.

Given my partial hearing loss from a beating I'd suffered a few years back, I was never certain that I was aware of everything there was to hear. I was more concerned that the killer would hear the pounding of my heart.

I forced myself not to react to the metallic clack-clack of the shotgun's pump action and the hit, bounce, and roll of the spent casing.

From the depths of the house, I heard Chuck approaching —ching-ching. He arrived in the room adjacent to the parlor, the room in which I assumed the killer was still standing with a loaded shotgun in his hands.

"What've you done, Bobby Jack?" Chuck asked the killer in a conversational tone of voice. He crossed the parlor, moved around the upset furniture, and looked out the broken window at Cecil's body. I saw his shoulders sag. "Aw, Christ, BJ. This weren't our idea, you know. Vahaska sent us out here."

Chuck turned back, his boots squeaking in the broken glass, and faced the maniac that had just murdered his friend.

"He's coming up. He's driving up from Beaumont and he wants you to lock your guest in the basement and meet him in Dallas. He said you'd know what to bring. His words. I'm telling you, BJ, he's coming out here hisself if you don't getcher ass back with me. Come on now. No more nonsense. Let's get on some clothes and get going."

No more nonsense? Unbelievable. I was in a mad house. I was already in up to my neck and there were still things to get done.

I listened hard as they returned to wherever they'd come from, Chuck continuing to chat with Bobby Jack as if he were a rational human being instead of a bloodthirsty murderer.

"Maybe Cecil didn't come atcha just right," Chuck was saying. "But ask yourself, was shootin' 'im the right thing to do?"

I remembered that the screen door squeaked, so I soundlessly moved into the parlor to look out the window at Cecil. I didn't know the ex-ballplayer. Still, I was sorry that every day had been painful for him because of his knees. And who was he to Bobby Jack that he should be gunned down in cold blood?

A second shotgun blast—from the interior of the house.

It was an unwelcome sound. Not a shock, though. Something had told me that Bobby Jack wasn't finished. And moments later another shotgun blast. Two violent sounds bracketed by a period of utter silence—eerie. I had to believe that he'd shot Chuck.

And then—a faint sound coming my way. I turned my head, used my best ear.

Footsteps. A floor squeak. The hall.

I moved instantly on tiptoe across the parlor, into the darkness of the adjacent room, into the original dining room. From there, I watched by the almost non-existent light from the porch as Bobby Jack entered the parlor from the hall. He was in more darkness than light.

I could just make out that he was slim, muscular, naked—late twenties maybe. He was carrying a short-barreled, pistol grip 12-gauge.

The sick animal went to the window and stared out toward the road for a few moments before raising the gun to shoot Cecil again. He pulled the trigger, but nothing happened. He'd used the three-shell capacity of the weapon.

I had earlier eased the hammer back on my revolver. I wanted single-action if I had to put that killer down. I was back in the dark room and hunkered down below the level of the dining room table, so I didn't think he could see me even if he looked in my direction.

He showed no emotion as he turned away from the window, stopped in the middle of the parlor, and just stood there. I could see the slight motion of his jaw. It was like he was grinding his teeth.

Hell, if I'd been Bobby Jack, I knew I'd be grinding *my* teeth.

Graceful as a panther, he moved through the archway and disappeared into the hallway. I stayed where I was without moving for several minutes and considered my situation.

I didn't think he knew I was there, but I couldn't be sure. *And*—he was moving on bare feet in his own house.

As Otis, my partner, would say, I had to double-watch my ass.

I wiped the sweat from my face.

Slowly, I took my purse off my shoulder, put it on the floor, and removed my boots and socks.

I had a job to finish.

I moved silently down the dark hallway with a cocked .32 in my hand. It was a small caliber, I knew. But up close and put in the right spot, it would do the job.

Light was coming from around the corner that I was

approaching. No sound—dead quiet. I noticed small spots of blood on the hall floor. I glanced back and saw the trail. Bobby Jack had cut his feet in the window glass—and hadn't seemed to notice.

On the far side of the hallway, there was something on the wall that didn't look right. It was a moment before I understood it. It was interesting how blood splattered on a wall could look so brutal.

Easy. Easy. I peeked around the corner and discovered Chuck on the hallway floor. He was face down in an expanding pool of blood, his legs splayed out, his feet pointing strangely. The back of his bloodied jacket was torn and riddled from the exiting slugs. His beautiful Stetson was crushed and stained beneath his head. He had an arm under him and one reaching forward. And at the end of his stretching arm, his finger pointed at his car keys on a silver ring.

Ching-ching.

Beyond his body there was an open door. A lighted bedroom. I could hear the low hum of an electric fan. I listened hard for any other sounds. Nothing. I looked behind me and got ready to go around the corner—

"Gotcha!" a male voice said from back there somewhere.

I froze. The voice was not close, not far away.

I heard whimpering. A girl.

That was a relief. I had begun to worry that she might be dead.

I wiped the sweat out of my eyes, stayed where I was, and listened some more. A slap. The girl cried out. The guy's voice again.

"What makes you so stupid? Try'n hide from me in my own fucking house."

Bobby Jack.

I stood there, around the corner, with my pistol at ready and listened to him force the crying girl up the hall from back in the house somewhere. From where I was, my view of the bedroom was narrowly framed by the open door. I could see a box springs and mattress on the floor through that doorway. Not much else.

When I heard Bobby Jack push the girl into the bedroom, I chanced a quick look and saw them, briefly. They were both naked. He shoved her onto the mattress and moved out of sight. She curled up and began sobbing.

It was Sherry Beasley: long brunette hair, seventeen years old, five feet tall.

Bobby Jack yelled at her from wherever he was in the room.

"Shut up your fucking bawlin' and getcher skinny ass over here. Get over here and do some of this, you lazy slut."

"No more, Bobby Jack." She sputtered through her sobbing.

"Yeah, more. This'll wake you up. Call yourself a good fuck. You don't know jack shit about how to fuck. Get over here."

"I'm gonna be sick."

Sherry saw Bobby Jack coming before I knew he was moving. She scooted off the bed and out of my sight. Bobby Jack crossed my doorframe view as he went after her. I heard him catch her and saw him drag her by her hair back past the open door.

"You get sick, I'll beat the living shit outta you," he told her from the other side of the room.

Sherry was growing hysterical. I could hear her crying and choking. Bobby Jack started snorting. I stepped around the corner and moved as fast as I could. I wanted to take a new position closer to the bedroom. I took care to keep my bare feet out of Chuck's blood as I passed him. I was almost to Bobby Jack's door when Sherry got slapped again. She fell to the carpeted floor in front of the open door.

I moved my hand holding the revolver behind my leg and kept moving toward her.

Sherry's eyes widened when she saw me. Her face went from wrinkled and panicked to stunned and disbelieving. Her nose and mouth were smeared with a pale colored powder. She had dark circles under her eyes. Her face was bruised and splotchy, not at all like it was in the pretty pictures that I had of her. She pushed her dirty, matted hair out of her face and opened her mouth to speak.

I brought a finger to my lips and showed her the palm of my hand.

I moved out of her sight as I positioned myself beside the bedroom door. I hoped that she would do the right thing. I couldn't count on it. I was just hoping.

I crouched down on my heels so that if he came to the door I would be below his natural line of sight. That instant might make the difference.

I heard Sherry get to her feet and speak to him using a calmer voice.

"I'll do you good, Bobby Jack. I will."

"Yeah?"

"I got scared for a minute. All those guns."

"What about the guns?"

"Nothing. Nothing about the guns. I just got scared, that's all."

There was a long awful silence before I heard struggling. Sherry sobbed and groaned and it was quiet again. I wiped the sweat out of my eyes and slowly—carefully, carefully, staying low—I peaked around the edge of the door.

Bobby Jack had his back to me. He was standing beside the bed on the floor with a hand holding Sherry by her hair. She was on her knees, her face to his crotch. His other hand held a nickel-plated Luger.

That was not good. I stood up and moved into the doorway just as he growled with disgust and pushed her away.

"You don't know what you're doing." He let go of her hair and jacked one into the chamber.

Sherry screamed hysterically and instantly back-pedaled away from him. He fell to his knees onto the mattress, grabbed her by her ankle, dragged her back, kicking and screaming, and pointed his pistol at her face.

I was going full speed by then, crossing the carpeted bedroom in giant strides.

Before anything else happened, I rabbit punched Bobby Jack with the butt of my snub nose. Solid. Right at the base of his skull.

He grunted loudly, fired a wild shot into the bed, and collapsed on Sherry.

The loud gunshot so near her face ratcheted Sherry into even more of a girl-gone-crazy mode. She screamed louder and began clawing and kicking her way from beneath Bobby Jack's limp body.

And then—Bobby Jack groaned, raised himself up, and gave his head a shake.

That really set Sherry off.

She yelped like she'd been jabbed with a cattle prod and pushed away so hard she launched herself off the low bed. She scrambled across the room on her hands and knees like some feral creature.

I gave my boy another hard smack on his brain stem. This time blood sprayed from the gash I opened and he fell face down on the soiled mattress, seriously unconscious.

"And stay there," I told him.

Sherry jumped up and dashed back to the bed.

"Hey, hey," I had time to say before she grabbed Bobby Jack's Luger and fired at him.

I moved at once and wrenched the pistol away from her. She grew hysterical again.

"Kill 'im! Kill 'im! Kill 'im!" she shrieked.

"You're beginning to piss me off," I told her.

That wild shot of hers had hit the electric fan and stopped dead the only decent breeze I'd felt since I'd come into that house. I stuffed the Luger in my belt, wiped the sweat out of my eyes, and looked around the dirty, disheveled room.

"Where're your clothes?"

Sherry Beasley, soon to be one of the richest women in Texas, stopped like she'd had a switch thrown. She just stood there, all ninety pounds of her, naked as a jaybird, her feet planted wide apart in a defiant stance, her nose bleeding slightly, her dilated eyes red and bloodshot. She wasn't herself and I knew it. God only knows what cruel indignities she'd had to suffer the past few days. She shook her head like she was denying a nightmare.

"It's all wrong," she said.

"You're right about that. Where're your things, Sherry?"

I thought I saw something hopeful in amongst the debris and clutter on top of the low dresser and went over to it. I picked up what had to be her pocketbook.

"This is yours, right?"

She snatched the Dior saddlebag from me, opened it, and dumped the contents out on the floor—the expected things, keys, money, lipstick. Taking her posh bag over to a side table, she dragged a pile of grayish powder into it.

"Forget that stuff. Let's get your clothes on so we can get out of here."

Her bruised face was flushed with anger and confusion. "Who the fuck are you to boss me around?"

"I just saved your ass, that's who. Get dressed. Let's move it."

She pointed at a soft leather travel bag on the floor by the dresser, near where the phone jack had been torn from the wall. "Get that," she said.

"Your clothes in there?" I stepped over to pick up the bag and saw movement in the dresser mirror.

It was Sherry with a glittery Mexican figurine in her hands. She was coming at me to use it like a club. I turned, brushed aside her attempt to brain me, and cold-cocked her with a right cross. With a little help from me, she toppled back onto the mattress next to Bobby Jack.

Glancing down at the shattered chalk and glitter—all that was left of Jesus of Nazareth—I wiped the sweat from my eyes and said, "Halleluiah."

Though BABY SHARK is Robert Fate's first novel, he has written scripts for network television and screenplays for feature films. He has been rewarded for his efforts as a Hollywood F/X technician with an Academy Award for Technical Achievement. He's a Marine Corps veteran who studied at the Sorbonne in France and has worked as an oilfield roughneck and a TV cameraman in Oklahoma, a fashion model in New York City, and a chef at a chi-chi L.A. eatery. Does it surprise you that now he's writing crime novels?

He lives in Los Angeles with his wife, daughter, and the requisite number of pets. He has completed Baby Shark's BEAUMONT BLUES, the second in his crime series, and is writing novel number three, Baby Shark's SOONER WEEKENDS.

Find out more at www.robertfate.com.